Ride a Dark Trail

Ride a Dark Trail

A Bounty of Shadows Series

Winter Austin

TULE

Dedication

For my beta readers Jenn and Rachel,
who have been with me
through the thick of it and the thin of it.
They're my frontline warriors.
If it doesn't agree with them, it won't agree with you.
Here's to a lot more books.

"A guilty man always has a fear on him which he cannot hide."
US Deputy Marshal Bass Reeves

Chapter One

H IS GHOST ALWAYS joined her for the final drag on an Ave Maria Dark Knight cigar.

He started appearing two months into her newly formed habit. Always in his sweat-stained, gray Open Road Stetson and wool-lined coat with a few less wrinkles in his face. Here, in the goats' lean-to, where she'd taken to hiding out to have her smoke so as to not offend her mother's senses.

At his first appearance, she swore it was a hallucination. The second time, she flipped out. With each appearance since she became more belligerent, while he grew more persistent.

"*Biloba*, why do you keep doing this thing?"

She blew out the smoke. "Go away, *Aitonatxo*."

Her grandfather shook his head. One of the goats meandered through his transparent legs, disrupting his stern reproach. *Aitona* turned his withering look to the red-brown doe munching on hay.

"Goats. She just had to get goats."

A smile twitched at the corners of her mouth as she drew on the cigar for the last time. One year after her grandfather passed, her mother had sold the last of the sheep, turned the ranch into an outfitter and hunting business, bought horses

1

and mules for it, then goats just for the hell of it. The small herd had come in real handy in keeping the overgrowth of underbrush and weeds under control, saving the ranch a time or two from wildfires. The milking goats also made convenient pack animals when there was need for nourishment up in the mountains.

Aitona didn't roll over in his grave. No, he came back to fucking haunt her and complain about the goats.

"Dorothy Ybarra, where are you?"

His specter vanished with her last puff of smoke. Before her mother could barge into the goats' lean-to and give her hell for smoking in the building, Dorothy ground the butt into the bottom of her boot. One disapproving *familia* was enough, even if *Aitonatxo* was an apparition of her mind.

Angela Ybarra rounded the edge of the lean-to's weathered support post, her pack of mutts in tow. The goats scattered, except for a leggy dark brown female who'd taken a liking to Dot and exuded copious amounts of stubborn. That doe would not be deterred by no dog.

Exactly twenty years older and just as whipcord lean as her daughter, Angela Ybarra was the polar opposite when it came to Dot's tornado in a trailer park personality. But that didn't stop Angela from pulling the matriarch card every chance she got.

Angela wrinkled her nose and gave Dot a pointed look but held her tongue. Dot hadn't burned down any buildings. Yet.

Her mother reached out and scratched the doe's withers. "I've got a new elk hunting party coming in later today. We're taking them out to that nice valley for their hunt. I need to grab a few supplies for the trip. In the meantime, would you round up your gear and check it over?"

"You sure you want me up there with you?"

"I need you, Dot. This is a new group to me."

In other words, *Ama* wasn't comfortable being on her own with this bunch. Most of the hunters Angela outfitted were longtime customers she had built a strong rapport with and trusted. She took on new clients only if there was a long lull between her regulars and funds were tight.

Since Dot's return to the ranch, she'd been her mother's backup when one of the local sheep herders wasn't available to ride out with Angela. Dot's presence on hunts was a good deterrent for wannabe suitors or general dickheads. Not that Angela Ybarra couldn't hold her own—she was Samo Ybarra's daughter after all and had sent many a man intending ill-intent back to civilization with a limp and severe damage to his manhood. Dot, on the other hand, was less accommodating. The pervs usually woke up in the hospital, cuffed to the bedrail.

"*Ama*, you don't need to earn the extra cash. I can spot you."

"No." Angela sliced the air with a disapproving finger. "Your army and pilot funds are yours. Don't waste them on my business."

"Come on!"

"I'll hear no more of it." Angela checked her watch. "I'm going. Be ready." She slipped from view, her canine pack following.

Dot's guard goat gave a very goat-like nicker as she munched on weeds bold enough to dare grow in their pen.

It might have been a year since the crash. She might have been released from physical therapy with a clean bill of health two months ago. And she might be in the best physical shape of her life since basic training and flight school. Still, Dot hadn't spent more than two hours horseback in the last six months. Riding into the foothills of the Payette National Forest and getting to that valley her mother spoke of meant at least an eight-hour ride. Probably longer if this new hunting party wasn't used to long hours in the saddle.

Dot groaned. Good thing she loved her mother.

She rose from the goats' favorite climbing stump and vacated the lean-to. At the corner, she glanced back at the spot where *Aitona* had appeared.

He'd died while she was away at training. It ate at her for years that she hadn't been here to see him crossed over to the other side and be with his beloved Dorothy—Dot's namesake. Though somehow he hadn't quite left the ranch.

He wanted to know. Or maybe she was using his specter to ask herself the question.

Why did she do this thing? She was hale and hearty, ready to get back in the air. God knew the forest service hadn't stopped calling. Yet she couldn't pull herself away from her current predicament.

Why?

"I'm doing it for *Ama*," she said to the air.

ALONE IN THE barn, Dot worked the bowstring for her

recurve. The tang of warm horseflesh and sweet summer hay soothed her. In the paddock beside the barn, a horse gave a low throaty greeting to a friend and was answered in kind.

Dot lifted the tightly woven string and inspected it. The best way to ensure reliability was to nock arrow to string and let it fly at a target. Her earliest memory was standing with *Aitona*, his muscular arms haloing her tiny form and helping her draw back a bowstring on an equally tiny recurve. Hunting and fishing in all their forms had been ingrained into Dot from the moment her small hands could navigate the intricate details of each instrument. When not advocating or educating for the Basque community or tending to his beloved sheep ranch, her grandfather was hunting or fishing.

During her years as an army aviator, she'd fine-tuned her tracking and aiming skills in a different way. She now possessed uncanny abilities that made hunters visiting their outfitting business envious.

Dot checked her watch, a parting gift from her squad commander the day she DD214'd out of the army. Mom should be returning soon. Hopefully, she would be bringing something from Euskadi to eat. Dot was starving.

She was repacking her gear when the dogs started up a ruckus. She set aside her equipment bag and rose from the makeshift haybale seat.

A stranger was near.

Dot emerged from the barn's darkened interior and leaned a shoulder into the wall. Beneath her cream-colored, felt Stetson she scanned the drive. Nothing.

One of the blue heelers shot past her pos, toward the dirt path ringing the homestead. Fast on the bitch's trail came the rest of the pack.

Intrigued, Dot left her spot and followed the dogs. If no one was coming up the drive, then what did they hear and smell? She passed the house and the goat pasture, where the Great Pyrenees and Anatolian guard dogs' deep barks echoed over the valley. Dot stepped out from under the low branches of the shade trees and spotted the pack running to the wood fence separating the yard from the empty summer pasture.

With the start of elk season, there were times when hunters—on their own—would get lost or turned around in the forest and somehow end up here. On a few occasions, they would mistake the Ybarra ranch animals for the prey they hunted and take shots.

Dot scanned the horizon. A black shadow broke the pristine lines, wobbling about through the pasture's long grasses. She tilted back the brim of her hat and let her hawk eyes take in the sight coming toward her. The continued barking grated on her already frayed nerves.

"*Nahikoa!*"

The pack fell silent, but the dogs were not done. They kept their collective gazes trained on the oncoming intruder.

Dot lowered her right hand to her hip and removed the ever-present sidearm strapped to her leg. The intruder was too far away to tell if this was a predator or not. Wild animals were known to venture out of the Payette National Forest in search of easy game if conditions forced them.

She closed the distance between her position and the fence.

"*Itzalita,*" she said, ordering the dogs off.

They scuttled back to the trees, refusing to leave her alone. She never had anything to fear with those four-legged wingmen.

A cry echoed over the wide span of ground—a very human cry. The figure took shape as they raised an arm. Another cry went up right as the person floundered and went down, disappearing behind the waist-high grass.

"Shit." Dot rushed to the fence and vaulted over it.

The dogs once again started up their chorus of *intruder alert*. Dot snarled at their persistence.

She raced across the field, keeping her sidearm ready, straight for the spot where the figure had gone down. The faint cries increased in volume and distress the closer Dot drew.

She slowed her pace and lifted the pistol, searching the tree line for any signs of a threat of the four-legged or two-legged kind. She parted the grass, revealing a pitiful creature in the fetal position on the ground.

"What the hell?"

The creature's body jerked, and a disheveled head the color of dried wheat lifted from the ground. A pair of red-rimmed doe eyes peered up at Dot.

"Don't shoot," she pleaded, raising bloodstained and dirty hands.

Dot lowered the weapon. "Who are you?"

"I need help. He took her." She gathered herself and pried her trembling body up from the earth, still keeping her hands raised. "He took her."

"Who took who? How did you get out here?"

The woman—if she could be called that; she didn't look

a day over seventeen—continued to give mewling sounds.

Assured she was alone and nothing dangerous would come blowing out of the forest, Dot holstered her pistol. She catalogued the girl's features—the skewed flannel shirt, the dirty and ripped jeans, the piss-poor excuse for shoes, and the bleeding cuts joined by a large purple bruise under her left eye. She had obviously been in the rocky areas past the Ybarra ranch, hiking or camping in the Payette. Something was off. Really off.

"My ex," she blurted. "He took my daughter."

"And why would he do that?"

Through the blood and bruises, sheer terror appeared on the girl's face. "I don't know."

"Were you in the Payette?"

"Yes. I was hiking with my daughter. I don't know how he found us."

What she didn't say was broadcast all over her face and body. He'd beat the shit out of her before running off with the kid.

"What's your name?" Dot asked.

Giving a great shudder, the girl swiped away snot, blood, and tears from her face with the cuff of her torn sleeve. "My name is Ashley." She flinched at the sight on her sleeve. "Ashley Cooper," she added, her voice almost childlike.

Dot reached out and pulled the girl toward her. "Well, Ashley, looks like I'm about to disappoint my mother today."

Chapter Two

T HE PACK STARTED up their rendition of *Halt! Police!*
Dot, leading her sure-footed gelding out of the
barn, stopped to watch a pair of dark gray trucks with large,
yellow, six-point star decals announcing Pyrenees County on
the doors and gleaming aluminum trailers pull into the drive.
Clear to the back of the parade of dust-coated vehicles
followed her mother's ancient Ford.

Dot glanced at Ashley. "Anything you'd like to tell me?"

Ashley, clutching the reliable mule's reins, shook her
head. The blood-crusted hair hung in clumps around her
scratched features, giving the impression the woman was
Jamie Lee Curtis à la *Halloween.*

"No," she said, stroking the mule's nose and inching
back to use his neck as a shield.

Dot eyed the young woman but held her tongue.

Once the duo parked along the side of the gravel lane,
Angela maneuvered her 1965 robin's egg blue F-100 around
them and parked in the drive. She was out of the cab in a
flash and marched back to the lead vehicle.

Dot dropped the gelding's reins, officially ground tying
him where he stood. She left Ashley and crossed the yard.

The lead truck's driver's side door opened, and a beefy

man decked out in jeans and a dusty-brown uniform top and Stetson emerged. A pair of reflective aviators blocked his eyes, but his head swiveled—he was surveying the lay of the land. Until he spotted Dot. He shut the door and was about to take a step forward when Angela waylaid him.

"Richard T. Ford, what the hell do you think you're doing on my land?"

Dot managed to intercept her mother before all five-feet-four, one-hundred-twenty-five pounds of angry Ybarra was unleashed. She propelled *Amatxo* behind her back, putting herself between the sheriff and his pending doom.

Sheriff Richard T. Ford was one of those men Angela had always loathed and never divulged a single justification for her animosity. For whatever reason, Ford had been nothing but respectful and cordial toward Dot and barely tolerant toward Angela. *Aitatxi* used to say it was because there was history between the two, refusing to elaborate any further.

"Sheriff." Dot blocked her mother's attempt to get around her.

"Dorothy." He was the second person on earth who used her given name, Angela being the first. Ford probably did it to get a rise out of his tiny adversary. "I'd heard you were still at home." He tilted down his aviators and peered over the tops at Dot. "I figured you'd gone back to flying the wheelie birds."

Angela began muttering in Basque. Dot did her best to not laugh at the curses her mother rained down on the sheriff and certain portions of his anatomy.

"Haven't had any callouts," Dot interjected over her

mother's mutterings. "Why are you…" She pointed at the second truck and trailer. "Out here?"

A horse whinnied from the trailer. Dot's gelding answered.

"You taking someone for a ride?" Ford asked, nodding behind Dot.

She glanced back, noting that the mule was alone with her gelding … Ms. Ashley had pulled a Houdini. Dot returned her attention to Ford. "Nope. Just me and Ma here getting the animals ready for another hunt."

"You don't mind if we use your access into the forest for a look-see?"

"I mind," Angela barked. "You will back on out of here and go beg entrance somewhere else."

Dot refrained from making an exasperated face. "Gotta reason you need to ride into the Payette, Sheriff?"

"We got a report of an attempted kidnapping and a runaway. Potential kidnapper was last seen headed in the direction of your ranch."

That shut Angela up.

"Is that so?" Dot regarded Ford. "Sheriff, if you don't mind my asking, who reported all this?"

It was Ford's turn to consider Dot with a little extra scrutiny. Angela pinched the fleshy part on the backside of Dot's hip right above her waistline. It took a powerful amount of self-control to not flinch or reach back and swat her mother's hand.

"Well," Ford said, resettling his aviators firmly on the bridge of his sun-damaged nose. "Some campers along the trail heard a commotion. Checked it out and found two individuals fighting. Both broke up the fight when the campers intervened and then took off. There's claims of a child involved."

"Got any descriptions of these two individuals or this supposed child?" Angela pinched her again, and Dot twitched.

Boy howdy, if she didn't love her mother…

"Male and female. No one could give us details. And the gender of the child is unknown, if there was one. Me and my deputy here planned on riding up there to meet up with the campers. Two other deputies are taking the roads as far as they can." Ford gave her a level look.

At least that was what Dot figured he was doing behind those shiny lenses.

"Do we have your permission to leave our vehicles here and ride up?"

Angela poked her head around Dot's shoulder. "Over my dead body. I've got customers coming in, and I ain't catering to your nonsense."

Both Dot and Ford sighed simultaneously.

"*Ama*…"

Angela darted around Dot and wagged a finger in Ford's face. "Shove off."

"*Ama!*"

Angela's disapproving finger jabbed Dot's way. "Not another word, *alaba*." The stern finger returned to Ford. "Take your man and leave." Angela stormed off toward the house.

Ford ripped off his aviators and watched her go, then turned a beseeching look on Dot. "You and I both know this is the fastest way to campgrounds."

Dot shrugged. "It is. But I'm not the owner. Angela Ybarra has spoken. Her word is law." Pasting on a smile she did not feel, Dot gave Ford a nod and trailed after her mother.

As she passed the second truck, she sensed the hostile observation coming from within the cab. She slowed her gait and peered inside the open window. The deputy was unfamiliar to Dot—she'd grown up here and knew or knew about everyone who lived in the 3,734 square miles of Pyrenees County—but the disdain was all too recognizable. He was not from Idaho. His skin was too flawless. The prerequisite fawn-colored Stetson sat awkwardly on his head.

Dot halted. She returned his hard glare with one she'd perfected on recalcitrant soldiers who thought a female copter pilot would be a pushover.

The deputy used the good sense God gave him to relax his features and look away. Dot moved on, returning to her freestanding gelding.

A truck door slammed as she caught up the mule's reins. She turned and watched the sheriff and deputy swing their rigs around in the roundabout behind the house and rumble off the Ybarra ranch. The moment the dust settled Dot led the equines into the barn.

"You better get your sorry ass front and center," she snapped at the darkened interior.

A shuffle of bedding alerted her to Ashley's emergence from one of the empty stalls. The whites of the young woman's eyes gleaming in the shadows.

"Are they gone?" she whispered.

"Mind telling me why you lied?" Dot countered.

"I didn't lie." Ashley's objection sounded more like a whine.

"Girl, I'm this damn close to putting ass to leather and runnin' down the sheriff to hand you over. There will be no games played here. Out with the truth."

"What I told you is the truth. I took my daughter on a hike and my ex found us, beat on me, and ran off with my daughter."

"What's your daughter's name?"

Ashley's face contorted. "What does that have to do—"

"Damn it, answer me." The whiplash retort startled the horse and mule.

Her chin trembling, Ashley took a shuddering breath. "Bethany," she croaked. "Her name is Bethany. She's six years old."

"Why would you take a six-year-old on a trail meant for experienced hikers?"

"We were only staying near the campgrounds." Ashley hung her head. "I had no idea he'd found me. I don't know why he found me." Ashley sank onto a stray hay bale and started crying. "I'm sorry. I didn't know what else to do." She flung her hand in the direction of the mountains. "I don't even know how I came down from there and made it here."

"How did you get there in the first place?" Dot pressed.

"My car." She buried her face in her hands. "I think he slashed my tires."

"And you're certain he took off on foot with your daughter?"

Ashley looked up. "He walked into the campgrounds. I

don't know if he had a car."

Dot mulled this over. This part of the Payette National Forest was rough terrain, mostly forested, and smack dab in the middle of the busiest hunting season. The roads leading in and out of the park and campgrounds were a mix of gravel or dirt and very few were paved, like the one Ashley was most likely to have taken. ATVs and horseback were the only means to get into the forest from the Ybarra ranch. And *Ama* didn't keep ATVs.

"You've gotten me caught up in a real mess," Dot ground out.

The barn's back door rollers squalled as it was pushed aside, putting a stop to any answer Ashley was about to give. Angela's silhouette stepped into the center of the picturesque scene of pasture and timber.

"Who is this?" she demanded, crossing her arms.

"Trouble," Dot answered.

"I'm not," Ashley protested, rather weakly.

"Is she the reason Ford came out here to bother us?" Angela asked.

Dot pointed the gelding toward the stall where Ashley had been hiding out. "Appears so."

Outside the dogs started up again. Angela grunted and left the barn doorway.

Ashley bolted upright. "Who's that?"

Without being commanded to do so, the mule followed the gelding's lead and headed to his own stall. Dot was of half a mind to scrap her original plan to help Ashley out, let the chips fall where they may and all that shit. Dot had gambled enough of her life away for other people, and every single time had left her with nightmares and battle scars.

"Probably my mother's clients," Dot said.

Ashley darted past her to the doorway, gasped, and flung herself back toward the now-occupied stall. The gelding snorted at his space invader.

Dot refused to play into Ashley's melodramatic antics. She'd been spared the agony of a long ride into the mountains to track down God knows what with an unreliable girl. Knowing the sheriff and his crew were on the hunt for Ashley's kid was enough assurance to not go out on a seek-and-find mission of her own.

"He found me," Ashley blurted from her hidden spot.

Dot fisted her hands and ground her molars. *What the fuck.* She would not ask. She would not ask.

"He found me," Ashley wailed in a reedy voice.

Dot let out a low-timbered growl and stalked over to the barn door.

Angela was greeting the occupants of the first truck hitched to a utility trailer. Right behind the city boy getup was a light gray, dual cab heavy-duty truck.

Dot peeked over her shoulder. "Those are elk hunters."

Ashley keened but remained hidden.

Rolling her eyes, Dot gave up on the girl. Her fits of flightiness were a stark reminder of why Dot preferred solitude over dealing with people. She exited the barn just as the driver to the heavy-duty emerged. Dot put on the brakes.

Dark hair curled under the wide brim of the black hat. The once clean-shaven face was covered in a dark brown beard sprinkled with silver. He was thicker in the upper body, carrying a bit of a belly around the midsection, but still as imposing as he'd been the day she first met him. He'd traded in army fatigues for jeans and waffle-knit, long-sleeved shirts.

Angela ceased her conversation with the city boy and swung her focus on the bearded intruder. She wouldn't know him. Dot made certain her mother was not privy to any of her life during her stint as an army aviator.

"Can I help you?" Angela called out.

He spotted Dot and the rounded edges of his beard moved. Was he smiling? Dot couldn't tell for sure from this distance.

"Still like to blare *Highway to Hell* over the sound system?" His question rolled over the yard.

His voice, still as rich and deep as she remembered, took her back to a place she'd tried so hard to forget. He hadn't been there in her final days flying helicopters out of Afghanistan, during the chaos of a botched pullout. He'd gotten his DD214 a year before.

"Only on days when I had to haul your sorry ass anywhere," she shot back.

He removed his wraparound sunglasses and hung them by the ear from the top button on his shirt. "Hey, Flygirl."

"Danger Ranger."

If he was here, something was up. By the way Ashley reacted, things were serious. It was one thing for Sheriff Ford to come to the Ybarra ranch and ask questions—it was his job. T.J. Roman was a whole different ball of wax.

Angela had left her client and made her way over. Dot noticed the driver of the tricked-out city boy truck trailed after.

"*Alaba*, you know this man?"

"I do, *Ama*. He's an old army friend." Dot moved to the edge of the barn lane. "Though I'm not sure what he's doing in Idaho. Or why he's here."

"You didn't double-book our weekend?" The snide undertone in the client's question called for Dot's full focus. He glared back, but he lacked the intensity Dot would expect from a big game hunter. An experienced hunter.

The fucking new guy tried to dress the part. Yet everything looked recent, top of the line. Like he'd been sold on this idea from a commission-happy clerk at a big chain outdoor retailer.

No. Her mother was not taking this FNG or his buddy—who had rounded the front end of the spotless truck and looked more out of place than his partner—into the mountains. Neither one of them looked prepared for an hour-long horseback ride, much less a four-day trip into the Payette and back out. Even with Dot riding along.

"Name?" Dot barked.

FNG flinched, glanced at his buddy, and then back to Dot. "Brady."

For the love of God, he even had a dippy name. Dot had to get these city slickers out of here and away from any blowback. She met her mother's searing look. Angela shook her head.

"*Barkatu*," she apologized.

"*Ez!*"

Ignoring Angela's protest, Dot moved closer to Brady, pointing at his truck. "Get back in your vehicle and leave. We'll send your reimbursement."

"Wait! What?" He looked back and forth between mother and daughter. "I didn't just drive hundreds of miles here to not go on a hunt. I'll get what I paid for."

Dot dropped her hand next to her holster. "Like I said, you'll be reimbursed."

His face flushed deep red. "Is this how you do business?" he asked Angela. "You some kind of scammer? Steal people's money under the pretense of a business deal, and when they show up you send them packing after pocketing their money?"

Dot stepped back as her mother forced her way into Brady's personal space.

"You will not insult me to my face. I run an honest outfitting business for authentic hunters. You"—she looked him up and down—"are nowhere near authentic."

"This is bullshit. I'll sue you."

"For what?" Dot threw out. "For returning your money?"

"False pretenses," he countered.

T.J.'s low chuckle made Brady's face turn purple.

"Boy, if I was a smart man—and you strike me as someone with some intelligence—you'll do as the ladies say and hightail it on outta here."

"I don't have to do a single fucking thing." Brady spat and reached for Angela.

Dot drew her firearm and leveled it against Brady's cheek the moment his hand clasped Angela's arm. He stiffened, giving Dot's Colt 1911 the side eye.

"Guess I read you all wrong," T.J. said.

"You have one second to unhand my mother," Dot said,

her voice dipping into her lethal tone.

The deep red flush seeped from Brady's face.

He released Angela's arm and slowly lifted it in surrender. "I did nothing wrong." His voice cracked prepubescently.

"You touched my mother. In my world that constitutes as assault, and as such, warrants certain measures." Dot leaned into the 1911 a smidgen, indenting Brady's fleshy cheek. "We can deal with this in one of two ways. You leave and accept a modified refund, or I call the authorities and have you arrested for assault and trespassing. Either way, doesn't matter to me."

"Modified refund?" Brady asked incredulously.

"I can make it so there's no refund and tack on a lawsuit if you want."

He gave a curt shake of his head, then stepped away from the barrel. Once free of her weapon he backpedaled, keeping his hands up and facing Dot. When he felt he had enough distance between them, he turned and hurried over to his truck. His pal said something, and Brady barked at him to get in the truck.

Dot holstered the 1911 and waited for the pickup and trailer to leave the ranch before turning to T.J.

"*Ama*, meet Titus Jethro Roman, formally of the United States Army Seventy-Fifth Rangers."

He removed his hat and respectfully nodded at her mother. "Ms. Ybarra, good to meet you."

Angela looked from Dot to T.J., then back. "Old army friend. Right."

Dot ignored her mother's subtle tone. "Why are you here

in Idaho? I figured you'd returned to Oklahoma and gotten yourself set up with a Mrs. Roman there."

"I tried to go home. Didn't stick. Ain't no woman wants to be a Mrs. Roman." He looked back at the mountains and took in a deep breath. "Always did like hearing your stories about your home and decided to give it a try." He looked over his shoulder at Dot. "Liked it a lot."

"Just what is it you do for a living, Mr. Roman?" Angela pressed.

T.J. faced them, resettling his hat on his dome. "I'm a fugitive recovery agent now." One side of his mouth quirked up. "And I'm hunting down that little lady right behind you."

Chapter Three

Dot found Ashley standing a yard or two behind, gaping with those doe eyes at T.J.

"You're a fugitive recovery agent?" Dot looked to T.J. "And you're looking for her?"

What the hell had she gotten herself caught up in?

"I'm not a crook," Ashley protested in that girly voice.

"Don't matter, honey, you're the cosigner on the bail. We've got a failure to appear, and people want their money one way or another," T.J. drawled.

"I don't know what that means. I did not sign any papers."

"That's not what the bail bondsman says."

"I still don't understand what you're talking about," Ashley said, in such a pitiful tone it made Dot want to shake it out of her.

Dot held up her hand before T.J. could answer. "You're going to arrest her for someone else's screwup?"

He gave a half shrug. "Not arresting. I'm seeking payment or a warm body."

Ashley cried. "I don't have any money. I just want my daughter back."

T.J. scowled. "What do you mean, you want your

daughter back?"

"Seems the asshole in question caught up with Ashley and her kid up at a campground," Dot provided. "He beat the shit out of her and took off with the kid. She came stumbling down from the mountain and found me."

"Oh, this ain't good," T.J. said. "If he's up there with a hostage, I gotta involve the five-o's."

"They're already involved," Dot said. "We just ran off the sheriff and a deputy, told them to find some other way up there." She jerked a thumb over her shoulder at Ashley. "What she failed to mention was that her scumbag ex might have a getaway vehicle, and he could be halfway to Boise or heading north."

"You still fly?" T.J. asked.

Dot stiffened. She did. Well … she could, but she couldn't. She hadn't since the accident. She wasn't cleared yet to get back in a chopper.

Angela cleared her throat, sparing Dot from having to answer him. *Ama* clearly was none too pleased with this line of conversation.

"How about you two bring me up to speed on what the hell is going on and why I just lost clients?"

"Those two idiots deserved to be sent packing," Dot replied. "I just saved you the agony of putting up with a couple of whiners who didn't look like they'd last the night."

"Not your decision to make, *alaba*."

"You made it mine when you demanded I come along on your merry little trip before the blonde from a horror flick showed up."

"She does kinda look like the one the axe murderer goes

for first," T.J. added.

Angela leveled her infamous stern look, which had always been saved for Dot, on him. "Mr. Roman, kindly shut your yap."

Dot relished seeing T.J. put in his place. He'd been a pain in the ass for anyone who outranked him, and on more than one occasion mentioned how badly he behaved with his own mother. Her enjoyment was short-lived, as her mother pinned her with that particular skin-peeling glare.

"We will help this girl, and we'll do it the Ybarra way." Her dark blue eyes were hard as stone. "Now, you will tell me what I need to know."

Dot hung her arm out of the passenger side window of T.J.'s truck, hand surfing on the air currents as the heavy-duty sped along the last paved road heading up the mountain. Behind him, Angela followed with Ashley as her passenger, hauling the horse trailer with four of the Ybarras's best mounts and Angela's canine pack.

"I could get in all kinds of shit for bringing you and your momma along," T.J. said, slowing the truck for a snake curve.

"Like I said before, consider it a search-and-rescue mission. We're both qualified for it." She brought her hand back inside the cab and tucked flyaways behind her ear. "*Ama's* dogs are tremendous trackers. I'd trust them any day."

"A few of those dogs look like they'd eat a bear."

Dot chuckled. "That's their original purpose."

The truck cab was tidy in comparison to most of the men around the area. Ranchers and cowboys in general kept most of their tools of the trade shoved in the back seat or on the passenger side floorboard right along with discarded bottles of whatever, along with food wrappers joined by the occasional clod of manure and scattered grain or hay.

T.J. was hauling his trade tools in the back seat, but they were locked away in a special box designed to hug the floorboard. His to-go bag leaned against the seat behind him for an easy grab. There were no fast-food wrappers, no discarded coffee cups or plastic bottles, not even a smidgen of dirt to gunk up the interior.

"How do you transport your bond jumpers in this thing if you're alone?" she asked.

"If I know I've got my defendant, I have another vehicle for transporting. Occasionally, I'll ask a few guys in the business to help me out for a cut if I know I need assistance."

"Didn't think to drive the other one for this little foray into the wilds?"

"No time to switch out gear; I had to get up here. Craig Cooper is a flight risk. Once he leaves Idaho, I'm screwed. If he takes the girl with him, he becomes an FBI problem, and the marshals get involved."

Dot studied the yellow and orange leaves still clinging to the trees. Autumn in the mountains was beautiful. She'd missed it during her tours in the Middle East. "What's her story?"

"Who?" he asked.

Dot pulled her attention back to T.J. "Ashley Cooper. I'm sure you have details."

He kept his focus on the road. "What I have of her are bits and pieces. She's not my target."

"You have more than I do. Couldn't pull a hat trick with that one if you tried, she's so tightly wound."

T.J. drummed the steering wheel with thick, scarred fingers. His were the hands of a man who spent hundreds if not thousands of hours perfecting and greasing his ability to react correctly and shoot. Those hands had also found a few minutes in secluded areas on base to drive her mad.

"I really shouldn't be telling you anything until this bastard is caught and in police custody," he grumbled.

"Yet, here I am. We're not under the army's thumb. There's no red tape."

He glanced at her. "But there is. She has her right to privacy."

"She lost that right barging onto my family ranch. She's lucky she didn't get shot or turned over to the sheriff."

"You've gone soft in your old age, Ybarra."

"And you're growing a beer belly. So, cough it up."

His chuckle came from deep in his chest. "Shit." He gave her another side look. "Ashley's been with the scumbag on and off for the last six or so years. Craig Cooper's ten years her senior. Knocked her up when she was about sixteen. Two years ago, she got a break from him when he was in jail, and she ran. The problem was, he got out on a technicality. He got caught again, bailed out, used her as his cosigner, managed to actually make his court dates until sentencing."

"She's been hiding from him for the last two years?"

"That I'm not read in on. The bondsman who sent me out on this isn't the greatest with the paperwork. Which, in this line of work, you need to keep your shit straight. Either way, Craig found her and now he's got a hostage."

She peered at T.J. "Why take the kid?"

"Collateral. The poor girl is being used as a pawn to control her mother and a way to keep me and law enforcement at a distance. He's a criminal with nothing to lose looking at spending the rest of his life behind bars."

"If it's okay for me to ask, what did he do to get him a sentence like that?"

T.J. dug into his center console and pulled out a folded stack of papers, then passed them over to Dot. "Damn boy never learned his lesson all the prior times he got caught with controlled substances. Tacked on a few DUIs because he liked to sample his wares. Problem was, his last time out, someone died from whatever dope he was dealing. He ain't just going away for a few years this time."

She studied the mug shot and the arrest record on Ashley's ex. His history mimicked quite a lot of people from this part of the country.

"Armed?" Dot asked, setting the papers aside.

"Most likely," he said.

"Juiced up?"

"A high probability."

"Oh, goodie."

T.J. glanced at her. "This job is no different than what I was doing in the sandbox. I just don't get paid as well."

"And you don't have to kill them." Dot spotted their turn off. "On the right, dirt road. That's our way in."

"Won't the sheriff and his crew be there?"

"They'll be coordinating at the campground and using it

as their staging area."

T.J. eased his behemoth onto a dirt path just wide enough to accommodate the big-bodied truck. "Remind me again why we're not working with the sheriff's department and the forest rangers?"

"*Ama* hates the sheriff. Some of his deputies aren't the sharpest tacks in the box. And the only forest ranger I trust knows where we're at, and she knows how to watch my six." She pointed at the swing out where people parked their vehicles. "We stop here and let the dogs do their thing."

A lone vehicle sat on the opposite side of the lot. Dot noticed an odd tilt to it. "Someone's stranded."

T.J. swung his huge truck near the car and parked. "Well, ain't that just the shit. It's the same make and model Craig was seen driving." He exited the cab, leaving the door open, and circled to the front of the disabled car. "License plate matches too," he said loudly.

Dot hopped out of the truck and examined the deflated tires stripped down to the rims. "He's on foot." She surveyed the forest beyond. "With a small child who won't be able to keep up. Why would he not go back to the road?"

"Too risky. By now he's gotta figure Ashley's sounded the alarm on the kidnapping and law enforcement is converging on this area." T.J. placed his hand on the hood. "Still kinda warm."

"Even if he has an hour or so head start on us he's not going to make it far—not with the girl."

T.J. took hold of Dot's arm. "We need to be careful from this point forward. He's desperate, and he's got nothing to lose."

"So, what you're saying is, beware. I'm tracking a wounded grizzly." She winked. "Gotcha."

"Dot, I'm serious."

"Oh, believe me, I know. You're in my territory now, Danger Ranger. Don't forget, I'm not just a crack shot aviator."

Chapter Four

TITUS JETHRO ROMAN was no stranger to a horse. Growing up on a working cattle ranch in Woodward, Oklahoma, horses were the main means of traveling the wide-open grassy plains.

What he wasn't familiar with was being on a horse in the rocky terrain of the Idaho mountains. During elk season. With a slug of hunters roaming about. Though she said the gelding he was riding was an old hat, T.J. sagely decided to keep his mount close to Dot's. Ahead of them, decked out in hunter's orange, rode Dot's mother and right behind her rode Ashley, on a mule. Before them ran Angela's pack of dogs—also sporting the bright, neon orange—noses to the ground or up in the air, scenting for Ashley's daughter.

Dot had spotted the child's doll in the disabled car, and they'd broken in to retrieve it. The dogs were able to get a good hit from the scent-heavy toy and had taken off up the trail.

Angela had her own weapons slung to her saddle. T.J. carried his Glock 19 and rifle, along with his less lethal option, a shotgun that fired bean bag rounds. Dot was holstered with her 1911 Colt and a rifle, but she had also included a camo-painted compound bow and quiver full of arrows, which she had strapped to her back.

No one trusted Ashley with anything bigger than a knife, which she refused.

"Didn't peg you for a modern-day Robin Hood," he joked over the creak of saddle leather.

He noticed the upsweep of Dot's mouth.

"Bet you forgot I smoke stogies too," she said in a low voice, keeping her gaze drilled on her mother.

"A man doesn't forget a woman who handles tobacco better than he can." He jutted his chin at her bow. "Can you carry that out of season?"

"For me, it's always in season. For some predators, I prefer the arrow. I've heard of full-grown bears taking three rounds and keep on charging."

"Shit."

Dot glanced at him from under the brim of her Stetson. "Don't worry. I'm a dead shot no matter what I'm aiming at."

"Oh, believe me, I know it." He settled into the saddle, easing the ache starting in his lower back. "I know it all too well."

Back in their joint mission days—her flying his squad in and out of areas of Afghanistan—she piloted Black Hawks and, when necessary, Chinooks, which were always armed to the teeth. She typically had gunners watching their backside, but Dot was more than capable of handling her birds and manning the 7.62 machine guns at the same time.

Their path was narrowing the farther they headed into the mountains.

"We're going to have to go single file here soon," Angela

Ybarra called over her shoulder.

"*Ama*, I will take the rest of the way," Dot said.

The elder Ybarra woman halted her horse and reined around to face her daughter.

T.J. whoaed his mount and watched, a tingle of anticipation rippling through his veins. In the past, he'd taken a front row seat to Dot's bullheadedness. It was what had made her a great helicopter pilot in a war zone. She had a thread of cockiness to rival some of his fellow Rangers, but she was a woman well in control. She outranked every soldier to step on her helos, and those superiors she shuttled from base to base highly respected her. But that didn't seem the case with her mother.

"This I will not allow," Angela said.

Her tone brokered no rebuttal.

A smart man obeyed this woman, and T.J. was a smart man. He was a hellion with his own momma, but he damn well knew better when she meant business. Angela meant business.

Dot, on the other hand, was not a man and not him. She nudged her horse forward and stared down her momma.

"This one"—she pointed at Ashley, who had the good sense God gave her to look like she was in excruciating pain—"can't ride any farther. You insisted on bringing her along, you're stuck babysitting her." She jabbed her thumb back at him. "I'll take T.J., Gidget, and Zip."

The two dogs separated themselves from the pack, all of whom had laid down on their makeshift path. The wiry-haired heelers with dark tipped ears and dark-glinting eyes were the smaller of the bunch, which meant the quietest and quickest.

"Dorothy," her mother warned.

"*Amatxo*, I love you, but you need to trust me on this. Keep the pack with you, keep your eyes peeled, and keep her out of trouble."

T.J. watched in fascination as mother and daughter stared at each other. There was no shift in their features, but it seemed like they were having a telepathic conversation. Eventually, Angela threw her hands up and grumbled something T.J. didn't understand. Dot replied to her mother in the same language. This seemed to placate the elder Ybarra.

In the years he'd known Dot, not once had he ever heard her speak in this odd tongue that seemed to sound like Spanish one second and something entirely different the next. Whatever eccentricities she'd had—other than her unusually tougher-than-nails personality—were kept buttoned up under her uniform. This might be a handy trait.

Dot reined her horse to face Ashley. "Keep your mouth shut and stay with her. I'll get your daughter back."

Relief washed over the young woman's face. She didn't say a word, just nodded, her head flopping around like a bobblehead.

"Let's go," Dot called back to T.J. and took off, the two dogs sprinting ahead of her on command.

As T.J. rode past Angela, she shifted her horse to block his.

"You watch my daughter's back," she said. "She isn't fully in her right mind since the accident."

"What accident?"

Angela's eyebrows went up. "If you don't know, then

you best pay very close attention."

"Burnin' daylight," Dot said up ahead.

Angela swung her horse out of the way. T.J., with one last worried look at her, tapped his heels into his mount's sides and the horse shot forward, catching up with Dot.

"Easy on the heel. These horses were trained for knee and voice commands."

"Duly noted," T.J. said.

If she sensed what her mother had said to him, Dot kept it under her hat. Forward operation bases—or FOBs—and other army outposts were breeding grounds for scuttlebutt. Most bases were large, and one tended to stick to their assigned territory. FOBs were usually compact, where military personnel tripped over each other no matter which way they turned. But Dot didn't have time for tongue-wagging, even when her covert actions became fodder for gossip-seekers.

She would not talk about this accident her mother mentioned, especially not to him. Once this rescue mission was completed and he had Craig in custody, T.J. was pulling out the stops and putting his investigator skills to work.

He glanced over his shoulder to check on the two women left behind and saw no sign of them. Either he and Dot had ridden farther than he expected, or Angela had pulled her animals and Ashley from the trail into a secluded spot.

"You won't find them," Dot said.

"Why's that?" he asked.

"My mother is very good at finding blinds and blending in. We both were taught by my grandfather who was, among many things, an excellent hunter."

"Which is why your momma runs a successful outfitter operation."

Dot grunted. "You could say that."

Both dogs scuttled over the makeshift trail, noses seeking scent, their compact bodies in constant motion. Dot switched between watching them for indicators and doing her own searching. T.J. joined the trio in hunting instead of talking.

He figured they had gone at least two klicks, close to three. The constant winding and weaving through trees and around rocky outcroppings was deceptive. This wasn't a straight line from point A to point B. Their path was also going up. The higher they climbed, the thinner the air.

Craig Cooper was a lowlander. Along with his substance abuse, he smoked, like a chimney. His lungs and body had to be screaming in agony. From the looks of things back at the car, he hadn't brought any provisions for himself or his daughter. The trifecta was about to be his undoing.

"Drink," Dot said out of the blue.

T.J. shot her a reproachful look. "You act like I've never done something like this."

"You're out of practice." She chugged from her water canteen, then lowered it with a smack of her lips. "I haven't seen you drink once since we headed out."

"Yes, Flygirl," he remarked, and downed his own bellyful of electrolyte-laced water.

One of the heelers dropped to the ground, its body pointed to the right. The other dog followed suit. Dot reined in her horse, and T.J.'s stopped before he could muster the command in his head. He stashed his canteen.

Dot was looking uphill. "There's a path through the rocks." She twisted around. "We go on foot from here."

They dismounted and found a place to secure the horses. Dot activated a device attached to the saddles and then the one strapped across her torso. She dug into her backpack and held out one exactly like hers to him.

"GPS tracker. That way *Ama* can locate the horses or us if something happens."

He attached the blinking electronic to his body where it was least likely to get smashed or trashed. "Think of everything, don't you?"

"Army taught me a few tricks, but the forest service taught me more."

"You spend a lot of time with the forest service, huh?"

She called the dogs. "I worked for them." She headed up the path.

T.J. halted mid-step and gaped at her back. Worked for them. As in past tense. No longer. While his brain fit together the tiny pieces of the present-day puzzle that was Dot, he caught up with her.

"If he's aware, which I highly doubt," she said as they began to climb, "there's more horseback and hiking trails to the southeast. Directly east of here is another forest road."

"He's not that astute. It'll be sheer stupid luck on his part if he runs across any of those," T.J. answered.

Dot hunched forward into her climb. "Then we don't let him."

Neither spoke as they hiked upward as fast as possible. The dogs kept working, sniffing out the path taken by their target and his daughter. T.J. switched back and forth from keeping an eye on where he stepped to watching Dot's backside.

They reached a level area and paused. One of the heelers went stock-still, head pointed down and staring at something. Dot, drinking from her canteen again, moved over to the dog. T.J. remained in his spot, huffing and drinking his own water. Damn, he was not in shape for this.

"Good girl, Gidget." Dot praised the dog as she picked up a swatch of cloth.

"What is it?" he asked.

Dot held it aloft. "A piece of a shirt." She sniffed it and wrinkled her nose. "Male. An unwashed male at that."

He joined her and took the torn fabric. "How close you think we are?"

"Close," she said, replacing her water canteen with her Colt 1911.

A faint sound, like the cry of a small child, reached them. T.J. dropped the cloth and retrieved his rifle. The male heeler, Zip, let out a low growl.

Dot hissed a command in that weird language of hers, and the dogs circled around, bookending her legs. She gave them another verbal command as she stepped forward, raising her sidearm.

"I'd rather you not lead," T.J. said quietly, following her.

"Keep your male sensibilities in check, Ranger. You'll get your chance," she said over her shoulder.

The once small or medium-sized rocks increased in number and mass. He and Dot maneuvered through and over a field of boulders, some as large as a small cabin. Intermittently, between the stony outcroppings, bold trees had grown, casting shade over the ground. Far above them, a bird of prey screeched a call to the world below.

The bird's call brought on another fit of crying, closer this time.

"Shut up!" came the overly agitated answer.

T.J.'s heart hammered against his ribs. The customary buzz filled his head as his brain and body went into apprehension mode.

Dot pointed at a grouping of trees and boulders. T.J. tapped her right shoulder and moved to the other side of the cluster.

Once he rounded these boulders, it was game on. Whether willingly or in restraints, Craig Cooper was coming down this mountain. He would not escape T.J. again.

Chapter Five

D OT GAVE THE dogs a hand command to lie down and stay. They obeyed immediately. With her canines out of harm's way, she took position on the opposite side of T.J. as he headed toward the towering boulder.

The girl's crying intensified, and Craig's verbal abuse ramped up. Dot drowned out his words, or the minute she rounded the rocks she would shoot him on principle. Nothing made her blood boil more than hearing a human being abusing another, especially if the abused were a child. It certainly lent credence to Ashley's testimony of abuse at the hands of this douchebag.

Dot and T.J. reached the boulder at the same time. He gave her a hand signal she'd seen all of the Spec Ops guys use over the years and gathered his meaning. Hold, then go, on … he began counting down with his fingers. He made a fist for zero, and they both moved.

T.J. came around the rock, bellowing commands like he was kicking down insurgents' doors.

As Dot stepped into view, her sidearm leveled chest height, she felt the warm sensation of adrenaline pump through her veins. It was a familiar feeling. A welcomed one. Like an old friend returning after years of estrangement.

Then she saw the small, terrified girl wrapped in Craig's arm, a small pistol pointed at her head, and all that warmth fled replaced by cold fury.

The men were screaming obscenities and demands back and forth: Craig threatening to kill the child if T.J. and Dot didn't leave; T.J. refusing to leave and demanding Craig give it up.

A voice from the past penetrated the bellowing voices: *Aitona* whispering to her his old adage when handling a volatile situation. *When in doubt, sort it out.*

Even in the most adrenaline-charged moments, Samo Ybarra was always there. His aged voice, though ghostly, cut through the fog of anger, tamped down the chaos in her head, and settled her vibrating nerves. Dot holstered her 1911 and did the unthinkable—she stepped between two armed men.

"Craig. Can I call you Craig?"

His beady eyes darted from her to T.J. "Who are you?"

"Someone Ashley found to help her save her daughter. I'm not here for any other reason."

Craig spat, his actions making Bethany cry out. "That bitch! She's the reason they want to lock me up. I should have never trusted her."

Dot didn't flinch. She didn't dare look at T.J. She had to keep Craig's focus completely on her.

"I get that Ashley is the enemy here, but why take Bethany? She's just a child."

Craig made an error in looking down at the girl, which took his eyes off T.J. Dot sensed T.J. shifting, and she thrust her arm out to stop him. Her actions startled Craig.

"Stay back!" His arm slipped up around Bethany's throat and choked off the girl's next cry. He took a step back, dragging the poor child by her neck. "I mean it!"

"Craig," Dot barked.

Her command stopped him, and he gaped at her.

"You're hurting Bethany."

Without taking his eyes off Dot and T.J., he lowered his arm from Bethany's throat and a new sound escaped the terrified girl.

"Shut up!" he screamed at her.

Bethany clamped her mouth shut. Tears and snot covered her tiny face.

"Craig, I need you to listen to me," Dot said in a calm voice. "Bethany is not the enemy. There's no need to hold her hostage."

He laughed, the sound akin to someone who'd lost their sanity. "You don't get it. None of you get it."

"What don't we get?" Dot tried.

He aimed the pistol at Dot. "If I don't take her, they will."

His statement, said with such finality, hung in the air between them. Dot wanted to ask who *they* were, but she was certain Craig would either never tell or he couldn't fully identify the *they* himself.

"Craig, I can protect Bethany," Dot said. She held out a hand toward him. "Let me take your daughter, and I'll protect her."

He blinked. His gun trembled. He started to shake his head, then stopped.

Bethany held still, her gaze latched onto Dot.

"Craig, if you go with T.J., he'll help you sort out whatever is going on. I'll take care of Bethany," Dot assured.

Craig lowered the pistol a fraction. "I can't go back. There's nothing to sort out."

"Why?" T.J.'s deep voice rumbled.

"Man, you're an idiot," Craig snapped. "They won't let me live. Not after what I did."

"We can make sure that doesn't happen," T.J. tried.

"You can't," Craig shot back. "None of you can. I need to do this on my own."

"Going on the run with a child is harder than you think," Dot insisted. "Let me take her."

"She's right," T.J. added. "Let's you and I work something out. But first you need to let Bethany go."

"There's nothing to work out," Craig said, his voice losing its force. "I'm a dead man."

"Not if I have anything to say about it," T.J. replied.

"I don't know," Craig whined, shaking his head.

"Craig, please," Dot said. "Let me have Bethany. She doesn't need to be scared any more than she's already."

He dropped the gun to his side and stared down at his daughter, who'd never once stopped watching Dot. "You'll protect her?" he asked.

"With everything I have," Dot vowed.

A blink of an eye, then he released Bethany, pushing her toward Dot. The girl ran to her, and Dot swung her up in her arms. Bethany wrapped her legs and arms around Dot's torso like a spider monkey. T.J. moved to her right side but went no farther.

"Craig, set your gun on the ground and come toward

me," he said. "We'll discuss what to do next."

Defeated, Craig lowered his body, the gun out in front of him, and a crack rent the air. He jerked, then dropped to his knees and toppled over backward. T.J. shouted and took two steps toward the fallen man.

Movement from uphill caught Dot's attention. "T.J., stop," she barked.

Miraculously, he did.

With the child still clinging to her, Dot managed to draw her weapon and level it on the man lingering on the fringes of a stand of trees.

"Hold on there. I'm one of the good guys."

Emerging from the shadows cast by the trees came one of Ford's deputies. Specifically, the one who had shot eye daggers at Dot when she had sent them on their way.

"You didn't have to kill him!" T.J. shouted.

"He was reaching for a weapon at his back," the deputy drawled as he moved quickly toward the downed man, his rifle pointed at an unmoving Craig.

"He was doing no such thing," T.J. countered. "He was surrendering."

Dot, unwilling to put herself and the child at risk, kept a steady bead on the man.

The deputy reached Craig and kicked away the discarded pistol. "You two yahoos are too damn trusting." Without missing a beat, he set aside his weapon and knelt, then flipped Craig onto his stomach.

Dot tried to document his movements, but he was too quick. Seemingly out of nowhere, he produced another pistol from Craig's body.

"Told you." The deputy lofted the pistol, where it dangled from his finger by the trigger guard.

Before Dot could stop him, T.J. reholstered his sidearm and rushed the kneeling deputy.

Dot's frazzled brain went into combat mode. She returned her gun to its holster, and with her arm tight around the girl, hauled ass. She wasn't able to stop the first punch to the deputy's face, but she was able to glide between T.J. and the prone man before T.J. could straddle him and rain down hell.

"Roman!" Dot yelled, using her captain's voice, the one that always put insubordinate enlisted and underling officers on notice.

T.J. snapped to attention and backed off. His dark eyes glinted fire and brimstone, but he kept his mouth clamped shut. He glanced at the girl, whose head was buried deep into Dot's neck, and some of the fury drained from his face.

"I'll have you arrested…" the deputy was saying as he scrambled up.

Dot spun, cutting off his words. "Shut your fucking mouth."

"Whoa! Hold on here," a voice shouted from the direction the deputy had come.

Sheriff Ford and two other men emerged. One of the men wore the vest and adornments of a volunteer search and rescue team member. The other was decked out in tactical clothing covered by a blue government-issued jacket. Dot couldn't make out the shield on the left side, and the man made sure to not turn and reveal whatever alphabet agency name was printed across the back.

"Dorothy, we don't need a standoff here," Ford said.

"Fuck you, Ford. Your shithead deputy killed a man that was surrendering to the recovery agent."

"That's bullshit. He was reaching for a gun," the deputy snapped.

"You pulled that fucking gun out of your ass and planted it on him," T.J. snarled. "This dipshit didn't have two brain cells enough to spark that kind of preparedness."

"Fuck you!"

"Enough!" Ford yelled.

The child sobbed against Dot. Bethany's reaction seemed to bring tempers to a simmer.

Ford sighed. "Is that the kidnapped girl?"

Dot hugged the girl tighter. "It is."

Ford waved the search-and-rescue guy over. "We'll take her and get her back…"

"Over my dead body," Dot interrupted, her voice dropping to a lethal tone. "You FUBARed this enough. I'm taking her back to her mother. None of you will touch her."

"Now, Dorothy…" Ford started.

"Don't." She glared at Ford, daring him to try to ply his slick political bullshit. When he remained silent, she tilted up her chin. "T.J., we're going."

"Yes, ma'am," he growled and about-faced.

"You can't go. We need to get your statements and report back that the girl is safe," Ford stated.

"We'll do no such thing," Dot said. "If you make any attempt to claim contempt or whatever fucking nonsense you come up with, I'll sic my lawyer on you."

Ford shifted uneasily. The entirety of Pyrenees County

knew better than to cross swords with the Ybarras's legal representation.

"Why don't ya'll get your stories straight for the press. I'll have my lawyer contact you when we're ready to give our statements." Dot turned and walked away. "Gidget! Zip! *Orpoa!*"

The dogs emerged out of nowhere and joined her as she bypassed the large boulder.

"This ain't over, Ybarra!" Ford yelled.

Chapter Six

ASHLEY CRADLED HER daughter close the whole ride down the mountain and back to the trailer.

T.J. snarled the entire ride but kept the grumbling to himself. Dot got the gist: he'd lost the bond, and his defendant was dead. He was out both his time and major expenses trying to capture this guy.

After she heard about Ford and his deputy's disastrous intervention, Angela rode straight in the saddle the entire journey down. She would keep her comments tucked away, saving them for later when it was just her and her daughter. Dot couldn't disagree with *Ama* any longer on the lack of effective policing going on in Pyrenees County.

Back at the ranch, T.J. helped with the horses and mule. Once the animals were in their pasture and munching away on some grain, he pulled Dot aside.

"I don't like how any of that went down," he said in his rumbling Okie drawl.

"Neither do I." Dot crossed her arms and leaned into the barn doorway, watching the horses eat and flick at the flies. "Whatever that was, it's far from over."

"Agreed. Ashley and the girl aren't safe."

Dot looked up at him. "How so?"

He pushed up the brim of his hat. "Call it a gut feeling. Can they stay here with you and your ma? Until I can sort some things out."

"I don't know. That's really up to Ashley and *Ama*."

"I'd feel a whole lot better knowing they were under your supervision. I need to get back to Boise for a meetup, or I'd find a safehouse for them."

"I'll handle it." Dot rubbed the back of her neck, the day's tension pulling on the recovered muscles. "Did you catch who the blue jacket was with?"

"Couldn't make out the shield."

"Think he was a marshal? It'd make sense with a wanted fugitive."

T.J. shook his head. "I know all the marshals in Idaho. He ain't one of them. Coulda been FBI, since the kid was kidnapped."

Dot shrugged. "Maybe." She kept her personal thoughts tightly wrapped up. No sense in leading T.J. astray.

"Sorry I had to bring all this crap to your front door. You got a real nice spread here."

She smiled. "It's all *Ama*'s doing. I spent the better part of my adulthood flying guys like you into kill zones." She lightly punched his bicep. "Nothing to be sorry about. Ashley beat you to the punch with that burning pile of dog shit. Kinda livened things up around here."

They stared at each other. After a moment, T.J. shifted closer to her.

"It was still good seeing you again."

"Yeah, same here."

She had a split second to react when he bent forward,

cupped the back of her neck, and claimed her lips. After he pulled back, Dot scowled at him.

T.J. grinned. "Just as good as I remembered." He gave her a wink as he released her, then sauntered back through the barn and out the front.

Dot banged the back of her head against the wood frame and grimaced. Damn fool had to wake her long-neglected needs and walk away. If *Ama* saw him do it, there was going to be a major crap show followed up with a hell of a lot of questions.

The roar of his truck engine brought Dot out of the stupor, and she wandered through the barn and to the doorway in time to see T.J.'s heavy-duty leave the ranch yard and head out toward the road.

Dot spotted Angela standing on the porch, watching the truck leave. Ashley and her daughter were nowhere in sight. Dot strode toward the porch.

"Our guests are cleaning up," Angela said by way of greeting.

Maybe she hadn't seen T.J. kiss Dot. Good. No unnecessary conversations.

"I found some things of mine that will fit Ashley," Angela continued.

"What about the girl? We don't have kid clothes around here."

Her mother smiled. "I still have some of your old things tucked away."

"*Amatxo*, those old things? Those are so outdated."

"If you'd get out and about, you'd be surprised what kids are wearing these days." She gripped Dot's arm. "After we got back, I called Cousin Vivian. She'll be handling any legal details that will arise from this."

Their cousin from Angela's mother's side lived in Boise and ran a thriving law practice.

"I don't think we need to worry about that, but it's still a good idea." Dot crossed her forearms on the porch railing, bent over, and leaned into her arms. She scanned the horizon, looking for what she didn't know. "We need to keep the girl and her mother here for now."

"Your friend Mr. Roman asks this of us?"

"He does."

The sun slipped behind the mountain. Shadows danced across the wide valley, engulfing the ranch in their callous embrace. From the mountain came the ringing call of a bull elk. Tonight, at least, the big bastard would get lucky a time or two. No hunters to take him out before he increased his gene pool.

"What does your instinct tell you, *alaba*?" Angela asked.

"Something is coming. Something bad. We need to prepare."

LATER THAT NIGHT, after eating a hearty meal Angela had pulled together, Dot sat by the fireplace soaking up the heat and smoking a fresh cigar. Her mother had long gone to bed, so she wouldn't mind. Dot considered pouring a glass of red wine her mother kept tucked away for special occasions but settled on just smoking. She hadn't drunk a drop of hard liquor after the accident and wasn't up to restarting the habit. A beer now and then was fine, but it was the whiskey and bourbon she had to steer clear of.

The shuffle of feet against the worn wood flooring made her look over. Ashley hesitated next to the well-loved rocker sitting opposite Dot in the leather armchair.

"May I join you?" Ashley asked.

Dot gestured at the rocker with her cigar hand.

Ashley glanced at the fireplace then sat, tugging the edges of the old cardigan tight to her body. She set the chair in motion and swayed back and forth.

"I didn't thank you for getting Bethany back," Ashley said gently.

Never comfortable being complimented or thanked for doing a job, Dot just grunted, then drew on the cigar.

"You smoke cigars?" the young woman asked incredulously.

"Lots of women smoke them," Dot said, smoke tendrils escaping her mouth.

She peered at the end of the cigar, then knocked the ash into the waiting tray at her elbow. Ashley averted her gaze, staring at the crackling fire instead.

After a moment's peace, she spoke softly. "Thank you."

Dot shrugged it off. "Your girl sleeping?"

"For now. I don't know if she'll have nightmares." Ashley swayed harder. "I don't know what I'll do if she does. Or if I do." Her voice dipped into a whisper.

Having carried her load of nightmares past and present, Dot could help them. But she wasn't sure how close she wanted to get to the two. Which brought up the perfect opening.

"Where you from?"

Ashley tore her gaze from the fire and focused on Dot. "Rexburg."

"Got any family there?"

"None that would claim me." She fiddled with the edges of the cardigan. "It's just me and Bethany. I came here a few years ago to get away from Craig. Thought I was far enough away from Boise he wouldn't bother to look for me." She sniffed and pulled a tissue from a pocket.

"What have you been doing the last two years?"

"Working two jobs just to make ends meet. Bethany started school, so that helps, but I still can't pinch two pennies."

"Doing what?"

"Waitressing mostly." Ashley dabbed her nose. "I had a rare day off and decided to take her on a hike. She's been begging me to do it all summer and I just couldn't find the time. Should've just stayed home."

"He would've gotten to you one way or another," Dot said, knocking more ash from the cigar's end. "At least out here you found me."

"Guess you're right."

Dot let Ashley stew while she smoked her cigar and tried to figure out how to broach the subject she and Angela had agreed upon.

"What was he into?" she asked after a bit.

"All kinds of things, but drugs mostly."

"You do any of those drugs?"

"No. Never. I might be naïve, but I'm not that desperate."

Dot sensed the younger woman's scrutiny as she examined the end of her cigar and considered how much she had left to enjoy.

"Tomorrow I'll take Bethany home. Let you and your momma get back to your lives."

"Not an option. You and your daughter will stay here for the time being."

Ashley opened her mouth, probably to protest, but Dot kept right on rolling.

"My mother could use the help around the house. If you're confident enough, I might let you help with the choring. We'll figure out a way to get your girl to school, but I'd advise giving it a week before we attempt that." Dot jabbed the glowing cigar at the front door. "We've got a bunkhouse next to the barn you can stay in for now."

"What about my jobs? I can't just stay here."

"You're fucked two ways from Sunday if you leave here. What transpired with your ex didn't sit well with me or T.J. Whatever Craig was into and whatever was about to send him to prison made someone antsy." Dot looked squarely at Ashley. "If they so much as get an itch to push this further, they won't hesitate to do worse than kidnap your daughter."

Even with the weak light from the fireplace, Dot could see Ashley's features turn ghost white.

"I had nothing to do with him for the last two years."

"I doubt they'd care."

"How do you expect to keep me and Bethany safe? I don't even know if I can trust you."

Dot took a long pull on the cigar, let it sit in her mouth, then exhaled. "No, you don't. But right now, I'm all the options you've got."

Chapter Seven

A T PRECISELY TWELVE thirty, the back door locks rattled. Sloane Cross dragged her exhausted self from a pile of paperwork and watched through sore eyes as an imposing man entered.

"You're here late," T.J. said as he shut the door with SHADOW FORCE SOLUTIONS painted on the beveled glass and reengaged the locks.

Sloane rocked back in her chair and cradled her head with locked fingers. "Waiting on you to return."

T.J. hung his hat on the coat rack and wandered to the fridge they kept in their small office. "Just about didn't make it home." He yanked the door open and reached inside.

"That bad, huh?"

"That bad," he parroted, and pulled out a dark brown glass bottle.

Yeah, it was bad if he was breaking his vow to not drink after working a bounty.

Sloane wrenched her body forward, placing her hands on top of the paper pile. "The intel was solid."

"Didn't account for the sheriff and an idiot for a deputy." He popped the top under the bottle opener, the metal cap clanging inside the small metal bucket underneath.

"We're out the bond."

"Whaddya mean we're out the bond?"

"Craig is dead. Shot and killed by one trigger-happy deputy. The shithead about shot me." T.J. guzzled down a good sum of beer. When he pulled the bottle away, a few drops escaped and beaded on his beard. Those droplets glinted in the lamp light. "We're not Bass Reeves, and this ain't the Old West. No bringing 'em in dead or alive."

Sloane sighed, a snarl rolling out toward the end of it. This was not how she wanted her night to end. It was already a burning bag of dogshit after her daylong stakeout of an empty house. She'd been paid to hand over a subpoena to a deadbeat refusing to pay her portion of child support. The last known address was the house Sloane had spent the better part of a beautiful day watching. Then a nosy neighbor decided to take it upon herself to harass Sloane, and she learned that place had been abandoned weeks prior.

"Oh, I ain't done." T.J. slumped in the only chair in the office. He didn't keep a desk here, preferring to use his vehicles as his mobile office or let Sloane handle it.

"How could there possibly be more?"

"Remember that dude who came snooping around here a month back? Said he was looking for someone. Claimed he was with the marshal's office."

"Vaguely. If I recall right, you were the one who mostly talked with him," Sloane said.

"He was there. Tried to hang back, probably so I wouldn't recognize him, but I did. He was all decked out in one of those government-issued blue jackets, like the ones those alphabet organizations like to wear."

"Shit," Sloane spat out. "Why would the not-a-marshal be there in a situation with Craig? I thought you said he was looking for some girl."

"I did, and I have no clue why he was there. I don't think he expected me to be there, either."

"Before he was killed, did Craig talk?"

T.J. tipped the neck of the beer bottle at her. "Some. Still bothers me he ran and kidnapped his kid in the process."

"Hold up there. What kid?"

"Craig's daughter. His supposed cosigner—the ex, Ashley—had moved there a few years back, and he found them."

Sloane tried to wrap her head around this. "He was going away for involuntary homicide, and he decides he needs to skip bail and kidnap his daughter?"

T.J. took another swallow of his beer. "Boggles the mind, don't it?"

It did. Just like it had when she got the call from Craig's bail bondsman about him running. It was a bondsman she and T.J. occasionally worked with but not exclusively, due to his inability to maintain good business practices. But a paycheck was a paycheck. He was able to give them the gist of the situation, enough for Sloane to snoop around with and get more information, yet things weren't adding up. Craig was a sleaze, as evidenced from the mile-long rap sheet of drug charges, until he sold someone the wrong stuff and caused their death. This caused him to wise up, get his act together. Made all his court dates right up until his sentencing date, then he rabbitted.

"Something spooked him," T.J. said out of the blue.

"Obviously, if he ran."

"It was more than that. It's what he babbled on about when we caught up with him. Some gibberish about how he needed to protect the girl. If he didn't take her, *they* would."

It didn't pass Sloane's notice that T.J. mentioned *we*, but she stayed mum. "So, we got our not-a-marshal showing up. A bail-jumper kidnapping a kid to avoid prison? I got the raw deal on serving a subpoena—not. And while you were running that errand and I was getting swindled, I took some interesting phone calls today. Something's going on."

"What kind of interesting phone calls?"

Sloane explained the two separate calls. T.J. perked up at the mention of the man with serious cash looking for his daughter.

"We can decide what we're doing later," Sloane told him before he launched into a barrage of questions. "Where's Craig's ex and daughter?"

"Safe, for now," T.J. said. "Ran into an old friend up in the mountains, and she helped me out. She's the reason the girl ain't dead and I didn't get shot."

"Wait a minute. You know someone besides me in Idaho? And she's an old friend? How do I not know about this?"

"Because I'm a closed book. Knew her from my Ranger days. She used to fly the helicopters I rode."

Sloane snorted. "Lemme guess, between missions, the two of you were doing the horizontal mambo. On the sly."

T.J.'s eyes lit up and one corner of his mouth began to lift. He downed the rest of his beer.

Despite what people thought, she and T.J. were strictly business partners. The day they met, both of them were on the same trail of a female bond jumper with a bench warrant.

Instead of getting into a pissing match, they decided to team up and split the bond. After a wrestling match with the naked bond jumper in a pile of the grossest smelling trash, Sloane brought her in. To this day, Sloane still gagged every time she recalled that encounter.

"Who the hell is she?" Sloane asked.

"Dot Ybarra."

She startled. "No way."

He eyed her, setting his bottle down on the small magazine stand strategically placed beside the chair. "Why does it sound like you know her?"

"Because she and I grew up together, ya know, back in the Stone Age."

He grunted. "Small fucking world."

"So, she flew helicopters?"

"Damn good at it too. I was always a little less stressed about a mission when I heard she was taking us in and pulling us out." He crossed one boot over a knee. "Sounds like she kept it up with the forest service when she got out of the army. But her momma said something about an accident."

Sloane dragged her sleeping laptop closer. "Bet I can find out what that was."

Along with her bail bonds services, Sloane was a licensed PI. So was T.J., but he let her do the heavy lifting along those lines. He was more the muscle and tactician for bringing in the bail jumpers.

She was able to pull up the accident report quickly. She let out a whistle and rocked back in her chair.

"Damn. Dot's lucky to be alive."

T.J. kicked his boot to the floor and leaned forward, bracing his elbows on his knees. "What's the intel?"

"Last fall, she had to ground her chopper when the water bucket was blown into trees and tangled. She was able to control the crash, which is a miracle, because this has happened before, and the pilot died. She was in the hospital for weeks."

T.J. tapped the side of his head. "I think it screwed with her mentally. She avoided any talk of flying."

"Yet, she helped you out?"

"Glad she did. I'm a good tracker, but nothing like her. The woman is a damn genius." T.J. chuckled. "I'm giving her too much credit. The dogs did most of the work."

While he rambled, Sloane was surfing the web and found the Ybarra outfitters business webpage. By the look and feel of the site the business was doing well, or Dot's mother was able to fake it 'til she made it. Sloane reached up and rubbed the scar running out from the corner of her eye and across to her hairline. It was an old scar, dating back to her childhood of running wild in the foothills of the Payette National Forest with a certain dusky-haired girl who knew no restraint.

Dot Ybarra had fascinated Sloane, even back when Dot was bloodying the noses of ill-mannered boys on the school playground. Sloane, a book nerd from the day she could hold one in her hands, was the usual target of kids who were ignorant bullies or intimidated followers looking to one up someone else. Dot hadn't started school with the rest of the class until the second grade. She, like many of the kids raised on the far-off ranches, started out homeschooled. When

Angela Ybarra got a job in town, she decided a public education was needed for her wild child.

Sloane and Dot's friendship was cemented the second day of school when Dot laid out Tommy McGee with a right hook. Despite Sloane's testimony, the principal wanted to make an example out of Dot and suspended her for a week. Little girls were supposed to behave like ladies and not heathens. Two weeks later, Angela Ybarra's campaign to remove the principal succeeded.

The rest of their school years, no one crossed the Ybarra women. Woe to those who tried.

Sloane stared at T.J. as he wrapped up his story she'd heard not a word of. He needed a partner. Someone who was as capable of him in the physical aspects of this job. Sloane was not that person. He'd lamented off and on about maybe finding another recovery agent to bring into the fold, but he was so damn picky about who he worked with they never pursued it.

Maybe it was time.

"By your silence, I take it you're mulling over something," T.J. broke into her musings.

"I am." Sloane closed out the web browser and pushed the laptop aside. "Leaving the ex and her kid with the Ybarras was a good idea." She intertwined her fingers and placed her clasped hands on the top of her paperwork. "We've both said we need one more person to help out with the business."

"We have, but I told you I'm not impressed with anyone out there."

Sloane smiled. "How do you feel about bringing Dot in?"

T.J.'s gaze narrowed. "She's not trained."

"Won't take her long."

"She's too far away from Boise."

"I bet there's some office space up in Cascade or McCall we could find cheaper."

"She's got that business with her momma."

"Side income. We all need it."

"You've got an answer for every argument I can make," T.J. groused.

"They're not arguments, they're excuses," Sloane countered.

"Fine. I'm not keen on working with someone I've done up against the barracks wall."

Sloane laughed. "Hell, T.J., you've been a eunuch since I met you. Now, I think I know why."

He got up from the chair. "Not funny."

"Are you done making excuses?" Sloane asked his backside.

He threw his hand up in the air. "Do what you want. You always do." He turned back to point a finger at her. "Don't say I didn't warn you when Dot shoots you down. She didn't appear to be in a big hurry to leave the ranch."

"Give me more credit than that."

He shook his head at her, like she was a hopeless cause. Then again, she usually was.

Chapter Eight

FROM HER PERCH on the front porch, Dot savored her hot mug of joe and watched the sky lighten as dawn broke. The cool mountain air nipped at her nose and chilled her cheeks.

This was the time of the day she loved the most. When the world hovered on the brink of full awareness before it fully came awake. A stillness like holding one's breath, waiting for the burst of color when the sun topped the mountains.

Her morning meditation was interrupted as *Ama* emerged from the house with a squeak of door hinges. Angela's moccasins muffled her steps as she took a seat in the second wood-slatted chair and sipped from her own mug of coffee.

Mother and daughter sat in comfortable silence, watching the sun creep upward. When rays shot up from behind the jagged peaks, Angela spoke.

"You didn't sleep."

Dot nestled her mug between her hands. "It happens."

"Nightmares?"

She took a moment to answer her mother. "Not this time." And she wasn't whitewashing the truth.

After Afghanistan and after discharging from the army, insomnia had become a consistent visitor in Dot's life. It had taken up permanent residency while she recovered from the chopper accident. If it got really bad, she found relief smoking a joint or two, depending on the severity. *Ama* hated the stench of marijuana, and Dot usually had to take it outside.

Last night wasn't about the pain or the flashbacks. It had been the complete opposite. It was a night where Dot needed to clear her head and plot.

"I heard Ashley speaking with you last night," Angela said. "Did she agree to the terms?"

"She did. Probably scared her into the deal, but self-preservation is a powerful motivator." Dot lifted her mug to her lips. "So is that little girl."

"I'll teach her. What about school for Bethany?"

"Give it a week. I want to get everyone settled before we make any long-term decisions."

They resumed their morning vigil, enjoying their strong black coffee from a veteran-owned company. A fellow pilot had told Dot about the business and convinced her to buy in. She became a minor shareholder and major consumer and hadn't regretted her decision. It took some convincing to get Angela to switch from her usual brand, but she, too, enjoyed the brew.

From their sheds, barns, and pastures, the livestock began to stir. Soon they'd be singing for their breakfast.

"Should we get her started now?" Dot asked.

"Naw, let her sleep. Yesterday was harrowing for her and the girl. Lessons can start later." Angela stood and started for the door. "I'll get breakfast going."

"I'm going to head into Euskadi after choring. Get more supplies now that we've got two more mouths to feed."

Her mother looked down at her. "You haven't gone to town in months."

Dot lifted her gaze and met her mother's worried look. "I'll be fine."

"That's what you said the last time you went in and then came home looking like you'd gone ten rounds with a grizzly bear."

Dot tilted her head back and forth. "I guess, in a way, beating the shit out of Willy Donnel for smacking around his wife could constitute as a wrestling match with a grizzly."

"Dorothy, I'm serious."

"*Ama*, so am I." Dot rose from her chair. "I'll behave." She placed her empty mug in her mother's hands. "I'll get to the chores."

A FEW OF the old-timers paused in their daily gossip when the bell above the door jangled announcing Dot's entry to Hargrave's Diner. Those who'd known Dot since she was old enough to tag along with Samo gave her a hearty hail of *hi-o*. Dot returned their greetings as she slid onto a stool along the counter.

The proprietor, wearing a neon blue T-shirt, left her station at the register, grabbed a pot from the industrial-sized Bunn coffeemaker, and sashayed over to Dot.

"Black as sin?" Millie Hargrave asked as she flipped over

an ancient brown-rimmed and cream-colored mug.

"You know me too well," Dot said as Millie poured the dark brew.

Angela Ybarra had counted Millie as her one and only close friend. The two were thick as thieves, and just as devious. Dot had long suspected Millie was the sole person, other than Angela herself, who knew the identity of Dot's father. But just like Angela, there was no cracking that vault and learning the secret.

"Heard you had some shenanigans up your way yesterday." Millie set the pot down and rested her crossed arms on the counter to lean closer to Dot.

"Shenanigans is about how I'd describe it," Dot said, then tested the coffee. Fresh and dark, just how she liked it. "What's the scuttlebutt around town?"

"From some unreliable sources, the word is that dumbass new deputy saved the day."

"Unreliable, and dumbass about sums it up. Who is he?"

Millie dipped her red bandana-wrapped head closer. "You saying you were the woman they claim interfered with official *police* business?" The way she said police made it sound salacious.

"I can neither confirm nor deny those allegations. The new deputy?" Dot coaxed.

Millie swayed her ample hind end as she considered Dot. Slyness glinted in her world-weary eyes. She rocked forward, her posture beckoning Dot to lean in.

"His name is Cory Wall, from somewhere down south."

"Down south as in southeastern US or southwestern?"

"Utah or New Mexico. No one can get a bead on which

one it is—his story changes every five minutes." Millie tsked. "Anyway, Ford hired him on more than a year ago. The longtime guys weren't happy about it, but ain't a one of them quit, either."

"Is Matlock still a deputy?"

Matlock was Millie's one and only son, born smack dab in the middle of two sisters. He'd fancied himself a bronc rider at one time but gave up on the idea when the law enforcement bug bit him. Dot grew up with Matlock and liked him. Dragged him out on a few hunts when they were teenagers and had lost her virginity to him. Or had he lost his virginity to her?

"He is. And he's none too happy with some of the things going on. 'Course, he don't tell me jack squat. Guess he's afraid I'll spread the manure."

Dot chuckled. "I thought that was what diner owners did when they weren't slinging hash."

Millie swatted Dot's arm. "Shut your mouth, girl."

The bell jangled.

"You should go see Matlock before you head back to the ranch." Since they'd been knee-high, Millie had been conspiring to get Matlock and Dot together. It hadn't worked out exactly as Millie wanted, but then nothing much did these days. "He's been placed on permanent desk duty," Millie said in a hushed voice.

Dot frowned. In her experience, if one was shunted behind a desk, they either had been injured on the job and were recouping or they'd gotten themselves into a heap of shit.

Millie pushed off the counter. "You need to eat, put

some meat on those bones."

"*Ama* already stuffed me until I was ready to pop. Just keep the coffee coming."

Dot sensed the weighty presence at her back. She didn't have to look over her shoulder to know who stood there.

Millie nodded. "Sheriff." She snagged up the pot and hauled it back to the burner.

Ford settled on the stool to Dot's right. "Dorothy, I'm a bit shocked to see you alone in town today."

"Ford," she acknowledged and sipped her coffee.

She didn't grace him with a look. He had invaded her personal space, and he was getting a full dose of the cold shoulder. Angela Ybarra's daughter was cut from the same cloth.

"How are the child and mother?" he asked.

Dot took another sip of coffee.

"I need to get the mother's statement. And the girl's if she's willing," Ford continued, unabashed.

She kept on sipping.

"Dorothy, we really need to talk about what happened yesterday."

The mug came down with a hard clack against the counter. Some of the hot liquid splashed over the rim and hit her hand. She disregarded the sting, instead pinning Ford with a hard stare.

"Do you see my lawyer present?"

"Now see here..." Ford started.

"There will be no seeing here. There will be no more questions. In fact, until my lawyer has contacted you, there will be no discussions or conversations of any kind, including with the mother and the child."

Red edged along the fleshy jowls on Ford's face, and the corner of his left eye twitched. For a sixty-odd-year-old man, Richard T. Ford was still hale and fit, but age was creeping in, along with something else. Something that flashed in his eyes as he glared at Dot.

The little beast she kept chained up within grabbed up its pitchfork and Dot gave into the prodding. She bent toward Ford, her actions making his eyes widen, and he tipped back.

"Who's the alphabet work for? Why is he here?"

The red faded to pink, and the eye twitch stopped. Ford's nose flared, giving Dot a clear view of the too-long hairs. "I don't know what you're talking about," he growled.

Satisfied she'd gotten to him, Dot stood. "I've got errands to run." She pulled out her wallet and withdrew a five-dollar bill, then tossed it on the counter beside the mug. "Thanks for the coffee, Millie. Keep the change."

"Any time, sug."

Ford's steely voice joined the jingling bell. "This ain't over, Dorothy Ybarra."

Because she could, and because she damn well felt like it, she gave him the two-bird salute behind her head. The glass door sucked close in her wake.

Giving her Stetson a quick adjustment, she headed for the truck. With Ford here at Millie's and the possibility of Matlock being chained to a desk, Dot wondered what her chances of picking her old friend's brain would be. She reached for the door handle, then stopped as a door to the bed and breakfast across the street opened.

Dot propped herself against the truck and watched a man emerge from the interior. He paused in the doorway to look back and acted as if he spoke to someone inside. He gave a nod, then continued onto the sidewalk. Dot lowered the brim of her hat and tracked his progress down the block to an older model dark sedan. She waited for him to drive out onto the street, where he whipped a U-turn and then drove past her. Once he turned left at the next intersection, Dot decided a chat with the bed and breakfast's owner was in the cards.

The fragrance of apple and spice assaulted Dot the moment she opened the door to Cherry Valley B and B. Nothing announced the arrival of autumn and hunting season better than the manufactured scent of apples, cinnamon, and pumpkins. Dot left the door open lest she become overwhelmed and pass out.

A cheery hello came from the breakfast room.

"Cherry?" Dot called out.

The bed and breakfast's namesake emerged from the dining room, a huge smile on her lips. "Dot!"

Cherry Hargrave—soon to be Petersen—was Millie's eldest daughter and the least like her mother and two younger siblings. Where the others were more salt of the earth, Cherry was Eva Gabor of *Green Acres* minus throwing the dishes out the window. She loved adding glitz and glamour to her life, not so much cowboy chic but more uptown girl meets Hallmark.

Cherry wrapped up Dot in a Chanel No. 5 embrace. "What brings you to my little establishment?"

Dot forced herself to remain relaxed as the woman

squeezed the living daylights out of her. When Cherry thrust herself back and eyeballed her, Dot smiled.

"I was in town and thought I'd stop by."

Cherry's blush-painted lips twisted. "You're such a liar, Dot Ybarra." She released her hold and scurried over to the front desk.

She did not walk, saunter, or sashay anywhere. No, Cherry scurried like a mouse on a mission.

"Okay, you got me. I spotted someone leaving here and thought I recognized him. Before I could catch him, he left in his car."

Cherry pursed her lips and then smiled. "Might be you're talking about my newest guest." She angled her laptop toward her. "I have a couple of guys rooming here; some of them are hunters. What's his name?"

"That's the thing." Dot ambled up to the desk. "I'm having a hard time bringing it to mind. If it helps, he was the guy who just exited right before I came in."

Cherry beamed. "Oh! Mr. Cutie."

Dot wrinkled her nose. "If you say so." She frowned. "Aren't you getting married next month? I thought the engaged weren't supposed to notice guys like that."

The unladylike snort from Cherry made Dot smile. "No one said I can't admire a fine specimen when it walks through my door. Rowdy knows I'm his lock, stock, and barrel." She cocked her head. "Your guy's name is Charles Smith."

A name as generic as John Doe. Good God, he might as well have slapped a sign on his ass advertising he was made in the USA by good ole Uncle Sam.

"Recognize him?' Cherry asked.

"Not who I thought he was. Sorry about that."

"Ahh, no biggie." She closed her laptop. "I'm surprised your momma let you come to Euskadi after your last foray this way."

"I'll remind you like I reminded *Ama*. Willy Donnel got what he deserved." Dot rubbed her chin. "Too bad he wasn't laid up in the hospital longer."

Cherry snickered. "Actually, he got booted out, then Valerie ripped a page from your book and kicked him to the curb, too, with a loaded shotgun. He's been shacked up with his equally loser brother."

"Probably drunk and bitching about all women and how the world has gone to shit since they got the right to vote."

"Most likely." Cherry swung out from behind her desk and scurried over to a shelf displaying some of the local artists' wares. "Rowdy told me you and your momma had a dustup with the sheriff and some folks over a deadbeat who kidnapped his daughter."

"How'd Rowdy know?" Dot shook her head. "Never mind. Matlock told him."

Cherry's fiancé and her brother were rodeo pals and friends. It was how Cherry had met her soon-to-be husband.

"Rowdy was actually helping with the search too." She finished rearranging a line of blown glass horses. "Yeah, Matlock probably told him more details."

"Your mom said he's been chained to desk duty in the sheriff's office. Any idea why?"

Cherry faced Dot and planted her hands on her curvy hips. "Darn straight I know. That rotten sheriff of ours brought this new guy in, and the idiot picked a fight with Matlock over an arrest of some drug head. A literal fight, fists and all. Ford thought he'd make an example out of Matlock and kept Wall on duty."

The stench of rot running through the sheriff Dot had picked up on the day before was beginning to take on a stronger smell.

"I was going to stop by and chat with Matlock, but I might reconsider it," Dot said. "Since I'm on the sheriff's shit list, too, I don't need more of it rubbing off on your brother."

"You coming to the rodeo tonight?" Cherry asked.

"I hadn't planned on it."

Cherry glanced around, then bent toward Dot. "Come. Rowdy and Matlock are team roping tonight. It'll be a good chance to see him without worrying about the sheriff." She straightened. "Besides, you haven't been to one in forever. Please come. Have some fun. Like old times."

"In old times, I was usually racing."

A sly grin popped up. "There's still time to enter."

"Ha! I don't have a barrel horse."

Cherry squeezed Dot's forearm. "I'm sure someone has a horse you can borrow."

"I'll come, but just to watch, if it stops your conniving."

Cherry clapped her hands. "Good. I'll let Rowdy know, and he can give Matlock a heads-up." She rolled up on her tiptoes and planted a sisterly kiss to Dot's cheek. "I like having you home for good."

She and *Ama* seemed to be the only ones.

Chapter Nine

DOT RETURNED HOME to find a giggling Bethany riding one of the older geldings *Ama* had deemed a babysitter horse. Angela was leading the horse and singing one of the old Basque lullabies Dot well remembered hearing as a child. Circling the riding pen lay the dog pack, keeping an eye on their alpha and her new charge.

The dogs glanced Dot's way when she kicked the truck door shut, then went back to observing the events in the pen from their ringside seats. Dot hauled the loaded cloth grocery bags to the house. The moment her boot hit the first step the screen door flew open, and Ashley barreled out.

"Let me help you." She clambered down the steps, blocking Dot's progress.

"Don't bother." Dot grunted and managed to sidestep the younger woman.

Ashley darted past and yanked open the screen door in time for Dot to enter the house, then trailed her to the kitchen.

Dot hoisted the bags onto the butcher block counter in the middle of the kitchen—a counter that was miraculously clean. Dot marveled at how spotless the room looked. Hell, most of the house.

"You do this?" she asked, waving her hand about.

Ashley ducked her head as she removed the groceries from the bag. "Angela wasn't sure I was ready for any outside work. I told her I did a lot of house cleaning before I had Bethany, so I offered to tidy up."

"Girl, this is more than just tidying up. I can't remember a time in my whole freaking life the house was ever this clean."

Ashley blushed as she set fresh fruit in the ceramic fruit bowl.

Something warm, sweet, and yeasty filled the kitchen. Dot gaped at the top of the oven where an elongated baking sheet sat overflowing with sweet rolls. "You bake too?"

Ashley shrugged as she carried a few of the chilled items to the fridge. "It's the least I can do to thank you and your mom for helping me and getting Bethany back safe."

Dot watched Ashley continue to empty the bags and store the groceries where they belonged. She moved around as if she'd lived here all her life. Ashley was comfortable among the trappings of a common life. It was hard to connect the bloodied and battered woman of yesterday with this domestic goddess. Which struck Dot oddly. What little bit she'd gleaned from Ashley on her life before dropping into Dot's, she didn't seem the type to be this self-sufficient.

"I was thinking of taking you to your place and letting you get some of your and Bethany's things," Dot said, sidling over to the pan of sweet rolls.

Ashley clutched a package of toilet paper to her chest. "That would be so nice if you did."

"We'll go tomorrow. I got a lot of bad vibes in Euskadi,

and I'd rather you give it another day to settle." Dot poked at the closest roll. "Are these things ready to eat?"

"Yes." Ashley joined Dot by the stove. "What about my car?"

"I asked our mechanic shop to tow it their place, and they'll replace the tires."

Ashley blanched. "I can't afford new tires."

"It's covered." Dot pried a corner roll off the baking sheet. "Consider all the work you've done so far as reimbursement for one of the tires." She bit into the sticky roll. The sweet strawberry center melted on her tongue, and she moaned.

"I found the strawberry preserves in the pantry. It's okay for me to use them?"

Dot swallowed the mouthful and pointed at Ashely. "Use whatever the hell you want. *Ama* always puts up more food than either of us can eat in a year."

"I wish I knew how to do that," Ashley said softly.

"Stick around long enough and she'll teach you." Dot stuffed the last of the sweet roll in her mouth, then headed for the coffeepot.

Ashley resumed storing the last of the groceries. When she pulled out a small stuffed horse, she froze.

Dot, her mug of coffee halfway to her mouth, froze too. She met Ashley's gaze and felt the heat rise in her face.

She lowered the mug. "For Bethany," she said gruffly.

"Thank you," Ashley said, her voice catching.

Dot's throat tightened at the sight of the liquid pooling in the younger woman's eyes. She cleared it with a short cough. "Yeah. Sure. No problem."

Taking a page out of Cherry's book, Dot did her own scurrying out the door and made a beeline for the barn.

Inside, she found Angela instructing Bethany on how to take care of her horse after riding. The little girl's face was flushed, and she practically beamed in delight as she ran the soft bristled brush over the gelding's belly.

Angela glanced over when Dot came to a stop in the doorway. "She's a natural."

Dot leaned her shoulder into the frame and studied the girl. "All girls are natural horsewomen."

"*Amona* says I can ride every day," Bethany said, butchering the Basque word for grandmother.

"*Amona* said that, did she?" Dot asked, eyebrows lifted as she eyed her mother.

Angela lifted her chin defiantly. "You did a good job, Bethany. Why don't you put the brush away and run into the house. I think your mom made some goodies for us."

Giving a little cheer, Bethany skipped to the tack room to deposit the brush and then pranced out past Dot, who watched the girl in bafflement. This was not the same child who just yesterday had been kidnapped by her demented father, verbally abused, and borne witness to his death. Once she was out of earshot, Dot pushed out of the doorway and waylaid her mother.

"What are you doing? She's not your granddaughter."

"Don't start with me, Dorothy. She's a little girl who's been through hell."

"She's someone else's family, not yours. You can't swoop in and replace what's already out there. Ashley has parents."

Angela, her face mottling with red spots, glared at Dot.

"If her family was so damn interested in their own daughter, then where the hell are they?"

Dot leaned back from the force her mother's venom. "Oh, *amatxo*, you can't get attached. They're only here for a little bit."

"To Basque, what is more important?" Angela insisted.

Oh, God, here it comes. Dot was about to be put in her place for trying to protect her mother's heart.

"Family." She sighed.

"Exactly." Angela poked Dot's chest with a blunt finger. "Does it always mean blood?"

Dot looked to the shifting gelding next to them. *A little help here, buddy.*

Then she met her mother's hard stare. "No, it doesn't mean they have to be blood."

A squeal of delight echoed through the yard, followed by the sharp clap of the screen door. Dot swung back from Angela just as Bethany burst into the barn. The girl slowed her roll and then approached Dot, careful to avoid the gelding's legs. Dot gaped as the child slung her arms around her legs and hugged her.

"Thank you for the horse," Bethany said, then thrust up the stuffed animal Dot had found in Euskadi.

"Uh, you're welcome."

Bethany's bright face beamed up at Dot, a stark contrast to the tear-streaked, fear-stricken one Dot had been introduced to yesterday. After giving her another squeeze, Bethany released Dot and raced out of the barn once more.

Angela cleared her throat, catching Dot's attention. The anger on her mother's features was replaced by amusement.

"Not family, huh?"

Dot pointed back at her mother. "Don't get attached." She turned to leave the barn.

"I wouldn't have to worry about such things if you would just find a good husband and marry."

Ah, the same old argument. Dot rotated and backpedaled. "You never did."

"I had you."

Dot grinned and spread her arms wide. "And I'm all you'll ever need."

ANGELA WASN'T THRILLED with Dot going back into Euskadi for the rodeo, even if it was at Cherry's insistence. She was even less thrilled when Dot admitted it was more of a fact-gathering mission than an outing to watch her old childhood mate compete.

After a quick supper of venison chili Ashley had prepared, Dot changed from her work attire into something a bit swankier—which for her meant changing her current shirt into one that was clean, and swapping out her hat for a black felt with a silver concho hatband. Before she left, Dot pulled her mother aside and walked her out to the truck.

"Remember your idea once upon a time about running a hunt camp base here?"

"You shot the idea down because we didn't have enough people to help run it and we needed a camp cook."

Dot glanced back to the house. "You've got your cook."

"I thought you told me this was temporary."

Dot opened the truck door and climbed inside. "Things can change."

The side-eye she got from Angela made Dot grin, and she shut the door. "Don't wait up for me," she said through the open window.

By the time she reached the fairgrounds, the parking lot was overflowing with vehicles of all shapes and sizes and a stream of folks were headed for the gate. Dot took note of the deputies on duty directing traffic and spotted Ford's tricked out Dodge parked in a primo spot near the fence dividing the rodeo competitors from the crowd. Looked like all hands were on deck, and hopefully they'd be too busy to catch her sleuthing.

With the old Ford parked in the furthest lane from the entrance, Dot hiked up to the ticket booth.

"Dot Ybarra? Your ticket's been paid for," the gal behind the window said.

"By who?"

The woman tilted the paper. "Doesn't say." She laid the sheet down and grinned. "Must be your lucky day."

"More like a Hargrave is sucking up to me," Dot muttered as she accepted the inked stamp on her hand to indicate she was a legit customer. "Beer tent have wrist bands?"

"Does a bear shit in the woods?" the woman asked.

Dot snorted and headed into the rodeo grounds. The well-trod path between the food and commercial vendor booths teemed with bodies. It was like an undulating stream ready to break the banks. A writhing sensation like a knot of snakes slithering up her arms and legs hit Dot. She hadn't been in a place this congested since the withdrawal. She had to focus on the fact that these people were happy and wanted to be here for a good time. They weren't trying to flee for their lives.

God, she was going to need to get stoned tonight if she had any hope of getting some sleep.

Shaking free of her trepidation, she made for the red tent dominating the entire west side of the grandstands. After putting a fortune down on a neon green band, she headed for the bar handing out the tap beer.

With an ice-cold Coors in hand, she headed for her section of the stands. By the time she climbed the metal steps and found her seat among a sea of people, her crawling skin had turned to fire. She should have taken Cherry up on her offer to go behind the chutes and stick with the riders. At least there was open space out there versus up here.

One good thing about her seat—she had an open spot to her left and right. If it stayed that way, she'd make it through until Matlock and Rowdy roped.

Halfway through her beer, a figure appeared to her right. "I think that's my seat."

She tilted her chin up and peered at the familiar face. "Damn it, T.J."

He grinned and slipped past her knees, taking the seat to her left and exposing the redhead leaning on a cane lingering on the steps. Dot shot to her feet.

"Sloane."

Sloane Cross smiled. "Long time, Dot."

"What the hell?" She looked down at the seated T.J. "Do you two know each other?"

"We work together." He said it as if it was common knowledge, then took a swig of his beer.

Sloane, not waiting for Dot's invitation, slipped in and sat in the spot to her right. "God, it's been forever since I went to a rodeo." She wedged the cane under the seats in front of them and officially blocked them in.

Dot sank into her seat between the two. "What are you doing here?"

"Came to see you." Sloane winked. "And, of course, to watch some rodeo."

Dot eyed the polished wood with a comfortable leather grip. "That's new."

Sloane patted her right leg. "Got in an accident a few years back. Shattered my hip and my thigh. Haven't walked the same since."

Dot was stopped from asking more questions by a crackle over the PA system, and the talking heads began their open soliloquy. Dot drank the rest of her beer and let the announcers take control of the opening ceremonies. By the time the national anthem was announced, Dot and T.J. had finished their beers and stood along with the rest of the crowd.

Both removed their hats and stood at attention, saluting the American flag as it blew past carried by a star-spangled horsewoman on a fast-moving paint. An uproar rippled through the crowd as the flag bearer ran out of the arena and the announcer yelled out, "Let's rodeo!"

Once more seated and hats back on their heads, Dot leveled T.J. with a hard look. "How did the two of you end up working together? And you couldn't bother to mention this fact yesterday?"

"How was I supposed to know you two grew up together?" T.J. protested. "She's my partner."

The first event, bareback riding, got underway with the first bucking horse blowing out of the chute.

Dot, keeping an eye on the rider, tilted closer to Sloane. "You're a bounty hunter?"

"No, my official status is private investigator. T.J.'s the bounty hunter, but he's also a PI."

"She typically gets me the bond jobs and does all the legwork," T.J. said. "I'm more the muscle."

The eight-second horn blared, and a cheer rose up from the crowd.

Sloane tugged at her ball cap. "I run the business side of things really and leave the dirty work to him."

"Interesting," Dot said, then focused on T.J. "What happened to you getting back with me on the status of my guests?"

"This is me getting back with you on that." He pointed at Sloane and then himself. "We ended up with more questions than answers."

"We thought it best to come here and talk with you," Sloane cut in.

"Actually"—T.J. stood—"she wanted to talk to you. I'm getting another beer. Want one?" His question was directed at Dot as he pointed at her band.

"Sure, why not. Coors."

With a nod, he managed to navigate the seating arrangement without bumping into Sloane or her cane and headed down the steps. The next bronc rider didn't fare as well as the first, flying off his mount two bucks out of the chute.

"What kind of accident?" Dot asked.

Sloane clapped with the rest to encourage the no-points rider as he walked out of the arena. "Motorcycle. Some asshole didn't bother to pay attention to what he was doing and forced me off the road. Luckily, I wasn't going that fast and I just ditched it. Problem was, I ditched it on top of my leg and was trapped under it until first responders arrived."

"The asshole call them in?"

"Fuck no. He was long gone by the time I stopped sliding over the pavement. That was all me. Always prepared Sloane."

Another cowboy on a dark roan came bucking out of the chute.

"Before you were a PI or after?" Dot asked.

"After." Sloane waited for the eight-second horn to finish. "Dot, I know T.J. thanked you for helping yesterday, but I wanted to reiterate it."

Dot glanced at her old friend. "No biggie. Really."

"I read up on your accident," Sloane said. "You still with the forest service?"

"For now." Hopefully T.J. would hurry up with that beer.

"You ever going back?"

What the hell was taking him so long?

Dot watched as another bronc, with an arched back and stiff legs, came crow hopping out of the chute. The huge mare flung herself to the left and kicked out hard, throwing her rider forward over her neck. He was coming off, and the mare knew it. She plowed forward and whipped her hind end with a mighty kick, and off went the cowboy, face first into the dirt. The horn blared.

"And that, cowboys and cowgirls, is why she's the reigning queen of the bucking horses," the announcer declared.

"I don't know," Dot said as the mare trotted out of the arena.

"Ever thought about a new career path?"

This got Dot's full attention. "What are you driving at?"

Sloane shifted to better face Dot. "Hear me out. T.J. and I work great together, but I can't help him the way he needs. Most of the time he's out there catching our defendants alone. He needs someone out there watching his six, backing him up and bringing 'em in. He's had a few close calls where I didn't know if he was going to make it out alive."

"He told me yesterday he has some of the guys in the business help him when he needs it."

"Yeah, in dire circumstances ... but there's no connection, no trust." Sloane turned her head to watch the last rider take his turn at eight seconds. Her gaze swiveled back to Dot. "He trusts you. You've worked together before. Yesterday would have had a completely different outcome if you hadn't been there."

Dot checked her surroundings and made sure everyone near them was paying attention to the rodeo and not their conversation. "Sloane, I only ever flew T.J. and his men in and out of missions. I wasn't boots on ground with him."

A sly smile pulled at the corner of Sloane's mouth. "Oh, you two had some boots on ground."

"Sex and war are two different things," Dot shot back.

"Are they?" Sloane resumed her forward-facing position and let her comment hang in the air between them.

Dot, left to her own thoughts, watched as the tie-down ropers warmed up their horses while they waited for the crew moving the calves, got things sorted. Dot knew what Sloane was asking without asking. But was she ready for another change in her life? Angela had been pestering Dot about making a decision to leave the forest service or go back. Her mother's reasons had more to do with needing help on the ranch and the outfitter business than Dot's need of a paycheck. Yet, if she analyzed her mother's underlying message, Angela was worried sick over her daughter's choices in dangerous careers. Twice she had come close to losing her only child and her last connection to Samo Ybarra.

The ropers filed out of the arena and into their staging area behind the calf chute.

Before the first roper had his horse settled into the corner of the box, T.J. stomped up the metal grandstand steps, carrying three beer cups. He handed off one to Dot and kept the other two to himself.

"You're on your own for the rest," he said as he sat. "Those lines are too damn long."

"What, you're not giving one to Sloane?" Dot teased.

"She's DD," he announced.

Dot frowned. "Are you driving all the way back to Boise tonight?"

"Nope. Got us some rooms at the B and B here in town. Cherry owns it now, I see," Sloane said.

"What'd she say?" T.J. asked, looking around Dot at Sloane.

"I didn't get a chance to properly ask," Sloane replied.

"Ask me what exactly?" Dot insisted.

"Wanna get into the bounty hunting … excuse me, fugitive recovery business?" T.J. blurted.

Dot looked back and forth between the two. T.J. looked expectantly at her over the rim of his cup as he sucked down his beer. Sloane gave her the side-eye, a slick grin on her face.

"Don't you have to be licensed or something like that?" Dot asked.

"To be a PI, you do," Sloane said. "For fugitive recovery, not so much. It's more of a learn as you go and keep yourself up to date on the laws and your weapons licenses."

"And you two think I'd be good for this?"

"You'd be a fucking rock star," T.J. commented.

"What's the pay like?" Dot asked.

"Lousy," Sloane admitted. "It's why I also do PI work and some pro bono tech work, keeps the bills paid. So, I'd keep your day job as a backup."

Dot snorted. "Listening to my mother coddle inept hunters. Grand."

"Hey, at least she has steady income," Sloane mentioned. "You wouldn't have to move to Boise. Hell, we could keep you here. Got a bail bonds group out of McCall that calls us up now and again. There aren't any agents up here."

"If I stay here, how am I supposed to learn from T.J.?"

"About that," he said and cleared his throat.

"Here's where my PI work comes in." Sloane leaned closer to Dot as the grandstands grew loud as the last tie-down roper finished his run. "I'm working a case that has leads coming from here. A certain person of interest keeps popping up in the oddest places at the oddest times, and he's here. Now."

Dot glanced at T.J., noting the gleam in his eyes that wasn't from his beer consumption. "You're talking about Mr. Alphabet Agency."

"Precisely," Sloane said.

"You realize he's staying at the B and B, right?"

T.J. chuckled. "Maybe she should get her PI license."

Sloane studied Dot. "Maybe." She nudged Dot's elbow with her own. "Whaddya think?"

The team ropers, Matlock on his flashy sorrel and Rowdy on his palomino among the group, were setting up for their run at the steers.

Dot straightened. "Lemme think on it," she said to Sloane. "My reason for coming here tonight is about to have his go in this round."

Chapter Ten

MATLOCK WAS WAITING for Dot by the bucking chutes. He took one look at the towering man behind her and made a face.

"You must be the troublemaker the sheriff keeps bitchin' about," he said by way of greeting.

T.J. gave his infamous Neanderthal grunt.

Dot rolled her eyes. "Could we move this along? Last thing I want is said sheriff seeing our little entourage."

"Don't worry about him." Matlock jerked his head to the side and led the trio back to his trailer. "Ford's too busy being smarmy with the purse strings. By now he's probably five cups deep and swimming in the shit."

"Doesn't account for the rest of his band," Dot remarked.

"Who are just as tied up in their own worlds to pay any attention to mine." Matlock stopped by an older rig where two horses stood tied to the side pulling at their hay bags. "Grab a chair, and I'll get the beers."

"None for me," Sloane said as she navigated the horse apples and the portable firepit with a blazing fire to a studio style chair.

"I need to pass on the beers," Dot said sinking into a

camping chair. "I've still gotta drive home."

Matlock paused beside a cooler. "I've got some of those girly drinks Cherry likes."

"It's like you don't even know me," Dot groused.

He laughed, a deep belly laugh that always put people at ease. Matlock was much like his father in that regard. A man everyone missed.

Matlock yanked up the cooler top and reached in to pull out two bottles of water, which he chucked to Sloane and to Dot. "Beer?" he asked T.J.

"I don't have to drive," T.J. rumbled.

"My kind of man." Matlock lobbed a can of Busch Light.

Once he had his own can, Matlock plopped into a camping chair beside the cooler and cracked into his beer. He tipped the brim of his Stetson back, pushing the hat to the back of his head. "See you've been poking the beast, Dot."

"I believe it's my middle name," she joked. "Can't let *Ama* have all the fun."

"Oh, it's worse this time than any past Ybarra transgressions. Ford's spitting nails, and everyone is paying for it."

"He's not taking special delight in you, is he?"

Matlock shook his head. "He backed off pissing on me after Momma burnt his steak and gave him a side of mashed crickets."

Sloane choked on a mouthful of water. Dot laughed.

"Remind me not to eat her food," T.J. muttered.

Dot lightly punched his rock-hard arm holding the beer can. "Don't cross swords with her kids and you'll be fine."

He took a swig of his beer.

"Cherry told me you wanted a chat," Matlock said pointing his can at Dot. "Didn't know you were bringing along company."

"I wasn't expecting them," Dot answered, crossing her right boot over her left knee. "But I guess they have a stake in what I want to talk to you about."

"How so?" Matlock asked before drinking his beer.

"Your sheriff's antics yesterday cost us a bounty," Sloane said. "Which killed a lead on a case I've been working for the last year."

"Not to mention the man in black running around town and schmoozing with the sheriff," Dot added.

Matlock smirked. "Noticed the suit, did ya?"

"Kinda hard to miss him even if he was trying to stay in the shadows. How long has he been around Euskadi?" Dot asked.

"Coupla months. Figured he was a lawyer or some nonsense like that until I saw him wearing a blue jacket like the feds wear." Matlock drank some of his beer.

"Did he have the ABC org he works for on the back?" Dot pressed.

He shook his head. "Blank. But I noticed the emblem on his chest. Kinda like one of those US departments of something, but the print was too small for me to read exactly what it said. Course, he made sure no one got a good look at it."

"He stayed far enough back for us to not make it out, either," T.J. mentioned. "Not far enough for me not to recognize him."

Matlock shifted his attention to Sloane. "You mentioned a case. For what? You some kinda cop now?"

She smirked. "Something like that."

His gaze swung back to Dot. "What's your stake in all this? I figured with you hiding out at your momma's ranch, you weren't too interested in the world at large."

Dot merely took a swig of her water. Even after last night's mental gymnastics, she still couldn't bring herself to come up with a solid reason why she was doing all this. Maybe it was for Ashley. Or maybe, for real, it was for the girl, Bethany.

Dot hadn't known a maternal bone in her entire existence. She'd been raised tough and rough-hewed. Samo Ybarra brought up his granddaughter the way he brought up his daughter, carving out an existence in the mountains and sustaining a life through trial and tribulation. Protect those you love and those who couldn't protect themselves. Do right and fear no man was Samo's life motto.

"Still as buttoned-up as ever," Matlock groused. He tossed back the rest of his beer, then crushed the can against his knee until it was flattened.

"Noticed that too," Sloane said. "I think the army reinforced the trait. Tall, bearded, and broody is just as bad."

T.J.'s grunt resembled an annoyed bear.

"You seem more interested in the man in black. I figured you wanted to know about all the sketchy shit going on for the last few years," Matlock said.

They all three leaned closer to Matlock.

"Sketchy shit like what?" Dot asked.

"Like billionaires with more money than common sense coming in and buying up land, forcing generational ranchers and farmers out of their livelihood. Companies from God knows where asking about development opportunities. And, worse, undocumented people flooding in bringing their shit with them. In the last three months, we've had ten overdose deaths. All kids. All too ignorant to know better." Matlock rubbed his face, then tossed his crushed can into a pile near a trailer tire and reached into the cooler for another beer. "That's just in a three-month span."

Dot hadn't paid attention to the pile before but noticed it now. With the new addition, there looked to be about eight or nine crushed cans. "Matlock, how many beers have you had tonight?"

"What's it matter?"

She met T.J.'s gaze. He shook his head and drank the last of his beer. They'd seen this same song and dance before, especially after returning from bad deployments, of which there were many. The moment anyone got near alcohol, there was no self-control. Dot had played the game a time or two until she regretted waking up the next morning. She still struggled to not crawl into the bottle and enjoy the sweet relief of oblivion.

T.J. had moved with a rougher crowd until he'd had his comin' to Jesus moment at a bar in Savannah years back, and he said nothing more about it.

Matlock was giving off all the red flags. He walked the path of destruction brought on by bad experiences.

"It matters," Sloane said as she leaned toward Matlock. "Because you're running headlong down the same path those kids did." She reached out and snagged the beer can from his hand. "Ask those two what self-destruction does to you." She tapped her bad leg. "Ask me."

The heated sap and burning wood popped while the distant cheering rodeo crowd filled the air around them.

After the drawn-out silence, Matlock pushed from his chair and stalked to the back of his trailer. Dot popped up, gesturing for T.J. and Sloane to remain in their seats. She swung wide of the horses' backends, holding out her hand and speaking to them.

"Matlock," she called out, just in case he came back here to piss.

"You're good," he said softly from the dark.

She inched to the corner of the trailer and peered around, finding Matlock sitting on the running board. She leaned against the trailer and looked up at the sky, relishing the sight of all those stars above.

"How many did you lose on your watch, Dot?" he asked.

"Whaddya mean?" She wanted to hear him say it.

He tilted his chin, the shadow cast by his hat brim receding to show the stubbled jaw. "Did you lose any of your people when you flew for the army?"

"I didn't lose any of my guys. T.J.'s one of them, and he can confirm that." She shifted and pressed her back into the trailer wall. "When we pulled out of Afghanistan…"

She didn't want to relive those moments, but the mention of it brought forward the reverberating concussive explosion and the screams that followed. Dot squeezed her eyes shut as the remembered stench of burnt flesh and the tang of blood filled her nostrils.

"Dot?" Matlock's voice grounded her.

She opened her eyes but didn't look at him. "You've been keeping count."

"Damn hard not to." Matlock ripped his hat from his head and swiped his shirtsleeve across his face. "Makes me glad Ford got pissed at me and shoved me behind a desk. I don't have to keep watching those kids being zipped up in body bags."

Dot gripped his shoulder.

They stayed that way for several minutes, until the rodeo had concluded. The announcement for the fireworks echoed over the grounds, making Dot stiffen.

Matlock stood abruptly, shoving his hat on his head. "You better get out of here before those go off."

"I ain't going to make it back to my truck in time."

"Dot," T.J. called from the other side of the trailer.

"He knows," she said softly to Matlock.

He drew closer, hemming her in. "Knows what?"

"Explosions trigger things in me."

Matlock smelled of horse flesh, sweat, and beer. He inched closer, his scent engulfing her. "How does he know so much about you?"

Dot placed a hand on his chest and pushed him back. "Because he's a Danger Ranger." She lightly patted Matlock's stubbly cheek. "You're drunk and emotional."

The first screeching rocket went airborne, then exploded overhead. Dot jerked involuntarily.

"I gotta go," she said and slipped past Matlock.

T.J. was coming around the back end when she emerged. He caught her elbow as another firework detonated. She had to squelch a shriek.

"Sloane's got us parked not far from here," T.J. said, adjusting his hold on her when she stumbled over an indentation in the ground.

"I'm not going to make it." She gasped.

The earlier memories were crowding in. The sound of her heavy breathing was replaced by the screams. She shouldn't have come. She shouldn't be there. A trio of explosions overhead brought Dot to a halt, and she ripped her arm free. She no longer saw the towering man or the sea of rigs and horses.

She was staring into the fiery pit of hell. Metal and fiberglass screeched and cracked all around her. The constant thumping of rotary blades were silenced.

She suddenly felt light. Something wrapped around her legs, and she was thrust over a solid wedge. Blood rushed to her head, and she blinked at a jean-clad backside.

T.J. carried her that way right up to Sloane's SUV and deposited her into the back seat, climbing in behind her.

"Take me to her truck. I'll drive her home," he said.

Dot barely registered what he said before another round of fireworks went off. God, save her from this hell.

Chapter Eleven

T.J. KILLED THE headlights as he drove the old Ford into the ranch yard. He parked and turned off the engine.

Huddled against the passenger door, Dot stared out the window. She hadn't said a word since he'd bundled her into the truck and pried the keys from her clammy hand. He hadn't seen post-traumatic stress this bad since one of his old squad mates lost his shit right before getting his DD214. Last he heard, the guy had gone AWOL, and his family believed he'd committed suicide because they hadn't been able to find him.

T.J. reached out to grasp Dot's hand lying in her lap. She jolted and slapped at his hand.

"Flygirl, it's me, Danger Ranger."

After a hesitation, she slumped. "What the hell," she rasped.

"Where'd you go?" he asked, his voice rumbling through the truck cab.

It was common knowledge that vets tended to relive horrifying moments in their service when they fell into the PTSD abyss. T.J. wasn't aware of any situations in Dot's career while he was in where she dealt with explosions, if one eliminated the RPGs slung at the helicopters when she flew.

He had heard her unit was near Abbey Gate. Had she been there too?

She didn't answer, only continued to stare ahead.

"You had a bad one," he said.

"Fuck." She rubbed her face, then seemed to realize her hat was gone and patted her head. "My hat?"

He picked it up from between them and held it out to her. She snatched it from his hand and resettled it on her head.

"Where we at?" she asked.

"Your place." He peered at the house. "Looks like all is quiet and everyone's in bed."

"How the hell are you getting back to town?"

"Figured I'd just camp out here. I don't think your momma needs to cope with the fallout from your episode."

She twisted to look at him. "More like you figured we'd pick up where we left off as fuck buddies. Go fuck yourself," she snapped, and exited the cab.

T.J. snarled. Yeah, like fucking her after she lost her shit even crossed his mind. Damn it. Why'd she have to be irrational *and* strung out? He jumped out of the truck and circumvented the front end.

"Dot, what the hell?"

"Leave me alone, T.J.," she snapped over her shoulder as she stalked to the barn.

He jolted at the deep, menacing barks coming from somewhere in the dark, then heard Dot ordering the dogs to shut up. At the sound of her voice, the guardians backed off, uttering low growls as a reminder to T.J. they were watching.

T.J. followed her right into the barn, where she flipped

on a light, blinding them both and disturbing the sleeping horses.

Dot recovered from her momentary stun and marched into the tack room. T.J. spoke to the animals as he passed and stopped in the doorway.

From a spot above the saddle rack, Dot pulled down a baggie full of a dried green substance with white papers stuffed inside and a lighter. She had the bag on the desk wedged in the corner of the room and was fumbling with the items to roll herself a joint.

"That's how you cope?" he asked incredulously.

She ignored him, lining paper with the marijuana, rolling the tips, and lighting it. She took a long drag on the joint and let the smoke sit in her mouth. After what seemed like an eternity, she exhaled the smoke through her nose.

T.J. winced as the stench of the weed hit him. It didn't deter Dot as she took another long drag, burning the joint halfway.

He propped himself against the frame and watched her. It took a bit, but the weed's effects began to kick in. Dot practically unwound right before his eyes.

"You got a doctor's script for that?" he asked, half joking.

"Fuck 'em," she said languidly.

He scratched his eyebrow. "You sure that's pure marijuana? It's not laced with anything?"

"It's clean."

"How do you know?"

"I grew the shit myself." She sucked on the last of the joint. "Just enough for me." The smoke rolled between her lips.

Well, that was one way to keep the feds off her ass and keep a steady supply of unadulterated weed.

"Stop worrying. I only smoke it when things get really bad."

"What constitutes as really bad?"

She held up her hand and counted off with her fingers. "Pain, no sleep, and flashbacks."

"Have you been trying to muscle through this on your own?"

Her gaze bore into him.

"Damn, Dot, they have groups to help people like us get through shit. This ain't like the old days."

"What about you?" She jabbed the stubbed joint at him. "You go to those groups?"

The question hung between them like a rappelling soldier.

"I did," he said slowly.

"Well, bully for you." She smashed the last of the joint into the scarred desktop, then pulled together her paraphernalia and returned it to her hidey hole.

"Your momma know about the weed?" he asked.

"She does and doesn't care as long as I don't smoke it in the house and don't burn the barn down." She turned back to face him, shoving her hands in her back pockets. "I'm not the bare-my-soul type."

"It doesn't have to be like that."

Dot snorted. "Get real, T.J. You and I both know it would. No therapist is going to let me slide in and out of their domain without ripping out a piece of my soul." Her shoulders dipped. "I've already given away too much of it."

"Is that why you won't go back to the forest service? You have to pass a psych eval before they let you back in the sky?"

Dot pulled her hands free and crossed her arms. He was well-versed in her stubborn posture. Silence and a stare-down was all the answer he was getting on this matter.

"Is it just explosions?" Maybe a different approach was the ticket.

"Yes. Gunfire doesn't bother me."

"Abbey Gate?" he pressed.

T.J. knew he was going to go too far with her. At some point, he'd push too hard, and Dot would come back swinging.

"Don't harsh my mellow," she countered. "I'd rather not get full out stoned, but you're seriously making me reconsider it."

He grinned. "Thought I'd try."

Dot dropped her arms and moved closer to him. "You should know better than to push me." With that she walked on past him. "I don't know about you, but I'm starving."

He rotated. "Am I allowed in the house? Or do I sleep out here with the goats?"

She circled her hand above her head and kept on walking.

T.J. bid the horses a good night and doused the barn lights, then followed her into the house.

IN THE THREE-BEDROOM home, Dot was stuck sleeping out in the living area. Angela had long taken over the master bedroom and confiscated a second for storage. Ashley and her daughter were camped out in Dot's.

T.J. made himself comfortable on the beat-down sofa in front of the crackling fireplace Dot had stoked to life and fed more wood. Dot was sprawled out in an armchair, her blanket-draped legs propped on a huge footrest.

She'd plowed through three sweet rolls and was enjoying a late-night smoke on a sweet-smelling cigar.

"Still can't get over you liking those," he said.

"Want one?" she asked.

"I'm good." He braced an elbow into the sofa's armrest and stared at the fire.

After a prolonged comfortable silence, Dot spoke.

"Why me?"

T.J. looked at her, waited for his eyes to adjust to the dark background without the bright spots, and studied Dot's fire-lit profile. "Why you what?"

She considered her cigar, then knocked the ash off the end and snubbed it out in the tray beside her.

Satisfied the cigar was doused, she shifted in her chair to face him. "Bounty hunting. Being your partner. Why?"

He took a long moment to sort through his thoughts and held her gaze. Sloane's idea and the reasons for asking Dot to come on with their little agency had taken T.J. some time to digest. Once he'd analyzed Sloane's bill of sale, he came to the same conclusion. Dot fit the criteria.

It was up to Dot to realize this herself.

"I trust you," he said.

It was her turn to mull over his answer.

She didn't take as long. "That's what Sloane said. Is it

what you want?"

T.J. straightened, taking up the center of the sofa, and draping his arms over the backrest. "Sloane was a good backup partner out in the field, but she's a better skip tracer. She's damn good at finding the unfindable. Most of the guys in this business are competitive and like to work on their own, and they usually don't like to share."

"But why me?"

He brought his arms down and clasped his hands between his knees. "Why not you? Yesterday was proof enough for me to know you're the right person to have my six. Or take the lead. Sloane'll be the first to admit she's never had the strength to help wrestle a defendant into custody. Since her accident, she can't do the fieldwork, and she feels bad about it, but there's nothing we can change.

"Dot, you have the scope and the ability to read all angles in a situation that means life or death. You have the training and know-how to defuse a tense showdown. Or ramrod a subject into submission. And you sure as hell can keep up with me."

She smiled at that.

"I have feeling you're never going to back to the forest service," he said.

She looked up at the ceiling.

"If tonight was any indication, I don't think you're planning to get back in a cockpit any time soon, either."

Dot shook her head. "You know me too damn well, Titus Jethro Roman."

"I really hate that you know my full given name," he grumbled.

"You know so much about me." She tilted her head, her braid sliding along her shoulder. "Tell me why you got into bounty hunting. Didn't you have a big family ranch to go back to after you got out of the service?"

T.J. felt a pang in his chest. He missed Oklahoma and his family sometimes. What he didn't miss was the smothering. "Wasn't my shtick. My sister and her husband have it well in hand. No need for a big lumbering ex-Special Forces guy mucking it all up."

"Why not law enforcement? Or contracting your skills out?"

"Hell no. I was finally free and able to make my own decisions and my own hours. I'm my own boss, and I like it that way."

"What about Sloane?"

"I like Sloane. She and I work well together. But we're partners in the biz—neither one is the boss over the other. It'll be the same if you decide this is what you want. Believe me, you'll catch on quick." He dipped his chin. "You're already in the game as it is. Might as well keep the test drive going."

"I wouldn't call what I've been doing in the last thirty-odd hours a test drive."

"You got your pal Matlock to talk." T.J. pressed into the sofa back. "Speaking of which, what did he tell you behind the trailer?"

"Nothing I didn't already suspect. He's hurting. Bad. Whatever is going on around here is taking a toll."

T.J. noted the change in her voice, and a part of him soured. "Just how close are the two of you?"

Dot regarded him. "Jealous?"

"No."

She broke out in a grin and flipped off the blanket.

T.J. shifted on the sofa as she climbed out of the chair and prowled the few feet between them. Dot swung her firm body over his legs and straddled his lap. She towered over him, forcing him to look up at her.

"You're a bad liar," she said, her voice dropping into a husky tone he was all too familiar with.

"You're a damn tease."

Dot lowered her head, stopping an inch from his lips. "What I said out there in truck earlier."

"Telling me to fuck off and we weren't fuck buddies anymore."

"Yeah, I shouldn't have said that."

T.J. hooked his hands on her hips and trailed them up her torso. "I'm not here to piss you off more, Dot."

"I think we're far past that point," she said, then pressed her lips to his.

Chapter Twelve

DOT BECAME AWARE of the softest shuffle of feet against the threadbare rug. She peeled one eye open and spotted the disheveled blonde in a pair of oversized flannel pajamas looming over T.J.'s sleeping form on the couch. The stuffed horse hung over Bethany's forearm, its glossy black eyes staring at Dot in her armchair. Slowly, Bethany squatted down until her head was level with the snoring man. Her small hand rose from her side and inched toward his bearded face.

Smiling, Dot drew her blanket up to her chin and waited for the show.

Bethany poked a finger into T.J.'s cheek.

He startled. "Holy shhhh…"

His scramble to get upright jostled Bethany, and she flopped back onto her rear. A giggle erupted from the girl and Dot joined her.

Fully awake, T.J. scowled at Dot. "Hey … kid," he said.

"You're loud," Bethany declared.

Dot snorted at the girl's bluntness. "I think he rattled the windows."

Bethany's bright face turned to Dot. "Yup!"

Ashley blew into the living room from the hallway.

"Bethany, you know better." She sent a pleading look at Dot. "I'm sorry. She's better behaved than this."

"She's fine," Dot rebutted. "His snoring probably woke everyone up."

"Not funny," T.J. growled.

Bethany popped to her feet, swinging her horse by its hind legs. "Mommy's making pancakes. Want some?"

"I could eat," Dot said, scooting her body out from under her pile of blankets to the edge of her chair.

Bethany danced over and leaned on Dot's legs. "Why are you sleeping out here?"

Dot stared at the peaches and cream face staring up at her. The kid was damn cute. "'Cause, kiddo, you and your *amatxo* are using my bedroom, remember?"

"Oh, yeah." Bethany's small hands pushed off Dot's knees. "Mommy, can we have bacon?"

Ashley glanced at Dot. "Is there any bacon?"

"Back porch, deep freeze. You might have to dig for it."

"Yes!" Bethany danced a weird jig. "I love bacon."

"So do I," T.J. piped up, a bemused expression crossing his face as he watched Bethany.

"Come on," Ashley beckoned her daughter. "Let's get you dressed and find the bacon."

As the pair left the living room, Angela emerged from the back rooms. Her gaze flicked from Dot to T.J.

"Good morning, Mr. Roman," she said curtly and strode to the kitchen.

"Mornin'," he said, a bit sheepishly.

Dot snickered as she rose from her chair. By the tone of her mother's voice, Angela had figured out what the two of them had been up to the night before. It amused Dot to no end to see T.J. embarrassed.

"Good thing your room is at the *back* of the house," Angela commented.

"Oh my God," T.J. groaned, the skin above his beard turning pink.

"*Ama*, stop making him uncomfortable."

Angela glanced over her shoulder as she prepared the coffeemaker. "I didn't think it was possible to embarrass an army man."

"Not true," Dot said as she passed T.J. on her way to the kitchen.

She didn't move fast enough before he playfully swatted her backside. She glared back at him and continued on. Admittedly, Dot hadn't planned on taking a middle-of-the-night romp with T.J., and she didn't think he had planned on it either. But it had been nice to release some long pent-up tension. Dot actually got the best sleep in forever.

She joined Angela in the kitchen.

"I got a call yesterday from one of my longtime clients. He's got a group who wants to come hunt this week," Angela said as she poured filtered water into the coffee maker reservoir.

Dot grabbed a hairband from the catch-all dish they left near the front door and began to braid her hair. "When will they be here?"

"I asked him to come today."

"I was going to take Ashley to her place to get some of their things today. I don't want Bethany with us, just in case."

WINTER AUSTIN

Angela closed the reservoir lid and started the machine. "When were you planning to do that?"

"Anytime. But I need to get T.J. back to Euskadi."

Angela's gaze darted to the man inching into their perimeter. "Mr. Roman can't have someone come get him?"

"I guess Sloane could come."

Angela frowned. "Sloane? Like Sloane Cross? The girl you used to be friends with?"

"One and the same."

Myriad emotions and thoughts rippled over Angela's features until she settled on indifference. "Very well. But who will watch Bethany? My client likes to show up early and get a start to the hunt."

Dot eyed her mother. "I'm not taking Bethany with us. Besides, we don't have room in the truck."

"Then you don't go today."

"We can't go as long as you're on a hunt. Those two need their clothes and things."

Angela scowled. "I need this contract, since you chased off my last one."

"Maybe you shouldn't be going out there right now."

"Maybe you should mind your manners."

"I'll watch the girl," T.J. cut in.

Dot and Angela directed their attention toward the man.

"Have Sloane come out here with our SUV, then the three of you can get Ashley's gear. Ms. Ybarra can do her thing. I'll keep the kid preoccupied. I can take her for a ride or something."

Angela sniffed, her nostrils flaring like an agitated horse. "Fine. I'll be too busy preparing to leave. I've got chores."

With that, she exited the house.

Dot glowered at the closed door. It was a damn good thing she loved her mother.

She turned to T.J. "You shouldn't have let her bully you into that."

"It's fine." He looked toward the back of the house where the screech of a screen door came from. "Besides, between you and Sloane, you might get better info out of Ashley without fear of her daughter hearing any of it."

"This have to do with what Sloane said last night about an ongoing case she's working?"

He nodded. "Might be best she explain that to you."

Bethany burst into the kitchen. "Found it."

She wore the same pair of jeans she'd had on yesterday and a half-faded black hoodie with the whirling Basque cross. Dot recognized the old hoodie as one of hers from way back in the day.

"Can I feed the goats?" Bethany asked.

"If you hurry, you can help. *Ama* just went outside."

The girl bolted for the door and ran outside, slamming the screen door in her wake.

Ashley's exasperated sigh proceeded her emergence into the kitchen. "I swear my daughter isn't usually like this."

"You worry too much," Dot admonished. "She's actually acting like a girl her age should."

T.J. poured himself a mug of coffee. "Being out here has certainly helped her cope well after her abduction." He tested the coffee.

"She likes it here." Ashley set the fat package of bacon on the counter next to the stove. "She keeps asking me if we have to go back to our home. I don't know what to tell her."

The young woman managed to keep her face schooled to hide her emotions, but Dot heard the agony in Ashley's voice.

T.J. met Dot's gaze and then meandered back to the living room.

Ashley whipped around. "Are you still planning to take me into town?"

"I am. We'll have an old friend of mine come get us." Dot nodded toward T.J. "He's planning on staying here with Bethany to babysit while my mother gets ready for a new hunting party coming in today."

"Are you sure you want to babysit?" Ashley asked T.J. "We can bring her with us."

"No." Dot poured her own mug of coffee. "It's still not safe. I don't have enough eyes in the back of my head to watch out for you and her. Bethany stays. You go."

"I don't know if Bethany will be okay staying here alone with a man." Ashley wrapped her arms around herself. "She's always been wary or scared, and after the other day..."

"She's had no problems so far this morning," Dot interjected.

"I was there to rescue her," T.J. added. "She knows I'm okay."

Ashley still looked apprehensive.

"If it makes you feel any better, my mother will still be here. She just won't be able to keep an eye on Bethany and pack up for a hunting trip." Dot gripped the younger woman's forearm.

"We won't be gone a long time?" she asked.

"We'll make it quick," Dot assured.

After another pregnant pause, Ashley nodded her head. "Okay."

"I'll call Sloane," T.J. said, disappearing down the hall with his phone in hand.

Ashley watched him go, then began pulling out ingredients for the pancakes. "Who's Sloane?"

"His partner."

She paused and gaped at Dot. "The bounty hunter has a partner?"

"Oh, yeah. And she's a doozy."

Chapter Thirteen

RICHARD T. FORD wasn't a man many believed capable of anything remotely close to being a Benedict Arnold. For thirty years, he'd run on the slogan of being the sheriff's people of Pyrenees County, and the voters ate it up. Not many had tried to run against him each election cycle, and those who did lost by a landslide. For most of his career, he'd practiced what he'd preached.

Until he'd been offered a business proposal he would have been stupid to refuse.

Sitting in his truck, sipping strong black coffee from a Yeti thermos cup, he watched the front door of Cherry's bed and breakfast from three buildings down. Yesterday afternoon he'd spotted the huge SUV roll into Euskadi and park outside Cherry's. When he saw the hulking figure of the man who'd partnered with Dorothy the day before exit the vehicle, Ford's apprehension went through the roof. It'd ratcheted up another step when Sloane Cross emerged.

A light knock on the passenger side window and Charles Smith, if that was his real name, settled into the passenger seat with a fancy to-go cup in hand.

"You city slickers and your need for some damn highfalutin' espresso."

"Don't knock it, Ford," Smith said, then drank from the cup. "Any change?"

"None." Ford gave the man the side-eye. "You sure she came back alone last night? Her partner could have hopped out a mile back and reconned his way into the house without you noticing. He crossed me as military."

Smith returned Ford's skeptical look with an irritated one but said nothing.

The front door opened, and Cherry popped out to set a potted plant on the porch then slipped back inside.

Charles Smith was a self-centered prick with a special knack for making things happen quickly or making people disappear. Smith had been sent here after Ford was initially approached. He lingered long enough to ensure processes were completed and things were in place and then returned to his masters. Each time he came, shit hit the fan in Pyrenees County. When Smith left, Ford found himself standing a pile of dirt with more than a few bodies buried beneath. Still, no one was the wiser as to what was going on.

Smith's return this time was due to a major fuckup on the part of Ford's newest deputy, Wall. The deputy had been brought on because the handlers wanted a consistent plant in the department. Ford suspected they were finding him lacking and needed an informant.

Problem was, Wall had run afoul of Matlock Hargrave, Pyrenees County's favorite hometown boy. Not only did Hargrave begin to play detective into the clandestine goings-on in the county, but he also copped an attitude that grated on Ford's pride. If given half a mind to do it, Hargrave would run for sheriff in the next election, and Ford would lose his position. And the powers that be would have to run a scrub mission.

"You need to handle the woman," Smith said.

Ford dragged his attention away from the bed and breakfast to glance at the man next to him. He knew full well who *the woman* was.

"She's not someone you trifle with. She and her mother would eat us alive." Ford shook his head and resumed his watch. "No. I'm not going that route."

"You have no say in the matter. She goes. The girl and her daughter go too."

Ford felt the blood seep from his face. "A child?"

Smith drank his fancy coffee.

"I don't hurt children," Ford insisted.

"Then you shouldn't have entered this world."

The Yeti trembled. Gulping against the tightness in his throat, Ford shoved the thermos into the cupholder and gripped the steering wheel.

"The girl and her kid aren't part of this," he said. "They're not part of the deal."

"The deal was to be flexible to whatever needed to be done to keep the project on track." Smith crushed his now-empty cup. "You know the cost if you can't uphold your end of the bargain."

The bed and breakfast door opened again, and this time Sloane Cross exited. She shifted her cane to her left hand to slide her sunglasses down, then returned the cane to her right and hobbled down the steps.

"Follow her," Smith said, then exited the truck cab.

"Where are you going?" Ford demanded.

Smith slid his own sunglasses on. "Your job is not to ask questions." With that, he shut the door and walked away.

Ford watched Sloane climb into the large SUV, indecision waging a war in his mind. He had to obey the command. He'd thought that by being involved with the project, he'd have a way to control certain aspects.

The taillights snapped to life on the SUV, then it slowly pulled away from the curb.

Ford had willingly kept his head in the sand as parts of the project spilled over into the populace of Pyrenees County. But the issues were starting to make themselves more prevalent, and people were noticing. People like the Hargraves.

Things had already gone badly with them, and they were becoming even more involved.

Now Dorothy had entered the mix.

Sloane's SUV crept down the street. Ford started his truck and pulled out. When the SUV turned left onto Jefferson Street, Ford sped up. He made the turn and spotted the SUV heading for the edge of Euskadi.

Ford had a suspicion he knew where Sloane was going. But he couldn't break off after being ordered to follow.

If he had only listened to his conscience and refused the offer.

Chapter Fourteen

S LOANE DROVE ONTO the Ybarra ranch, slowed the SUV, and studied the quaint scene before her.

T.J. stood in the middle of a round pen with a dark gray horse walking around him. On the back of said horse rode a little girl who looked for all the world like she belonged up there. Standing along the fence, her foot propped on the bottom rung, Dot watched the goings on, with a younger woman Sloane assumed was the girl's mother right beside her.

It was a homey scene. Picturesque if one had to label it. It reminded Sloane of years past when it was Dot's grandfather Samo teaching her how to ride, with Dot doing her own crazy stunts in the next paddock over.

Sloane parked the SUV along the lane and hopped out. The door slam drew Dot's attention from the chittering girl.

Dot said something to the other woman and then moved to meet Sloane across the yard. As Dot's jacket shifted around her, Sloane spotted the holstered sidearm.

"Thanks for coming out," Dot said by way of greeting.

"No problem." Sloane nodded at T.J. "Would have needed to come get him eventually." She looked pointedly at Dot's right hip. "Expecting trouble?"

Dot settled her hand on the pistol butt. "I always carry." As if that was the only reason.

"Always knew T.J. was good with kids," Sloane redirected.

"Definitely makes it easier for her mother to leave her here with him."

"Your mom not able to watch her?"

Dot's face screwed up in bemused scrunch. "I scared off her last paying customers, and this is a longtime client she trusts. Gotta let her do her thing without a kid underfoot." She contemplated Sloane. "I mentioned you this morning, and she seemed curiously weird about you."

Sloane flashed a grin. "Is that so?"

Dot narrowed her eyes. "Did something happen I don't know about?"

Oh, something had happened all right, clear back in the days when the two of them were getting out of high school. Angela had cornered Sloane and demanded she convince Dot to find a different path—one that didn't send her into the army—and Sloane refused. Dot was never the wiser to her mother's attempt to sabotage her future career, and Sloane earned Angela's lifelong ire for not siding with her.

"Never you mind what your mother thinks of me," Sloane said. "I'm used to people dissing me because of my line of work and my opinions."

Dot stared at her a moment longer, then rolled her eyes.

"We're burning daylight," Sloane said.

"Ashley!" Dot's barked order drew T.J.'s and the girl's attention to them. The little girl waved wildly at her mother as Ashley walked away.

The three of them climbed into the SUV. As Sloane navigated the vehicle along the drive and pointed toward the road, Angela Ybarra stepped out of the house. She paused on the porch to watch them leave. Sloane noted the scowl that crossed the elder Ybarra woman's face as they passed.

Never let it be said a Basque woman didn't hold a grudge.

A mile down the road toward Euskadi, Sloane broke the silence.

"Where is it we're going?"

"I have an apartment in that complex on the northside of Euskadi," Ashley said from the back seat.

Sloane glanced in the rearview mirror, the woman's face filling the majority of the view, except for the black smudge in the distance.

"Anywhere else?" she asked, returning her gaze to the road before them.

"Nowhere else," Dot said.

"Uhhh," Ashley started.

Another glance in the mirror showed a flushed face before Ashley leaned away and revealed a full picture of the roadway in the rear. The black smudge had the distinct shape of a cow kicker grill.

"Uh, what?" Dot asked, twisting in her seat to look back.

"Would it be okay if we stop at the restaurant where I work and get my last paycheck?"

Dot's pensive face didn't seem promising.

"I don't see why not," Sloane said. "We're well prepared."

Dot eyed Sloane, then sighed. "As long as you're quick about it."

"I should probably tell them I'm quitting, too."

This threw Sloane. "Why would you quit? You need the job."

"Angela asked if I would like to be a camp cook for her hunters." Ashley ducked her head and faced the window, getting out Sloane's line of sight. "It would be good for Bethany and me."

The satisfied look on Dot's face when she resumed her forward-facing position intrigued Sloane.

"I'd still hold onto your job," Sloane said. "Hunting season is a short time, and you'll need something on the offseason."

"I'd bet my best bow Cherry would love to have help during the tourist season," Dot mumbled.

After what T.J. had told Sloane about Dot's reaction to having Ashley around, her sudden desire to help the woman out was unnerving.

"Are you feeling alright?" she asked.

Dot's side-eye brought back a lot of memories. "I'm right as rain."

She certainly looked it. In fact, she seemed more chipper than she'd been last night. In a really good mood considering how she looked when Sloane parted ways with her and T.J. Then it dawned on Sloane.

"Picked up right where you left off, huh?" she teased.

Dot shrugged and left it at that.

"Is it going to be a problem for me to stay on your ranch?" Ashley asked, her voice holding a hint of trepidation.

Dot slumped in the seat, tilting her hat forward. "It was my idea. Why would it be a problem?" She crossed her arms and let her chin sink to her chest. "Wake me when we get to town."

Sloane watched the dark vehicle gain on them. "Sure thing," she said.

She caught Ashley's gaze in the mirror. The younger woman must have seen something in Sloane's face, because she twisted in her seat to stare out the back window. Ashley suddenly whipped around, her eyes glinted with fear. Sloane pressed a finger to her lips and hushed Ashley before the woman could raise the alarm.

At this point, Sloane wasn't certain if the truck was purposely following them, or it was just coincidence they were traveling the same route.

Ashley's fear was justifiable after what she'd gone through in the last few days. Hell, for the last several years of her life. This would be a good time to get the woman's mind off her fear.

"Ashley, do you care if I ask you a few questions?" Sloane caught a twitch in Dot's arm.

How long would she feign sleep before becoming involved?

"I guess," Ashley ventured.

"When you were with Craig, did he ever have people come over who seemed … out of his league?"

"What do you mean by out of his league?"

"People he didn't want you to see or be around."

Ashley seemed to mull on this. While Sloane waited, she kept glancing at the mirrors and tracking the vehicle trailing them. It was another ten miles into Euskadi.

"Right before he went to prison, before I moved here,

there were times he made me go in another room and shut the door. Made me keep Bethany quiet so no one would hear us." Ashley peered at Sloane curiously. "Why are you asking?"

"It's kind of a long story," Sloane replied.

"But you're a bounty hunter. Right?"

"I'm also a private investigator. Coincidentally, Craig's bounty and a case I'm working have intersected."

This roused Dot. She flicked her hat brim up and stared at Sloane.

"You knew this last night," Sloane stated.

"All you said was you had a killed lead on a case. You didn't specify that Craig was your lead."

"It was implied."

Sloane focused on the vehicle trailing them. It was clearly a truck, but she couldn't make out the front plate. The driver was maintaining minimal speed and distance to avoid indication. She'd gone out of her way to slow down then speed up, and still the truck tailed.

Ashley must have noticed her hyper awareness. She twisted around. "It's getting closer."

"What's getting closer?" Dot demanded and looked back herself. "It's just a truck."

"A truck that has been following us," Sloane said.

"For how long?"

"The moment we left the ranch road and got onto the pavement. I think it might have been following me when I came out to your place, but I wasn't paying attention then. Can you make out the model and maybe the driver?" Sloane asked.

Dot was quiet, then shook her head. "Too far back. It looks exactly like any of a hundred trucks with cow kickers driven by everyone in this damn county."

"Now what?" Ashley asked.

"We're going to find out if this asshat really is following us," Dot said. She pointed at a lane jutting out from between a patch of scraggle pine and fir. "That's a private drive. Take it."

"Whose private drive?"

"Don't worry about it," Dot barked.

Sloane slammed on the brakes and took a hard right onto the drive. She gunned the engine, and the SUV barreled down the gravel lane. Dot pointed to a two-track dirt road merging on the right-hand side.

"Pull in there and go until you reach the trees."

Sloane did as ordered and halted the vehicle between the trees. Dot had the door open in an instant.

"You got a pair of binos?"

"Glove box."

Dot pulled out the binoculars. "Stay put." She didn't give Sloane a chance to protest before she slammed the door and took off.

"What is she doing?" Ashley asked, a tremor in her voice.

"Whatever the hell Dot wants."

"And that is?"

"Pissing people off," Sloane groused.

"Aren't you going after her?"

Sloane gaped at the woman, then jabbed a finger at the cane and her leg. "Does it look like I can go after her?"

Ashley turned a bright shade of pink and sank into her

seat. "Sorry," she croaked.

Sloane rolled her eyes. "Never mind." She popped the top on the console and removed her sidearm. "If it's a legit threat, we're well protected." She stared hard through the passenger side window in the direction Dot had disappeared. "Not that she'd allow them to get to us."

DOT RACED OVER the flattened terrain, heading back to the road. She kept to the cover of the intermittent patches of firs and sagebrush scattered through the empty pasture. Seeing the paved road in sight, she slammed down onto her belly.

With binos pressed to her face, she found the truck. It was parked along the side of the road, a patch of sagebrush obscuring the door panel. As Dot was adjusting the binos for the distance, the truck began backing up. It picked up speed then swung around to face east and peeled out, smoke rising from the tires burning rubber to find purchase.

Everything happened too fast for Dot to make out the words along the side of the truck or the plate.

"Fuck!"

Dust puffed into the air from her fist.

She gave it a few more seconds, then climbed to her feet. Brushing herself off, she stared at the empty roadway. With a grunt, she turned and headed back to Sloane's SUV.

She pried open the door and chucked the binos inside.

Sloane pounced. "You see who it was?"

"Fuck no. We spooked them bad when we turned down here. They cut tail and ran back the opposite direction."

"Just confirms we were being followed. Even with the binoculars, you didn't see anything worthwhile?"

"Only what I said before, it's a make and model of truck nearly everyone drives. It did have something on the door panels, but I couldn't adjust for the distance in time to make it out."

"A truck with a decal or wording on the side narrows it down."

"By half," Dot remarked. "Too many people put their ranch or farm name or brand on their vehicles."

"Who would know about me? Or be able to spot me in this vehicle?" Sloane asked.

Dot gave her a wry smile. "Agent Alphabet. You and T.J. are staying in the same damn B-and-B he is."

"And he's buddy-buddy with the sheriff."

Dot pulled herself into the cab. "Or a particular deputy. We can't be too certain it wasn't someone else."

"It thins out the suspect herd," Sloane said.

"Absolutely does." Dot turned to Ashley, noticing the lack of color in the younger woman's features. "You now have less time to get your things. The longer we take in town, the more likely we're going to be cornered."

"I really need my paycheck."

"We'll get it. You don't go anywhere alone." Dot faced forward as Sloane backed out of the dirt lane and headed back toward the paved road.

"Who do you think they were really following?"

Dot glared at the windshield. "It could have been any one of us. But they know about you." She swung her narrowed gaze to her old friend. "Which means you've worried them about something."

Sloane nodded at the rearview mirror. "They know about her too. Probably thinking she knows more than she does or thinks she does."

"I don't know anything about Craig's business dealings. Or who he dealt with."

"Doesn't mean a damn thing," Dot said. She focused on the passing scenery. "Craig didn't just try to take Bethany."

"What are you saying?" Ashley demanded.

"What she's saying is, Craig was making a run for it with the only thing of value to him and he was leaving you for the dogs," Sloane said.

"The dogs? Value to him? What are you talking about?"

"Damn it," Sloane snapped.

"What?" Dot asked.

"I think this is more connected than I first thought." She sighed. "T.J.'s not going to like this."

Chapter Fifteen

T.J. SETTLED INTO a wooden chair on the porch with a fresh mug of joe. Out in the yard, the swirling pack of dogs surrounding her, Bethany pranced around like she was still riding a horse. The herding dogs would bark at her now and then, trying to steer her, but Bethany paid them no mind and continued on her merry way.

Angela's hunting client and his friends had arrived thirty minutes ago, and she was busy finalizing the details for the hunt.

T.J. sipped the coffee. He was liking this brew. Better ask Dot where she got it.

Bethany halted mid-prance, about-faced, and, with a wide grin, bolted. The dogs veered direction and took off after her, joyous barking included. She made it as far as the porch and abruptly changed direction, colliding with one of the bigger dogs. She toppled over and fell to the ground, laughing. The dogs swarmed, a few getting a chance to lick her face.

From somewhere behind the house, Angela appeared.

"Off!" she commanded the dogs.

The pack left the giggling girl on the ground. Angela walked over to Bethany.

"Aren't you supposed to watch the girl?" she asked T.J.

"I'm watching her play with the dogs."

She shook her head and reached down to haul Bethany to her feet. The girl babbled to Angela about whatever it was little girls babbled about.

Angela smiled and picked out the leaves in Bethany's hair. "Sounds good to me. Why don't you run into the house and clean up. Let's see if we can find some lunch."

Bethany squealed with delight, ran up the steps, and blew into the house. Angela followed, pausing next to T.J.

"Be honest with me, Mr. Roman."

He looked up at her, but she kept her gaze trained on the door. "What's that?"

"Have you involved my daughter in something dangerous?"

He considered her a moment, wondering what it was Angela Ybarra really wanted to hear.

"Do you know what it was your daughter did while she was in the army?" he asked.

"She flew helicopters." Angela looked down at him. "And that's all I know."

That was all Dot wanted her to know. Angela seemed levelheaded enough to T.J., but she was a mother. T.J.'s own mother hadn't been thrilled when her boy joined the army, nor was she happy that he kept secrets from her. What mother did? The type of missions he'd been on—the type of missions Dot flew him in and out of—were not for public consumption.

"There's always a certain level of danger in a war zone, Ms. Ybarra. And, as we both know, she was in the thick of it when she flew for the forest service."

Angela looked away.

"You raised one helluva tough woman," T.J. said.

"Her *aitatxi* raised her to be tough," Angela stated.

"She still had her momma to teach her the ways of a woman."

A soft smile revealed a different side of her T.J. wasn't sure he was supposed to see. The harsh reverberation of a gun discharging shattered the moment.

T.J. looked in the direction of where Angela had left her clients. Another weapon fired, making all the ears twitch on the dog pack now lying about the yard.

"Zeroing in the sights?" T.J. asked.

"I had a firing range built up behind the old bunkhouse. They get to use it with the expectation of cleaning up after themselves."

"Mind if I have a go at it when the crew gets back?"

Angela glanced down at him. "Be my guest." She placed a hand on the screen door. "Dorothy will probably come out and have a shoot off."

She had the door partially opened when T.J. asked, "When do you plan to leave with your clients?"

"After lunch. We'll ride up to the campground and camp tonight. Hunt tomorrow and the next day."

T.J. finished his coffee. "Do you trust them?"

"This man, yes. He doesn't bring along anyone he doesn't trust himself. Alcohol is never allowed on my hunts."

Another weapon discharged, the boom echoing through the valley.

"I have my pack." Angela patted her side. "And my protection if there's any trouble."

"Never second-guess a pistol-packin' momma."

"Mr. Roman, I think I might like you," Angela said and walked inside.

T.J. wiped away his grin and rose, leaving the mug on the chair's wide armrest. The dogs' heads popped up as he descended the steps, and they tracked his progress toward the trucks Angela's clients had parked at the edge of the drive. He was waylaid when his phone rang.

He retrieved the phone from the case hooked to his belt on his left hip, glancing at the caller ID before answering. "If you're calling me, something has gone down," he said to Sloane.

"It has. We were followed on the way to Euskadi. Couldn't tell who it was. Dot's insistent we stay at the ranch."

T.J. scanned the perimeter. "We need to get a handle on this."

"I know. Soon as I get back there, I'm making a call to the client."

She wouldn't say his name in front of the uninformed. It wasn't Sloane's way.

"No. I'll call him. You worry about getting all our gear and keeping your guard up."

Another gunshot echoed around him.

"Was that gunfire?" Sloane asked, a hint of panic in her voice.

"Angela's outfitting clients, just making sure their guns are ready for a hunt."

There was a noticeable sigh over the line. "Call him. I'll

probably still have to explain things later." She ended the call before he could respond.

T.J. rerouted and headed for the barn where he could make the call undisturbed. The heady scent of hay and horseflesh called to him as he entered. He knew Dot's weed stash was in here, and she'd smoked it last night, but he couldn't smell it. Probably a good thing she'd chosen here to hide it.

He entered the tack room and closed the door. If Angela came in here, she might wonder why it was shut, but it gave him the extra layer of soundproofing he needed for this call.

The client picked up on the third ring.

"We have a problem."

WHILE SLOANE MADE her call to T.J., Dot entered Cherry's bed and breakfast.

Cherry popped out from behind her front desk. Today she was decked out in a purple and black flannel button-up under a black vest, snug blue jeans, and dark-brown leather paddock boots. She looked better suited hanging out with all the high-born equestrians instead of in a cowboy town.

"Dot?"

"Hey, Cherry. I need you to check out Sloane and her partner. Today."

Cherry's smile faded. "Why?"

"Long story. Don't worry about payment. They plan to pay for the entire stay even though they won't be here."

"Payment isn't an issue." Cherry slapped her hands on

her hips. "What's going on? Does this have anything to do with why Matlock was drunk off his ass last night and too hungover to go to work today?"

"Come again?"

"What did you all talk about last night? I've never seen my brother so … so … not my brother."

After her catastrophic bout with flashbacks and panic attacks, Dot hadn't really thought much on Matlock's mental state when she left him.

"Ah, shit," Dot muttered.

"Ah, shit is right," Cherry chided. "Rowdy had a difficult time rounding up Matlock and getting him home last night. Apparently, my brother was so far gone he passed out before Rowdy could get him in his house."

Dot ran a hand down her face and groaned. "Cherry, I'm sorry. Your brother is going through some shit and…" Dot sighed. "I don't know if you should be privy to all that."

"Don't really have a choice. He's my brother."

A brother who was bound by the law not to reveal what he'd witnessed or had dealt with in the last year or more. Matlock was, by nature, closed off and protective of his family. He'd spun a special cocoon around himself when his dad was suddenly taken from the earth, hiding behind those delicate folds while becoming more hyper vigilant in watching over his mother and sisters. It was now coming back to bite him in the ass.

How well Dot knew the feeling.

"Look, Cherry, Sloane getting out of here has nothing to do with Matlock. There's other reasons."

"Sure?"

Dot couldn't tell if Cherry was asking or being sarcastic. Her tones were beginning to meld together. Or Dot was more exhausted than she realized, and she was letting her imagination run wild with her.

The door banged open, and Sloane hobbled inside. "Got that handled," she said and smiled at Cherry. "We all set?"

Cherry gave Dot a particularly hard stare, then looked to Sloane. "Yeah, we're all set. I'll keep the rooms open in case you change your mind and come back."

"That would be awesome." Sloane headed for the staircase. "Follow me."

Dot leaned toward Cherry. "I'll check on Matlock after I get Sloane back to my ranch. Okay?"

"You better. Momma doesn't know about his episode. Yet."

God forbid Millie Hargrave find out her son took a headfirst dive into the alcohol pool. Millie became a hard-on teetotaler after it was suspected alcohol may have contributed to her husband Quincy's death.

"If she does, you get to play referee," Dot stated.

Cherry shook her head. "Not in a million years."

Even her grown children refused to cross swords with their mother.

Dot rushed up the steps, catching up with Sloane as she was opening a door halfway down the hall.

Sloane chucked a replica skeleton key at Dot. "T.J.'s room is this one." She pointed at a door across the hall.

Dot was inserting the key when Sloane stopped in the doorway.

"What the ever-lovin'…?"

Dot crowded in behind her friend. Sloane's room was ransacked. What few belongings she'd brought were dumped on the bed and scattered. The mattress was skewed, the bedding dangled from the edge.

They found the same carnage in T.J.'s room.

"Are you fucking kidding me?" Sloane snapped.

Cherry appeared at the top of the steps. "What's wrong?"

Sloane swept her arm back and forth between the rooms. "Some asshole went through our stuff."

"What?" Cherry's voice rang with incredulousness. "That's impossible. I would have heard it." She poked her head into Sloane's room. "Oh!"

"Exactly," Sloane snapped.

Dot pushed between them and studied the room. "Someone probably picked the locks." She glanced at Sloane. "Any idea what they were looking for?"

Their gazes locked. Sloane didn't need to verbalize in front of Cherry what Dot suspected. There was some sense in why Sloane was being followed. Whoever did this needed to know they had time.

"Anything of interest was not left in our rooms," Sloane said.

Dot resumed her study, but movement outside the windows caught her attention. The room faced the street where the SUV was parked. A dark-gray truck with a huge grill and SHERIFF scrolled across the side panel had parked alongside the SUV. The driver's side door opened and out slid Deputy Corey Wall.

"Sloane," Dot said.

Cherry moved with Sloane to the window. The trio

watched Wall look about and then amble over to the SUV.

"Shit," Sloane muttered. "Ashley."

They'd left the younger woman in the SUV.

Dot reeled back from the window. "Gather up your stuff. I'll go run interference."

She didn't give either woman a chance to rebut. Dot was down the hall and racing down the stairs. She pulled up fast at the door and, with a casualness she didn't feel, opened it and sauntered onto the porch.

The clack from the door shutting jolted Wall from his snooping. He about-faced faster than a private caught dicking with his buddies when the First Sergeant arrived.

"Can I help you, Deputy Wall?" Dot asked, stepping off the porch.

He pointed at her. "Dorothy Ybarra, right?"

"I could be. Do you need something?"

He glanced at the SUV. "Well, I was driving by and no-ticed..." He flashed a smile at her. "Maybe I was just seeing things."

"Like what?" Dot invaded his personal space. He wasn't much taller than she was, and there was a spearhead of black ink peeking out from behind his shirt collar on the right side. The shiner T.J. had given him covered nearly the whole left side of his face.

"Like someone getting inside the vehicle," he stated.

Dot looked around him. His truck was pointed right. The SUV was pointed left. The windows on the back half of the SUV were tinted darker than the windshield and front two. When they'd vacated the car, Dot had ordered Ashley to get further into the back and lie down on the bench seat.

It was possible the woman had moved around, but how had he seen it? Had Ashley gotten out?

Wall was now gripping the straps of his utility vest. "I guess I should have thanked you for not letting that hothead shoot me the other day."

If he thought he was going to make small talk with her, he had another think coming.

"Deputy Wall, what are you doing?"

"My job, Ms. Ybarra."

"And that is?"

His gaze narrowed; the muscles in his face twitched. "I heard stories about you," he said in a lowered voice.

She smiled, baring her canines. "I'm sure you did. Fairly certain the most recent one was how I handed Willy Donnel's ass to him after I caught him beating on his girl. Or maybe it was the one where I told the sheriff to go fuck off."

"You and your momma think you're something in this county."

"How would you know? You're not from here." Dot leaned closer. "Just where is it you come from, Wall? Nevada? Utah? California?" She growled out the last word.

"I know that girl is with you. She needs to come in."

"Why?" Dot shot back.

"You know why. She's an eyewitness."

"She's six years old and saw nothing. Thank God for that. I've seen enough shit in my life; I can't begin to imagine what it could be like to watch some dipshit shoot my father dead in front of me."

Wall's features tightened, and a red-purple hue seeped in, matching the color of his bruise. His dark eyes turned hard.

"Someone needs to shut your mouth."

"Wanna try?"

Dot tapped a fingernail against the Colt's gun butt under her hand. The loud click dragged Wall's gaze down, then it flicked back to her face.

"Open carry. Conceal carry. I've got it all covered," she said.

The bed and breakfast door squeaked open, drawing Wall's attention away from her.

"Deputy." Cherry's voice was like a whip crack. "Is there something I can help you with?"

His cold eyes slithered back to Dot. "Not really, Ms. Hargrave. I think I figured out what's up."

"Yes," Dot said coolly. "You most certainly have."

He sidestepped, getting past the SUV, and then back-pedaled to his truck. "If you need any assistance, Ms. Hargrave, you just call."

"I'll be sure not to do that," Cherry said.

Dot watched him climb into the truck and drive away. Once the dark vehicle disappeared around a corner, she yanked open the back door. Ashley tumbled out, wrapping her arms around Dot's midsection.

"Oh my God. I thought he was going to see me and haul me out."

She trembled hard enough to make Dot shake. She gingerly patted the other woman's shoulder.

Sloane's cane clapping against the porch steps dragged Ashley away.

"Everything seems accounted for," Sloane said as she hauled two backpacks to the SUV. She chucked the bags into the back. "Dot, make sure the creep didn't tag my vehicle."

"Did you see him try it?" Dot asked, pushing Ashley aside. "'Cause I sure didn't."

"He stayed upright the whole time," Ashley said. "I didn't see him bend over to look under the car."

Sloane took an elongated hard-shell case from Cherry. "Don't mean crap. There's fucking trackers the size of your fingertip now. They can be placed anywhere on the vehicle and will blend in."

Dot ran her hand over the panel on the driver's side of the SUV. "You didn't keep a gun case in your room?" she asked as Sloane slid the case into the hatch area.

"Hell no. I had Cherry lock it up."

"Smart." Dot felt the slightest bump on the underside of the mirror encasement. She got a fingernail under the edge and pried off whatever it was. The thing stuck to the tip of her finger once it came free of the framework. "Got it."

"Told ya."

Dot peered under the mirror. A neat circle surrounded by dust was left behind where the tracker had been placed. "Uh, Sloane." She stepped back and examined the tiny black spot on her finger. "I think this has been there a while."

Sloane marched up, scowling. "Can't be. I always do a sweep."

"Is it possible to have a bug that's not detectable by normal measures?"

"I mean, it is, but that's like big-time spy craft..." Her features turned crimson, making her freckles disappear. "Give me that."

Sloane snatched the tiny bug. She pinched it between her

finger and thumb and crushed the device. "They wanna do a li'l F-A? Let's do some F-O."

"Mind telling me what is going on?" Cherry insisted.

Dot wanted to know herself. Seemed like Sloane knew more than she was willing to reveal.

Sloane shook her head. She navigated around Cherry, leaning heavily on her cane in the process, and hiked to the back end of the SUV. "For your sake, it's best you know jack squat."

Cherry's frown turned to a scowl. She turned that scowl on Dot.

Dot's instant reaction was to shrug. Sloane had always been closed off and difficult to read, even when they were kids. Intelligent and book smart, she came across as a nerd, but underneath the shell was a badass with a sharp tongue. She'd ruffled more than feathers in her younger years. It was one of the main reasons she and Dot had gotten along so well. Yet, there were a lot of years between their youth and now, leaving Dot to wonder what made this Sloane tick.

Sloane slammed the hatch shut. Ashley jerked.

"She's right," Dot soothed. "Keep an eye out and Rowdy close."

Cherry's scowl faded.

A wariness appeared in her eyes. "Does this have anything to do with Matlock's current state?"

"I really don't know." Dot gripped her friend's arm. "I'll talk to him. Promise."

With an acquiescing nod, Cherry returned to her business. Dot motioned for Ashley to get back in the vehicle as Sloane stormed toward the driver's side.

Dot stopped her. "Let me drive."

Rage radiated from Sloane. "Are you coddling me?"

Dot eyed Sloane with her don't-bullshit-me look in place. Sloane rolled her eyes and dug out the fob.

"I hope you drive better than you fly," Sloane snarked as she rounded the front end.

"Better than you can drive a bike," Dot shot back.

From her rooted station beside her opened door, Ashley gaped at Dot. "Did you just…"

Dot flung open the driver's side door. "Insult her? Sure as hell did. She insulted me."

Ashley's eyes widened. "I don't—"

"Stop, right there. You don't know me or Sloane's history. If you so much as cry foul on us, especially her, she'll rip you a new one. Get in. We don't have time to debate."

They were back on the road and halfway out of town when Sloane spoke again.

"What did he say to you? Wall, that is?"

"He gave a piss-poor excuse as to why he was snooping around the car. Then demanded we bring Bethany in."

"Why?" Ashley squeaked from the back.

"Because they think she saw Wall kill her father." Dot glared out the windshield as a thought occurred to her. "Or she saw or knows something before that." She looked at Sloane. "This was why you were questioning Ashley about Craig's business dealings when they were together."

"Exactly."

Dot gripped the steering wheel, grating the leather casing against her palms. "Shit."

"What does it mean?" Ashley asked.

"It means we have to dig deeper into this and close ranks."

Chapter Sixteen

T.J. MOMENTARILY LOST track of Bethany. He found her in the goat pasture among the herd, casually petting one of the guardian dogs while she talked to the animals. The two other dogs wouldn't allow T.J. anywhere near the goats and the kid, so he had to coax Bethany out. Once past the fencing, he hauled her up and carried her back to the house.

"What are you, some kind of animal whisperer?" he asked.

Bethany bobbed her head, making her hair fly. "Mommy says I'm trouble."

T.J. chuckled. "Trouble sums it up."

"Where are your kids?" Bethany blurted.

"Don't have any," T.J. said without missing a step. "Just nieces and nephews."

"You should marry Dot and have kids."

He stopped walking and nearly choked on his tongue. He looked at the girl, and her wide, beguiling eyes stared back at him.

With a shake of his head, T.J. laughed. "Kid, I can barely take care of myself some days. A family is the last thing I need."

They rounded the house in time to see the SUV pull in.

Bethany squirmed in his arm when Ashley emerged. T.J. set her down, and she took off for her mother.

He ambled up to the SUV as Dot slid out of the driver's side and Sloane the other. Both women looked perturbed.

"What's up?" he asked.

"Someone broke into our rooms at the B and B and ransacked them," Sloane said, moving to the hatch.

Panic hit him. "They didn't take the guns?"

"No, I had those with Cherry. Far as I can tell, nothing was taken," Sloane answered.

Relief washed away the panic. No sense putting themselves further into trouble without suitable firearms.

Dot bypassed him, stopped, and about-faced. "For now, you two can hole up in the bunkhouse. Might need the cobwebs knocked down and swept, but it's functional."

"As long as there's a bed, table, and internet access, I don't care," Sloane said.

"I'm heading back to Euskadi," Dot said.

"What for?" T.J. asked.

She grimaced. "Apparently, Matlock had a really bad night after we left. I need to run interference."

"Check your truck!" Sloane hollered.

"Duh!" Dot shot back.

T.J. felt like he was being whacked around in a dryer barrel. "Check your truck for what?"

"Bugs," Dot said, and walked away.

Sloane poked her head out from around the hatch. "Someone tagged the SUV."

Heat surged through T.J.'s veins. "How the fu—" He made eye contact with the scowling Ashley still holding her daughter. "How?" he amended.

Sloane emerged with a pair of packs. "No idea. And no clue how long it's been there."

He moved to take the bags from her and spotted his gun case in the back. "Whoever tossed our rooms knows who we are."

"Exactly." Sloane dragged a hard-shell case where she kept her laptop and devices to the edge of the back end. "The only thing I can think they'd want to steal other than the guns are my case notes."

"Did they succeed?"

"No." Sloane removed a plastic cover, where normally the car manufacturer left a cheap set of jack stands and a lug wrench for tire repair. Sloane had retrofitted it as a portable safe. "Never leave information or evidence where someone can access it." She removed the contents.

When she went to reach for the other bags, T.J. stopped her. "Let me handle this. You get set up in the bunkhouse."

Sloane looked ready to argue, seemed to reconsider, and then took the hard-shell case. Without a word, she headed off toward the bunkhouse.

T.J. loaded up on their gear while Ashley pulled her own things out.

On his way to the bunkhouse, Dot waylaid him.

"*Ama* gone?" she asked.

"Left about an hour ago with her hunting party."

She considered the foothills, her features pensive.

He rotated to stare out in the same direction. "There going to be a problem?"

"Shouldn't be. She always carries a satellite phone with

her for emergencies. If something comes up, she'll call. Besides, she's safer out there."

"I'd say so. She took the whole damn pack of dogs, save for those two heelers you had the other day. According to her, those are your dogs."

"They've adopted me." She moved to her truck. "No bugs. I'm going."

"Armed?"

She lifted her coat to reveal the holstered pistol on her side. "Always."

He watched her leave. A niggling feeling in his gut didn't sit well with him. He shrugged it off. It was Dot. She was fine.

THE BUNKHOUSE WAS a typical throwback to the Old West concept of one large room divided into sections. One side held five racks of bunk beds. The center was the kitchen dining area. The last section was a small seating area to relax before a fire and chat or read.

After a quick cleaning and locating bedding for the bunks, Sloane set up her equipment all over the table and parts of the seating area. She was punching the laptop keys with a fury T.J. hadn't seen in her in a long while.

With the background of angry clacking, he examined the guns and ran an oilcloth over them to ensure they were prepared.

"What did he say?" Sloane asked out of the blue.

He glanced at her, took a moment to figure out who she

was asking about, then continued his duties. "He's coming here."

Her furious typing ceased. "Why?" she asked.

"He wants to help. Apparently, we're going to need him."

She shook her head and resumed her work.

"He's not our only concern," T.J. added. "I got a call from the other client. He knows."

Sloane swallowed, refusing to stop her typing, but she kept faltering and having to hit the delete key. With a groan, she shoved the laptop away from her.

"I can't have them all here at once."

T.J. packed away the cleaning kit. "You don't have a choice. We had no clue any of this was going to intertwine when we took the cases."

She groaned again and scrubbed her face. "We need more people."

"Did Dot agree?" he asked, setting aside the gun he'd been cleaning and stood.

"Not yet." Sloane slumped in the chair. "We didn't have a chance to talk about it. I think she will, she just needs to say it."

He crossed the room and took the chair next to her. "Bounty hunting will be good for her. Work out all the broken parts."

Sloane eyed him. "I didn't think the PTSD was that bad." She sighed. "Guess I was wrong. Maybe she shouldn't do this."

"She's got a handle on it. Don't worry. We all have fucked-up heads."

Sloane rolled her eyes. "Oh, what a team we'll make."

There was a knock on the door.

"Yeah?" Sloane shot out.

The door opened and Ashley stepped inside with Bethany in tow. The little girl had her nose practically pressed to a handheld device. Sounds of a child's game came from its speaker.

"Can I speak with you two?" Ashley asked.

"Sure," T.J. answered.

Bethany's head popped up over the game and she grinned at him. T.J. gave her a wink, and she went back to playing.

"Sweetie, would you go sit over there and play your game?" Ashley asked.

"Sure, Mommy," Bethany said without looking up, then wandered over to the bunkbeds.

Once she plopped down on the farthest one—ironically, the one T.J. had claimed as his own—Ashley took a seat across from him and Sloane.

"The client you mentioned," Ashley pointedly asked Sloane. "It's my father. Isn't it?"

Whatever preconceived notions or facts they had been given about Ashley Cooper were straight-up lies. This chick was more observant than she led on.

"I never said anything to you about a client," Sloane said.

Ashley bowed her head in shame. "I heard you on the phone when we were at the B and B."

Sloane glanced at T.J. He shrugged. What was he supposed to say?

"How do you figure it's your father who is the client?"

Sloane asked.

Ashley tipped her chin up and looked between the two of them. "He's been chasing after me for years. It's why I stayed with Craig longer than I should have." She peered at Bethany, who continued to defeat animated foes. "Why I keep her close." Her gaze swung back to the pair of them. "My father is a lawyer. If he can't do it himself, he'll get someone who can."

Sloane shifted in her chair. T.J. noticed her attempt to muffle a moan. She was hurting, but she would never admit it.

"As I said before, we are private investigators," she explained to Ashley. "We tend to have more than one client at a time, and some of them are lawyers. Keeps the bills paid when we're between bounty jobs."

"But you're not doing the regular job a lawyer would ask of you. My father aspired to a higher calling. He does his best work cleaning up scandals. And I'm the biggest one that can ruin the family if I'm not brought back into the fold."

T.J. stared at the girl, trying to decipher what she was saying.

"What do you mean, your father aspired to a higher calling?" Sloane asked.

"Exactly that. Something higher than what he currently does. I bet he's trying to run for attorney general." Ashley gripped her hands and wrung them until the blood was cut off. "It would give him the most access to squelch the rumors and the investigations." She focused on T.J. "You weren't really after Craig. You came here looking for me."

"Actually, we did have the bounty on Craig. You just

ended up being a bonus," T.J. told her. He bent forward, bracing his elbows on his knees. "Your dad doesn't know you're here. I aim to keep it that way."

"Why? I know he's paying you both more than your asking rate."

T.J. gestured to Sloane to explain this one. She made her, thanks-a-whole-fucking-lot face at him.

"Your situation with your family is way down at the bottom of the list of things we have to deal with right now," she said. "All my questions to you earlier were in regard to another client we have. Oddly enough, Craig was involved with that case."

Ashley considered what Sloane had told her. "So, the whole line about me being the cosigner was a lie? My name wasn't on the bond. You just said it to protect my father while you chased after Craig?"

Sloane stared at T.J. That had been his ploy to keep Ashley off-guard, and it worked. For a short time.

He sat back in his chair. "Pretty much."

T.J. studied Ashley as she mulled over their answers and confessions. From her corner, Bethany stopped playing her game and was wandering around the bunk beds, checking over Sloane and T.J.'s gear. Her movements caught her mother's attention.

"Bethany, come here."

The girl gave a longing look at one of Sloane's cases, probably the one with some of her *spy* equipment, as she was known to call it. When her mother called her again, Bethany hurried over to her side.

"I should let you two do whatever it is you do," Ashley

said and stood.

"Before you leave," Sloane said. "Deputy Wall. Have you had any interactions with him?"

Ashley stared down at her daughter, caressing the girl's wind-whipped hair. Bethany peered up at her mother, perplexed, then she smiled. Amazing how happy this girl remained despite her life circumstances up to this point.

Ashley looked at him and Sloane. "I have. He would come into the places I worked and always found a way to sit in my section, so I had to wait on him. Never passed up an opportunity to hit on me." She scowled. "He never left a tip."

"Mommy, isn't he the bad guy who scared us at our house?"

Ashley's features paled.

Sloane pounced. "Did he show up where you lived?"

Ashley nodded, wrapping her arms around her daughter. "I think he was looking for me today."

"What's she talking about?" T.J. asked, staring pointedly at Sloane.

"When we were at the bed and breakfast, Deputy Wall showed up and was trying to get into the SUV with me in it," Ashley blurted out.

Little red-hot pokers stabbed T.J.'s mind as he glared at Sloane. "You failed to mention this. You and Dot. Now she's back in town."

Unashamed, Sloane glared right back. "Okay, he-man, we did. Excuse us for being preoccupied with other problems."

"You don't get a pass on this, Sloane. Between the tail

and our rooms being rifled through, among the many other disturbing things going on since I came here to get Craig, this is not one for you to keep from me." He tried to keep his temper under control for Bethany's sake, but these three women were making it hard. "Ashley, get back to the house with Bethany."

Without a word, Ashley ushered her daughter, wide-eyed and curious, out of the bunkhouse.

T.J. rocketed to his feet and went to the door to make sure she and the girl were far enough away before he blew his top. Once they disappeared between the trees, he whipped around.

"You better start explaining yourself."

Sloane struggled to stand.

Her reconstructed hip was bothering her, but she wouldn't tell him a thing about it. "You're not my boss. You're not my dad. You're not even my brother. So can the macho protector act and shut up."

"I am your fucking partner. And I will not stop being who I am."

Their standoff carried on longer than T.J. liked, but there was no backing down when Sloane got in these moods. The minute he gave her any leeway, she'd lord it over him. He respected her for her independence, but she had a way of forgetting she was not invincible.

"I thought Dot would tell you," she finally said, relenting.

"Why would she be the one to tell me?"

"Because she's the one who saw him, and she's the one who had words with him."

T.J. relaxed, letting go of his frustration. "Are you sure Dot is going back to talk with Matlock? Not chase down the sheriff's department?"

Sloane's face danced with unspoken emotions, her eyes widening as she came to a conclusion. "I don't know."

"Shit." T.J. turned for the door.

"Wait! If you go after her, you'll just piss her off."

"So be it." He yanked open the door.

"T.J., she's more than capable of handling herself. She might even get better information if we're not there hovering in the background."

He put the brakes on, then stepped inside the bunk-house. "She doesn't know what to ask."

"Maybe that's the approach we should take. If we want her to join our ranks, she's gotta be able to handle field work. Pounding on doors and asking questions is more than sixty percent of our job."

He sighed and leaned into the framework.

"She's got this," Sloane assured.

"Still doesn't get you off the hook."

"Chalk it up to stubborn nature."

He glowered. "Stubborn about sums it up."

Chapter Seventeen

MATLOCK LIVED ON the northeast side of the county on the old Hargrave spread about fifteen miles from Euskadi. It took Dot a hot minute to get there, especially when keeping to the speed limit so as to not attract unwanted attention from Ford and his posse.

After Quincy's death, Millie had turned over the reins to Matlock and moved into town with Cherry. Matlock's youngest sister had married and moved to Wyoming, where her husband's family ran a well-to-do retail business. Matlock sold off most of the cattle herd—keeping only what he could manage on his own—along with some border sections of ground to neighbors to pay for his father's funeral and any debts. The Hargrave ranch was still plenty big and had prime hunting spots, and Matlock allowed Angela to bring certain hunting parties onto his land. Other than that, the place was left to run wild.

Dot gave him props for keeping the yard and nearby outbuildings in good shape. She did wonder if Millie had more of a hand in the day-to-day out here than she let on. From the barn out back, she could make out the horses lined up along the fence watching her pull in.

Dot parked the truck next to Matlock's, noting his sheriff's vehicle was parked combat style—backed in with nose facing out—in front of the utility shed. She exited the cab and paused to take in her surroundings before shutting the door. Everything was quiet.

Too quiet.

She left the truck door partially open and headed for the older two-story farmhouse. Before mounting the few wooden porch steps, Dot hesitated at the muffled sound of something thunking against the floor in the house.

Fearing Matlock had done something monumentally stupid and was now falling down drunk, Dot hurried up the steps and rattled the front door with her fist. When the door creaked inward on its own, she backpedaled, her hand clasping the butt of her 1911, and she flicked off the holster strap.

With weapon in hand and leading the way, she nudged the door open farther and cautiously entered. The first thing to greet her was the smell of burnt coffee and aged wood. Second was the toppled coatrack made of elk antlers; some of the tips had broken and scattered across the wood floor.

Dot brought her pistol to her chest and squatted down to examine the rack. One of the broken pieces had a small dark stain. Blood. She set the piece down and rose. The front hall divided the first story and led to the kitchen at the back. To her left was the living room, to the right the dining room, and five feet in front of her was the staircase leading to the second story.

Every nerve was on fire. Her brain buzzed from the spiking adrenalin. Something was wrong. She had to clear the house.

A normal person would call out, asking Matlock to respond. The hunter in Dot said that stealth and silence were her best friends.

Which room to start with?

The doorways to the living and dining rooms were staggered, the entryway for the living room being closer.

Living room it was.

She resumed her gun forward position and crept ahead, making sure to step over the broken antlers. She rounded the doorframe cautiously and then swept back and forth, finding no one in the room. The TV was on, paused on some documentary on a streaming service. Dot noted the half-empty bottle of adult Pedialyte and a toppled bottle of ibuprofen on a round table beside the well-worn leather recliner.

She backed out of the room and headed for the dining room. Stepping through the first of two entries; the second door was farther down the hall rounding into the kitchen. Dot cleared the room. A huge china hutch covered the entirety of the wall to her left. She circled the monstrosity, staying vigilant, and moved to the second doorway.

As she was passing through the doorway, a moan, heavily laced with pain, came from the kitchen. The warning stalled Dot just as a hand reached for her weapon.

Her opponent missed grabbing her hand but managed to take hold of the pistol's barrel. He slammed her hands into the doorframe, the shock of it making her grip loosen. He nearly had the weapon free of her hold when Dot flung herself forward and forced the gun back into a one-hand grip. She freed her left hand and jabbed her palm into the assailant's elbow, bowing it inward.

He let out a garbled sound then let go. Dot was raising her gun when he slapped it from her hand. The pistol flew to the floor and skittered under the table.

Pissed, Dot pounced, forcing him into the wider portion of the hallway between the kitchen and dining room.

The man easily deflected her strikes and was able to get past her guard and backhand her across the face. Rattled, she staggered into the gap under the stairway. Shaking her head free of the ringing bells, she brought her arms up as he came at her again, backing her into the door leading to the basement.

He moved to throw a punch, and Dot braced herself against the door, then kicked out and hit him flatfooted in the groin. He staggered back, giving her enough room to reach for the handle. He charged and she stepped aside, pressing into the wall and yanked the door open as she moved. He couldn't change course fast enough and slammed face first into the edge of the door.

Dazed, he lurched back a step. With him disoriented, Dot slipped from behind the door, grabbed his shoulder, and shoved him through the darkened portal. Off-guard, he stumbled forward, missed the top step, and let out a startled scream as he sailed down the stairs.

Over the sound of his fall, she heard the gut-wrenching crunch of bone and tendons popping. He stopped moving, and there was a long wheeze.

Rubbing her cheek where he'd hit her, she flipped on the basement lights and stood at the top of the steps looking down. Her opponent's body was twisted around the bottom support of the staircase, wedged between it and a stone wall. He had landed face up, staring at the ceiling with unseeing eyes. Blood trickled along his temple and cheek from gashes he'd sustained as he hit the sharp edges of the stairs.

She didn't recognize him. Hadn't been able to tell who he was when he attacked her. But whoever he was, he was no longer.

Another agonized moan rolled from the kitchen. "Shit, Matlock."

She raced into the dining room, located her gun, and with it in hand hurried into the kitchen.

The place was a war zone. Once-hanging cast iron skillets lay about the floor or on the counter. Broken dishes were scattered and crunched underfoot. The back door was wide open. There she found Matlock lying halfway out, his bare torso draped over the lone step into the yard.

Dot holstered her gun and moved to her friend's side.

"Matlock, it's Dot," she said in a soothing voice, one that had been trained into her during flight school.

He didn't say a word, just gave that horrible, agonizing moan. Large red welts marred his back, arm, and side. His sweats had slipped down past his hips, like he'd been trying to drag himself out the door.

She touched his arm to try to roll him up, and he cried out. Dot snatched her hand away and rocked back on her heels. The beating had gone to his face, and by the size of the bruises, Dot suspected the cast iron skillets had been used. She could only guess at this point, but she wouldn't be surprised if he had broken ribs, arm, and jaw.

"Matlock, I'm calling for the ambulance."

All he could do was expel a groan-riddled sigh.

She wished like hell she could beat the living shit out of the dead man at the bottom of the basement steps.

She located Matlock's Motorola and called dispatch.

"Who are you?" the dispatcher demanded.

"Dot Ybarra. A longtime friend of Deputy Matlock Hargrave. He's been fucking beat the hell up and might be dying. So fucking get an ambulance out to his place. Now!"

Chapter Eighteen

DOT HELD THE line until the EMS guys got Matlock loaded and were on their way to the hospital. The moment the ambulance turned onto the road for Euskadi, the sheriff's vehicle pulled in, followed by a deputy's vehicle. How convenient for Sheriff Ford to show up late to the crime scene. The deputy was parked and out of his vehicle before the sheriff. Dot leered at Wall as he positioned himself near the front of Ford's truck.

Ford exited the cab, and, after hitching up his pants, ambled up to the house, with Wall in tow. "Dorothy, what happened out here?"

She crossed her arms and stayed rooted, blocking his way into the house. "You can shove off, Ford. I've already called the state police. They'll be handling this."

"You have no authority to do that. This is my county and my jurisdiction. I call the shots. If I want the state police involved, I'll call them in," Ford barked.

"You have no jurisdiction over this," Dot said coldly. "A deputy was assaulted and nearly killed. This belongs to the state police."

Ford rammed a finger toward her. "You've overstepped your bounds, girl. Just like your fucking mother."

If the man thought he was insulting Dot by comparing her to her *ama*, he was sorely wrong. When Angela got back with her hunting party, Dot planned to corner her and make her explain why there was a long-standing feud between her and Ford.

Dot smiled, the one she loved to impart on assholes like Ford, the one that carried with it the venom of a rattlesnake. "Last I checked, I'm still employed by the state and the federal government."

"That don't mean shit," Wall said.

But the expression on Ford's face said otherwise. He lost the ego. He knew Dot was right. If she, a state employee, suspected anything foul, she had the authority to ask for the state police's assistance. And she didn't have to ask for his permission.

By doing so, she'd just removed Ford's ability to spin this situation any which way he wanted. Which brought on scrutiny to any of the activities going on here in Pyrenees County.

Seeming to gather what last vestige of bravado he had left, Ford sneered at her. "You just butted in where you shouldn't have."

"We're long past that scenario, Ford."

Any remark he might have added was halted at the sound of a heavy-duty vehicle pulling in. Ford and Wall looked back. The SUV parked beside Dot's truck, and two men emerged.

T.J. looked like he was prepared for war, decked out in his tactical gear. The man with him was more polished, clad in a crisp uniform of dark-blue jeans and a dark-tan long-sleeved button-up under a black denim vest and a black Stetson.

"This is beyond the pale," Ford snarled, turning back to Dot. "Your friend there isn't authorized."

"Actually, Sheriff Ford, he is," the newcomer stated as he approached.

He held up a badge hanging from a chain around his neck, and Dot watched with satisfaction as the color drained from Ford's face.

"Detective Sergeant Cassius Larrabee with the investigative division of the Idaho State Police." He slipped the badge behind his vest. "Don't worry, Sheriff, Mr. Roman will be aiding Ms. Ybarra here outside the residence while I conduct my investigation."

"Larrabee, huh?" Ford said. "I've heard about you."

Larrabee flashed a big smile. "All good things, I hope."

The statie's flippant response seemed to fluster Ford. He looked to Wall, who seemed equally put out by Larrabee's presence.

"Since this is a situation you would have had to call me in on, Sheriff, and I have no reason to step on anyone's toes, why don't we make a compromise here?" Larrabee suggested.

"I'm all aflutter with anticipation," the sheriff remarked. "What's your compromise, Detective?"

Dot noticed the slight twitch in Larrabee's features at the snide tone in Ford's voice, but other than that, the man seemed unfazed.

"We'll still need a sentry posted at the road to direct the rest of my people here and to keep out the riffraff. Think your deputy here can handle the job?"

Ford considered the suggestion, then moved closer to Larrabee. He said something to the statie, something Dot wasn't able to pick up on. Larrabee's single response was to grin again and give Ford the good ole boy slap to the shoulder.

"You do just that," he said, and stepped aside.

Ford turned to glare back at Dot, then motioned for Wall to follow.

No one moved until the two men were back in their vehicles and driving away. T.J. stepped into the center of the driveway and watched them go.

Larrabee thrust out his hand to Dot. "Ms. Ybarra, seems you and the sheriff have a history I'd be sorely tempted to hear all about."

"You'd be sorely disappointed, because it's not my story to tell." She took his proffered hand, hers getting swallowed in the big man's paw. "You the client Sloane keeps talking about?"

"One of them. But that's not public knowledge, so let's keep it to ourselves."

T.J. joined them. "You said there's a body in the basement?"

Dot jerked her head toward the house. "Matlock's attacker if I'm not mistaken. Decided I needed to join the injury list, and I disavowed him of the notion."

T.J. gingerly rubbed the side of her nose, making her wince. "He got in a few licks."

After his hand drew away, she spotted the flakes of dried blood on his thumb. "Like I said, disavowed him."

"Lead the way, Ms. Ybarra," Larrabee said.

"It's Dot," she corrected, and headed up the front steps.

T.J. followed to the front door and peeled off to take position as sentinel. Dot guided Larrabee down the hall to the open basement door. She'd turned off the lights when the EMS team arrived, wanting them to focus solely on Matlock and not waste time on a dead man. She flicked on the lights and stepped aside for the state policeman to take a look.

Larrabee peered down at the man, who was beginning to pale as the blood pooled to the bottom of his body. He let out a whistle and studied Dot, then turned back to the body. "If I don't miss my guess, that man is heavier than you by about fifty to eighty pounds."

"One may be heavier and muscle-bound, but they need to be smart and light on their feet too. He was neither." She rubbed her swollen cheek. "He got what he deserved."

"Where did you find Deputy Hargrave?"

She pointed him toward the kitchen and trailed him into the destroyed room, pausing just past the threshold.

"Ideas on the scenario that brought them here?" Larrabee asked as he picked his way through the debris.

"I'm not a cop, nor am I an analyst. Why are you wanting my thoughts?"

Larrabee paused, clasped his hands behind his back, making the sleeves of his shirt strain over the upper arms, and studied her. The brim of his black Stetson shaded his eyes. Dot wasn't able to get a read on him.

"Ms. ... Dot, take me through your arrival and entry into the house."

Wondering what he was driving at, she did, laying out each detail as best she could recall. When she reached the point in her account where she'd heard the *thunk* inside the house and feared her friend had injured himself, Larrabee stopped her.

"The *thunk*," he said. "You heard that all the way out there at the bottom of the steps? You're a helicopter pilot, correct?"

"I was, yes."

"Your hearing is good? Even after being in a war zone and working with the forest service?"

"I wore protective headgear all the time. I even do it when I'm on a hunt with firearms." She eyed him. "You questioning my account or what I actually heard?"

His face relaxed. "Neither. I'm fascinated with your ability to sense something was off by a single sound."

"Matlock's sister said he was in a bad way, and it's not normal for him. I considered the possibility he was still drinking and had passed out or tripped."

Larrabee resumed his study of the kitchen. "Thus leading you to hurry into the house."

"With considerable caution," she added. Dot resumed her report.

He let her finish this time, stopping at the spot where she'd found Matlock's severely battered body. "You have any idea what was used to beat him?"

Dot looked down at the cast iron skillet lying in front of her boots. "By the looks of him, the attacker used what was convenient."

Larrabee made a noise of approval. "Back to my original question. How do you think Deputy Hargrave and his attacker ended up in this room?"

Dot scowled at the man a moment, then decided to play along. She mentally backtracked out of the kitchen and retraced her steps.

Upon arriving, she hadn't seen any other vehicles, which meant the attacker's mode of transportation was out there somewhere. Had he walked to the house? And from which direction?

The TV had been on in the living room. Matlock was nursing his hangover by watching shows. He might have heard something at the back of the house and went to investigate. It would stand to reason why the conflict occurred here in the kitchen and not anywhere else in the house.

But the coat rack had been knocked down in the front hall, and there was blood on it.

Unless…

Dot strode back down the hall and stopped halfway. She looked from the door and the rack still lying on the floor and back to the kitchen.

"The attacker heard me coming and came to investigate," she said. "He must have tipped over the rack accidentally. That's what I heard outside."

"Go on," Larrabee pressed.

She pointed at the rack and then the dining room. "He probably went in there when I came into the house and waited for me." She strode back into the kitchen, pushing past Larrabee. "He came in through the rear. Made a noise to lure Matlock back here. Beat him. I bet the blood I found on one of the broken shards is Matlock's."

"But if he heard you coming, why not leave?" Larrabee

asked as he moved to the still-open back door. "He could have easily gotten away, and you would have been tied up with your injured friend, unable to follow."

"We won't be able to ask him that," Dot remarked, exiting the house into the backyard.

"Hey!" T.J. hollered from the front of the house. "Calvary has arrived!"

"Dot, you know this area well," Larrabee said. "Let me and my team do our thing here at the house. You and Roman track our assailant."

Dot surveyed the whole area. "I wouldn't have parked anywhere near the homestead."

"That's you," Larrabee said as he turned back to the house. "According to you, we're not dealing with the sharpest tack in the box."

Truer words had never been spoken.

"I hope T.J. brought extra gear," she muttered as she looked down at her appearance. She was not geared up for a trek through the foothills.

Chapter Nineteen

S LOANE GAVE HER phone rattling against the tabletop the side-eye. Should she look to see who was calling? Could be T.J. Or Dot. Sloane doubted either of them were taking the time to update her on their current situation. T.J. was especially tightlipped when in working mode. She chalked that up to his years doing special operations gigs overseas where he had to keep his mouth shut. Dot, on the other hand, was Dot.

The phone continued to buzz along the scarred wood. Sloane glanced out the windows, noting that it was getting later in the day. Ashley and Bethany were holed up in the house while Sloane kept watch. Except she'd gotten bored two hours after T.J. left with Detective Sergeant Larrabee.

Her phone refused to cease and desist.

Snarling, she picked it up and read the incoming caller's name. "Damn it." With a truckload of reluctance, she tapped the accept button and then the speaker. "Afternoon."

"Ms. Cross, glad you could take my call."

She rolled her eyes at the condescending voice. Why had she taken his case again? "Mr. Shumway, I'm a busy woman."

"It would seem so," he replied, leaving it at that.

Now that she'd met Ashley, Sloane was beginning to feel she'd fallen for Hyrum Shumway's money at the cost of her morals. She still wasn't aware of the whole story, but this was a family she shouldn't have put herself in the middle of. In fact, she'd never met Hyrum Shumway face-to-face, on his insistence. Every transaction, every conversation had been done via some form of technology. It had bothered her at first because Sloane liked personal interactions to make sure she was dealing with the right person. But she'd let it slide this time.

Damn the money.

"You obviously had a reason for calling me," she said, rising from her chair and grasping her cane. She needed to move. Everything was getting stiff and hurting.

"Of course. I'm calling to check on your progress with the search for my daughter." There was a weighted silence between them before he spoke again. "Need I remind you; the rest of your payment is pending due to the outcome of your search."

"Oh, Mr. Shumway, I'm painfully aware of that part of our agreement. But, as I explained to you on the day you hired me, I do have other cases with more age and more traction than yours."

"Yes, along with that little bounty hunting gig you do. One would gather with your skills and success rate you would have found Rebecca by now."

Speak of the devil and she shall appear. Rebecca—aka Ashley—emerged from the house and made her way through the yard toward the barn, her daughter holding her hand.

"True, one would gather." Sloane answered, watching

mother and daughter pause for Bethany to pick up a particular leaf flitting over the grass. "One would also be aware that, when a subject doesn't want to be found, they have all the resources in the world to remain unfound."

"I find such a notion ridiculous with all the technology available for even the average person to gain access to. It makes it impossible for someone to disappear. Rebecca is not that smart."

Once again, he sorely underestimated his daughter's determination. He'd lost her before, multiple times if he was to be believed, and yet he still considered her beneath him, unworthy of such skill and fortitude to elude him all this time. The fact he didn't know about her name change was a testament to his arrogance.

The woman in question disappeared inside the barn with her daughter. Sloane cringed at the thought of this man ever learning about his granddaughter.

"Mr. Shumway, I assure you, my partner and I have dedicated time to your case, and we are searching for your daughter. The minute we have any leads or news we will contact you."

"Your partner said the exact same thing to me earlier. Is this a little song and dance the two of you have cooked up to waylay your clients?"

Once a lawyer, always a lawyer. The man was pushing for some kind of confession. The gaslighting had been ongoing from the minute he sob-storied Sloane into taking his case. She had considered reimbursing him and dropping the case, but the money from the first half of their fees had been used up for expenses. They were too far into this to back out now.

Sloane ripped a page from Dot's book on confrontation and kept her mouth shut. It was a good policy to implement. Kept her from blurting out her honest opinion of the jerk.

Hyrum muttered something. "Ms. Cross, I'll be checking back with you in a few days. I expect results."

"Duly noted."

There was another muted response to her answer, and the phone went silent.

"Goodbye to you too," she snapped at the dead airspace.

Sloane stashed her phone and decided to get some fresh air. She didn't leave the bunkhouse until she was armed. The brisk autumn air was tinged with the heavy scent of pine and dirt. If Sloane had any regrets in her life, other than the fateful bike accident, it was not spending more time here on the Ybarra ranch.

After Dot enlisted and left for the army, Sloane had tried to visit Angela and Samo. But Angela's animosity toward Sloane drove her away until she, too, took off for greener pastures. Sloane learned of Samo's passing while slogging away through her first year toward law school. She touched base with Dot to send her condolences, but something in the way Dot spoke told Sloane that her old friend was different.

Sloane purveyed the ranch yard, taking care to notice the differences she hadn't paid attention to upon her first arrival. The sheep were gone, and there were way more horses. In place of the sheep was a herd of fat goats and a pack of dogs. For the most part, the main house looked the same with a few noticeable upkeeps. And the barn looked to have had an overhaul. Seemed there were fewer trees surrounding the property. Or was that the Mandela Effect doing its thing on her?

Enthusiastic shouts came from the barn as Ashley and Bethany reemerged. The two ambled back toward the house.

Sloane stepped off the bunkhouse portico and headed for them.

Ashley must have heard her coming and looked up. She flinched but stopped her daughter.

"Ashley," Sloane said as she joined the two.

Bethany was staring at the cane.

Shifting her weight to her good leg, Sloane lifted the cane and pointed at the damp spots on Bethany's pants. "How'd you get wet?"

"Dog slobbers," Bethany stated matter-of-factly. "I thought old people used those."

"Bethany." Her mother gasped.

Sloane chuckled, waving off the offense, and returned the cane to its place at her side to lean into it. "She's a kid. They're blunt by nature."

"She has better manners."

Get real. She returned her attention to the girl, now reaching to poke at the cane. Sloane jerked it, and Bethany snatched her hand back with a giggle.

"Not all people need canes," Sloane said, catching the girl's attention. "I happen to need one because I had a really bad accident, and it did things to my body where I can't walk like you and your mom."

Bethany tilted her head. "What kind of accident?"

"On a motorcycle. You know what those are?"

Bethany bobbed her head. "My daddy used to have one."

Sloane glanced at Ashley for confirmation. Kids were known to embellish for the sake of connecting. Ashley nodded.

"Did you need something?" Ashley asked Sloane.

They eyed each other. The two obviously boring Bethany as she slipped free of her mother's hold and wandered over to a self-formed leaf pile. She was joined by the two mutts Angela had left in Dot's care.

With the girl out of earshot, Sloane pounced. "I did." She gave Ashley a hard stare. "I think your father is onto us. I just got a call from him, and he's demanding updates. This is the second call today."

Ashley tensed, crossed her arms, and shifted to watch her daughter play in the leaves with the dogs. "He can't find me."

"I understand that."

Ashley whipped her head to Sloane. "No, you don't." A look of sheer terror crossed her features. "You have no idea." Her voice cracked.

When Ashley spoke to T.J. and Sloane earlier about her father, she had appeared composed—rattled but composed. This was not a side Ashley had planned to show anyone.

"What aren't you telling us?" Sloane gently pressed.

Ashley shook her head, freed strands of her hair flying about her face. She lifted her shoulders and tightened her hold on her body.

"I can't help you in the way you need if I don't have the full picture," Sloane said, inching a step closer.

"If he finds me, I have to run again." Ashley shuddered.

"All this time and you still haven't left the state. Why?"

Ashley lost her frightened child expression and glared back at Sloane. "I don't have the money to just disappear into another state. Craig was my only option for so long, and he controlled every aspect of my life. I left one kind of nightmare for a different one." She closed her eyes, her features pinched as if she'd sucked a sour lemon, then sighed. "I can't put Bethany through any more of this."

"Then maybe it's time to stand your ground and face him."

Ashley's eyes widened and the frightened deer returned. "No." She turned her back on Sloane and marched to the house, calling her daughter.

Sloane, standing under the tree with leaves fluttering down, watched them go, scrutinizing Bethany's features. A ghost of a thought tickled Sloane's curiosity.

There was something deeper to this. Something more sinister than a father searching for his wayward daughter.

Chapter Twenty

DOT AND T.J. tracked the assailant's mode of transportation to the far edge of the Hargrave ranch on a rarely used fire road. They had walked the path, instead of messing with Matlock's horses. T.J. wanted the advantage of seeing the path without worrying about controlling a horse who wasn't familiar with him.

A dust-covered gray Subaru Outback sat pulled off to the side of the dirt path. It looked well-maintained and out of sorts in an area dominated by all-terrain vehicles and massive, heavy-duty pickups. It was a car meant for campers and hikers and general weekend warriors. Not a would-be assassin.

While T.J. reconned the area for unwelcome guests or surprises, Dot broke into the car by smashing the driver's side window.

"Was that necessary?" he asked as he joined her.

"Faster and cheaper than waiting for a locksmith." Dot popped the locks and pried open the door. She swept the glass fragments onto the floorboard and began her search. "Besides, no one bothered to search the dead guy's pockets for the key fob."

T.J. was on the passenger side, working his way around

the interior. He popped the center console and found a phone. He played with it. "Bingo." He turned the screen toward Dot. "Face recognition passkey."

"You'll have to go back to the scene for that." Dot reached under the front seat.

"Won't have to wait for some encryption program to unlock it." T.J. stuffed the phone into a front pocket on his duty vest.

Dot's fingers brushed against something cool and smooth on the floor. She shoved her arm farther under the seat, and as she dragged the slim object out, her elbow caught on the sharp edge of glass. It ripped through the sleeve of her shirt and sliced skin. Wincing, she powered through the shard and pulled out another phone.

"Looks like we have a burner." She twisted her arm to inspect the cut but couldn't see it. "Of course," she snarled. It would be in the one spot on her elbow out of view.

"What?" T.J. asked.

She held up her aching elbow for him. He scowled.

"You'll need to bandage that." A slick smile popped up. "Teach you to break glass."

"Bite me."

Dot turned the phone in her hand; it wasn't as fancy as the other one T.J. had found. She tapped the screen, and it came to life. A keypad popped up and asked for a password.

"Will have to use an encryption breaker for this one."

T.J. paused as he was backing out of the door, then thrust himself inside. "Stash it. Don't show it to Larrabee."

"Why?"

"I'm betting the one I have is the private use one. What

you have for sure is a burner. Let ISP have fun with this one. We're going to have Sloane hack the burner and we're going to figure out who sent him to beat the hell out of Matlock."

"Aren't you supposed to be working with the police? Not against them?"

T.J. shrugged. "Sure. But Sloane's faster. We'd have to wait weeks if not months for the ISP crime lab to get around to the phone and what's on it." He tapped his watch. "We're running out of time here. Whoever is behind all this is in pressure mode."

"Fine." Dot slid the burner into a pocket of the vest he'd loaned her and backed out of the front half of the car.

They rummaged through the back seats and then the hatch area but didn't find anything more incriminating. The SUV looked like a rental. T.J. was certain he and Sloane could track down the information on the rental agency faster than Larrabee and his team, so he jotted down any info to pass along to Sloane. Since they were out in bumfuck nowhere, their phones wouldn't get service, so texting the information to her was out of the question.

"Now what?" Dot asked him as they closed up the car.

"Hike back to the house and tell Larabee where to find this. He'll send a crew out to tow it in." He shook his head. "He's going to be pissed you broke the window."

"And it affects me how?"

"He's a stickler for preserved scenes. No unnecessary changes are allowed on his watch."

Dot patted her vest where she'd stowed the burner phone. "Taking this and the one you have isn't changing the scene?"

"Different scenarios," T.J. sniped. "Hand him the golden egg and he'll forget about the goose."

"How do you know him so well?"

T.J. let his weapon hang from the shoulder strap crossing his upper body. "Sloane and I've worked with him before. He keeps us on tab. If there's any chance he can use our private investigative skills to double his chances of closing a case, he takes them. In return, he passes along any tips on bail jumpers and bail bonds agencies needing recovery work."

Dot frowned. "Why would a cop want a recovery agent to do their job?"

"Because they don't have time or the manpower to chase after every dickhead who decides to skip. Bench warrants are a dime a dozen. Cops willing to deviate from their normal shift patterns are not."

With a grunt, Dot started off in the direction they'd come from. A few meaningful strides later, T.J. caught up with her, his hands resting on his rifle, ready to lift it into action if the need arose.

"You haven't confirmed one way or another if you made a decision on Sloane's offer."

She kept walking. "There hasn't been time to consider it."

"Fine, I'll grant you that."

"Yes, grant me that. Changing careers isn't an easy thing."

"Does this reluctance to change careers have anything to do with your momma?"

She stopped, which made T.J. stop as well. He would

take her lax decision-making into the personal category. He had no right. None to call her out. Or to hit at the heart of the matter.

"Why is it so important for me to join you and Sloane?"

He studied her, his features a hard read behind the beard and shades. He didn't answer right away, and Dot let out a huff and resumed her walk. She'd gone at least fifty yards before T.J. caught up with her again. They continued their hike back to the Hargrave homestead in silence, Dot doing her best to stop spinning the hamster wheel of regret and self-incrimination.

Larrabee emerged from one of the parked vans when they hiked into the yard. "Any luck?"

"Found the dead guy's mode of transportation about two to three klicks northwest of here," T.J. answered. He dug out the guy's cell phone and handed it to Larrabee. "Found that in the car."

"It was unlocked?" Larrabee asked, taking the offered device in a gloved hand.

T.J. glanced at Dot. "Not exactly."

Dot met Larrabee's inquisitive gaze with a hard stare. "I broke a window to get in."

He looked down at her blood-streaked shirtsleeve. "Appears you need some medical attention, Ms. Ybarra."

"It's Dot. And no, I'm fine." She started to remove the duty vest. "If you are through with my assistance, I really need to get back to my ranch. With my mother gone, I'm sole caretaker."

"Uh, sure," Larrabee said. "We still haven't IDed the assailant." He wagged the phone. "This should help."

"When you're through here, have T.J. tell me. I'll have to get Matlock's family the heads-up."

"Yes, ma'am, I'll be sure to let you know," Larrabee said.

Dot glanced at T.J. and then left the two men for her truck. She dumped the Kevlar vest onto the seat beside her and started up the old Ford. Her elbow twinged—she'd have to get it looked at when she got back to the ranch. Sloane should be handy with first aid.

As she pulled onto the long lane headed back to the main road, a few of Larrabee's team scooted out of her path. She kept her eyes peeled for anyone not paying attention as she made the slow drive down the lane.

At the entrance, she spotted Wall's vehicle pulled to the side. Ford had decided to take off for better pastures, it would seem. She was near the mouth of the road when the driver's side door on Wall's truck flew open and he scrambled out. He hopped and skipped to stand in the middle of the way, blocking her from leaving. Dot slammed on the brakes, noting with smug satisfaction the huge roll of gravel dust that engulfed Wall.

Served him right.

He waved away the cloud in front of his head and marched over to her side of the Ford. Dot's hand slipped from the steering wheel and clutched the butt of the 1911. Wall tapped on the window, then motioned for her to roll it down.

Dot glared at him through the pane and did nothing.

"Roll it down," he said, loud enough to penetrate the glass.

Without batting an eye, she gunned the engine and shot

forward. Wall wheeled backward and nearly fell on his rear. Free of him, Dot pulled onto the road and sped off. She peeked in the rearview mirror.

Wall had run into the middle of the road and was watching her drive away. Whatever gave him the idea she'd be willing to speak to him must have come out of a fit of arrogance.

Chapter Twenty-One

F ORD HAD LEFT Wall to man the comings and goings of
the state police and eventually Dorothy when she left
the Hargrave place. Halfway along the route to the Ybarra
ranch, he'd pulled into a driveway and parked near the home
where a stand of trees blocked the westward winds. He found
a spot where he could watch the road, but those on the
pavement couldn't see him. Ford was privy to the fact the
owners were gone, living here only through the summer
months to get a break from whatever chaos they lived with in
Nevada.

So, should he do as he was ordered? Or grow a pair and
refuse?

He suspected Sloane Cross was on guard duty with the
woman and her kid. She'd be easy enough to overpower,
with her being crippled and all. Once she was out of the way,
he could round up the woman and her daughter. But he
couldn't account for Angela—she was not a woman he
wanted to double-cross, ever. It was Dorothy who gave him
ulcers, and no amount of antiacids would alleviate the
constant gnawing in his gut.

The sun began to dip down in the sky. It'd be dark soon,
and he could easily miss catching Dorothy on her way back

to the ranch.

His ringing phone nearly scared him into a heart attack. He hadn't thought he could get service this far out. Guess the owners had supplied some kind of booster tower to their home.

Ford checked the screen before answering. "Where the hell are you?"

"My whereabouts are none of your concern," the man called Smith said gruffly.

"You could have fucking warned me you were going to have Hargrave beat to death. If I'd been given the heads-up, I would have been able to control the situation."

Smith said nothing to this news.

"You gonna own up to Hargrave's situation?" Ford demanded.

"As I told you, Sheriff, my whereabouts and my business dealings are of none of your concern."

"You've damn well made it my concern. We have the state police crawling all over the place. Now Dorothy Ybarra is on the fucking scent."

"You were told to take care of her."

"It's not that simple. You don't know her like I do."

"Which is why you were tasked with eliminating her. Now you have a bigger mess to deal with."

Ford slammed his hand into the steering wheel. "I'm not the fuckwad who started all of this. If your man wanted so desperately to clean house here, he should have stayed far away from the Ybarras and the Hargraves."

"Sheriff, I'd be very careful how you speak with me and about him." The coldness that slipped into Smith's voice chilled Ford. "He's well informed on your lack of progress."

"Hargrave's not dead," Ford shot back. "Though I couldn't see it myself, I'm damn certain whatever man tasked with doing the deed is dead."

Again, silence met his news. Was it entirely possible that Smith and the man Smith answered to had nothing to do with Matlock Hargrave's attack? Or was Smith's boss moving behind his back?

Ford's radio squawked, and Wall called out to him on a private frequency.

Smith, probably hearing the call out, said, "You have twenty-four hours to decide how you're going to deal with this entire situation and then act on that decision. How you decide determines how we go forward with you."

Ford swallowed hard at this revelation. "Why?"

"Your place isn't to ask why, Ford." The connection died.

"Ford, do you copy?" Wall was saying. "The Ybarra woman has left."

Ford dropped the phone onto the seat and fumbled with the center console. When he finally managed to pop the latch and get inside, he pulled out a flask.

"Ford?" Wall persisted.

He cued his mic. "Damn it, Wall, I heard you the first thousand times. Now get off this line and do your job."

Ford dropped the mic and took a slug from the flask. The liquor burned the ulcer.

Another stiff drink, followed by a third, stronger belt, helped ease some of the tremors. He capped the flask and stared out the windshield, watching the sun slip past the mountain range.

What was he going to do? Twenty-four hours to decide what? Storm the castle and take the women by surprise? Out of the fucking question. Dorothy was a fair hand at the rifle or bow and arrow. Skills her grandfather had taught her well. Plus, there was no forgetting Dorothy's years in the army.

Which left the question of Sloane Cross's partner. What the hell was his name? T.J.? He'd carried himself like a military man. And if Ford didn't miss his guess, the man was hardcore. Probably did a stint in the Special Forces.

No wonder Smith and his boss wanted Ford to do the dirty lifting this time around. He had become deadweight. If they had any inkling about the type of people Ford was faced with, they'd know he was not long for this world.

He should have retired and sought out a warmer climate.

Chapter Twenty-Two

THE GOATS AND horses had a bale of hay to tide them over until Dot could get them their feed, and the chickens would put themselves to bed. The dogs had access to food and water for now. With Bethany having run of the place, she'd probably already browbeaten her mother into allowing her to do the chores as it was.

With that weight off her mind, Dot headed straight for the hospital.

"What's the word on Matlock?" she asked Millie and Cherry, who were standing in the lobby.

"They had to airlift him to Boise," Cherry said. "It's bad, Dot. Really bad." Her voice cracked, and she pressed her knuckles to her mouth.

Millie was like stone. The woman was made of stern stuff. But even stone would crumble under enough pressure.

"Rowdy is coming to drive us down there," Cherry was finally able to choke out.

Dot grasped a shoulder on each woman. "If there's anything you need me to do."

"You've done enough," Millie snapped.

Jolted, Dot released her and stepped back.

"Momma," Cherry pleaded.

"No, Cherry. It's fine," Dot said, her gaze locked with Millie's. "Now's not the time." Breaking eye contact with Millie, Dot gave Cherry a hug. "I just wanted to check on you all. Call me when you have more details."

She headed out of the hospital, back to her truck. Behind her the doors opened again, and Cherry called out. Dot turned as she caught up.

"I am sorry about Momma. She's not taking this well."

"I get it. Your daddy's death is still fresh on her mind."

Cherry looked back at the glass doors to the lobby. "I think I have an idea about why Matlock was attacked."

"You mean other than him being a stubborn cuss who kept poking his nose in the sheriff's business?" Dot asked.

Cherry's eyes widened. "You think the sheriff had something to do with it?"

"What do you think the reason was?" Dot pressed.

Cherry checked once again that her mother was still inside the hospital and gripped Dot's injured elbow, making Dot wince. Cherry released her arm and gaped at the blood streaking her fingers.

"What did you do to your arm?" Cherry asked.

"Never mind me. Spit it out already."

"Matlock didn't want to worry Momma or make her grieve all over again. But he told me he found evidence to prove Daddy was murdered."

Dot chewed on this. It would explain why Matlock seemed off-kilter. She could imagine him being affected by the drug-trafficking and human suffering he'd dealt with lately, but if he was digging up dirt someone didn't want dug up, it would elicit the type of response he had meted out on him today.

"Why would your father be murdered?" Dot asked.

"Matlock thinks it's because someone wanted the ranch. More specifically the ground the ranch is on."

"It's a huge swatch of land in the foothills. What the hell…" Dot's voice trailed off as something dawned on her. "Minerals?"

"That's what Matlock thought. When he took over, he kept dealing with these men coming out trying to convince him to sell." Cherry leaned in closer to Dot. "The scary part is those sections of the ranch Matlock sold off to our neighbors are gone. The neighbors took whatever bill of goods was sold them and hightailed it out of here. Matlock was looking into those business transactions, and I think he figured out something. It's why I wanted you to talk to him."

"He didn't tell me jack squat about this last night. How many other people are affected?" Dot pressed.

"I don't know. He refused to involve me any more than he did. And he sure as hell hasn't said a word to Momma."

"Damn it," Dot muttered.

"I'm sorry," Cherry said.

"Why are you sorry? This is out of your control."

"We shouldn't have dragged you into it."

Dot gripped her friend's shoulders. "Cherry, that ship sailed long ago."

A large dually rolled into the parking lot, and the driver honked the horn.

"There's Rowdy," Cherry said and raced back inside to get her mother.

Dot waved at the burly man behind the steering wheel as she made her way over to her truck. What Cherry told her gave her more to contemplate.

And plenty for Sloane to go dig up.

IT WAS FULLY dark by the time Dot returned to the ranch. The lights were ablaze in the house, and one lone light shone from the bunkhouse. T.J.'s SUV was not parked in the drive, which meant he and Larrabee were still busy at the Hargrave place.

Dot left the truck in her normal parking spot and headed into the house. Cherry had reopened the cut on her elbow, and she should take care of it before it got infected. It would have been easier at the hospital, but Dot had had her fill of hospitals to last a lifetime.

Stepping into the house, she was greeted by the laughter of a child and the guttural noises of dogs at play. The heavenly aroma of stew and warm bread engulfed her, making her stomach growl. She hadn't eaten since breakfast.

Sloane, sitting at the dining room table, looked up from her laptop when the screen door clapped shut. The proverbial feast was spread across the center of the table surrounded by empty bowls and silverware, waiting to be used.

From her spot on the floor sandwiched between the heelers, Bethany gave a shout of greeting and resumed her tussle with the dogs.

"What's up with your arm?" Sloane asked, pointing at the sleeve.

Dot glanced down, noticing how damp her shirt had become. "Cut myself."

Ashley appeared from the kitchen and handed Dot a towel. "You're dripping."

Beside her boots, dark red splotches lined the floorboards. Dot pressed the towel to her elbow. "I think it's deeper than I thought."

Sloane rose from her spot. "Got a med kit here?"

"One in the bathroom. *Ama* has the other one with her."

Ashley propelled Dot to a stool by the kitchen sink while Sloane went to the back of the house to get the kit.

"Let me," Ashley said as she pried Dot's hand from her elbow.

Dot grimaced as Ashley rolled up the shirtsleeve and began cleaning the cut.

"How did you do this?"

"Cut it on glass."

Ashley glanced up from her ministrations, then did a double take. "What happened to your face?"

Oh, yeah. Dot had forgotten about the few blows the dead assailant had managed to land.

"Nothing you need to worry about."

Ashley's eyes narrowed, and a hardness Dot hadn't realized the woman possessed seeped into her features. "I think we're far past handling me like a child."

Sloane returned with the softshell med case. "You might as well tell her." She set the case on the counter and leveled a piercing look at Ashley. "She's got revelations of her own."

Dot looked between the two women. "Maybe the both of you better tell me what's going on."

Neither woman took the chance to explain. Ashley got into the med kit and removed items to clean Dot's wound.

Their silence must have disturbed Bethany. The girl ceased playing with the dogs and wandered into the kitchen to lean on Dot's leg. She peered up at Dot, a worried bent to her brows.

"Who did that to you?"

Dot stared back at the girl, wincing when Ashley applied the wound wash.

"Did a guy like my daddy do it?" Bethany pressed.

"Sweetie, I don't think you should pester her," Ashley said.

"Mommy, she's hurt. Like what Daddy did to you."

"Bethany, it's not the same," Ashley countered.

"Actually," Dot broke in. "It is the same."

Ashley's grip on the gauze slackened.

"Bethany." Dot stared into the girl's wide eyes. "A bad guy, kinda like your daddy, did some horrible things to a friend of mine. Then he tried to do the same thing to me."

"Did he cut you?" Bethany gasped.

"No. I did this to myself." Dot pointed at the bruises on her face. "The bad guy did this."

The girl contemplated what Dot had said, sticking out her lower lip as she mulled. She straightened. "Did you kill the bad guy?"

Ashley made a strangled noise and dropped the items she'd held. "Bethany."

"What?" the girl asked innocently. "Daddy used to hurt you, and he got killed."

"That's not … Bethany, this isn't a conversation…"

"Don't bother," Dot cut off Ashley. "She's got things figured out." She looked down at the girl. "Yes, Bethany, the bad guy is dead."

After a few seconds of considering this, Bethany nodded. "Good." She patted Dot's leg. "We need you."

Taken back, Dot blinked at her. After she had her wits about her, she smoothed her thumb over the symbol on the hoodie Bethany wore.

"Did Ms. Angela tell you what this symbol means?" she asked.

Bethany looked down at the four swirling arms, then shook her head.

"In our home country, this is an important symbol called the *lauburu*. It has a lot of different meanings, but we use it as a good luck charm or to protect us. We carve it into our homes and on jewelry or wear it like this." She jiggled the hoodie sleeve. "You see it on the door and our barn?"

Bethany nodded. "Where's yours?"

Dot smiled and reached for the collar of her shirt to slip it past her left shoulder, revealing the *lauburu* tattoo on her collarbone. Bethany's eyes widened.

"I engraved mine on my body so I have it on me at all times."

Bethany looked to her mother. "Can I have one like that?"

Horror filled Ashley's face. "Absolutely not. You're too young."

Dot chuckled. "Wait until you're bigger like me." She ruffled the girl's hair. "I think we might have a necklace or bracelet you could have."

"Oh, please." Bethany clapped her hands. "Mommy should have one too."

Dot considered the other woman. "If she wants."

Bethany pushed away from Dot's leg and moved to Sloane. "Do you have one?"

Sloane grinned and rolled up her right shirtsleeve to reveal the large *lauburu* tattooed to the underside of her forearm. "Got mine the same day Dot did."

Dot smiled at the memory. Behind her mother's back, she and Sloane went to the nearest tattoo parlor the day before they graduated high school. Angela was livid when she saw her daughter's shoulder, but it was no different than any of the times before. The tattoo was minor compared to Dot's enlistment into the army.

"I think you're good," Ashley said as she began packing up the unused med kit supplies.

Dot examined the bandage the best she could and was satisfied. "Among your many talents, you can add nurse to the list."

The younger woman flushed at the compliment.

"Now that you're patched up," Sloane said and headed back to the table, "let's eat. I'm starved."

Dot rose from the stool. "While you're stuffing your face, you two can tell me what revelations I'm supposed to hear about."

Chapter Twenty-Three

NIGHT HAD STRENGTHENED, and an icy chill settled over the Ybarra ranch. Dot couldn't decipher if it was from the cold front moving in or her knowledge that things were about to get worse.

Ashley had refused to reveal anything in front of Bethany. In fact, she'd put the kibosh on all conversations that didn't relate to Bethany's adventures during the day. Dot, despite pegging Bethany as a child wise beyond her young years, understood. The girl would remain shielded from secrets.

Sloane had hiked back to the bunkhouse to fulfill Dot's written request to search for more details on what Cherry told her of Matlock's personal investigation. Dot also handed off the burner phone she found in the dead guy's rental. Sloane's eyes lit up when she took the device.

Currently, Dot was pulling sentry duty outside with the two heelers and one of the livestock guardian dogs who'd taken to patrolling the perimeter every night before settling in with the goats.

Inside, Ashley argued with Bethany over the age-old debate of cleanliness being close to godliness. Mother was losing the battle to daughter, who was sticking to her guns about wearing Dot's old hoodie with the *lauburu* to bed. Those on the next ranch over no doubt heard Bethany's protest of needing its luck.

Grinning, Dot, fresh cigar and a mug of coffee in hand, sank into the Adirondack chair, settling deeper into her wool coat. The heelers curled about her boots and watched the guard dog sniff the fence line. With her mother out on a hunt, Dot could use her bedroom for the night. But she doubted she would.

Too many people were after Ashley and her daughter. Nothing short of death was going to keep Dot from protecting those two. Once T.J. returned, she was going to set up an overwatch cycle between the two of them, and maybe Sloane if she was up to it.

Sipping the coffee, Dot considered the far-off mountain range, just a shadow in the dark. Angela was out there camping with her pack and her gun for safety. If *Ama* trusted the man she did business with on this venture, Dot shouldn't be worried.

Yet the revelation that Quincy Hargrave might have been murdered, Matlock had been brutally beaten, and Ford, with his lackeys, was acting all kinds of bad, made Dot want to saddle up and race into the Payette looking for her mother. She didn't have enough intel to decide one way or another. The obligations to the people here on the ranch and her deep-seated drive for all things *familia* tore Dot in two.

The guard dog stopped his progress along the pasture and looked toward the lane. About the second Dot heard the pop of gravel, the big male took up his intruder alert chorus. The heelers were on their feet and dashing down the steps to join him as they greeted the large SUV pulling into the yard.

"*Itzalita!*" Dot yelled at the dogs. "*Utz ezazu!*"

The three dogs ceased their barking and took position in the grass to stare at T.J. as he exited the SUV. He was alone, and even in the dark Dot could tell he was tired. Once he passed the dogs, the heelers and the Anatolian inspected the tires, and the two males took turns peeing on them.

T.J. mounted the steps and paused at the top to lean against the roof support. "Tell me there's food."

"Elk stew with bread. Ashley kept them warm for you." Dot took a drag on her cigar. "All alone?"

"Left Larrabee to hitch a ride with one his guys." T.J. yawned. "I'm done in."

Dot waved her cigar around, the end glowing red at the movement. "Not until we have a confab in the bunkhouse."

"I'm eating first."

A screech came from inside, and he pulled up short of grabbing the handle. "What the…" Another girly screech interrupted.

Dot chuckled. "Use caution when entering. There's one tired girl with an attitude in there."

"Guess I'll give it a few before going in," T.J. said, backing a step.

"Very wise of you, Danger Ranger."

He shook his head. "What's got her all pissed off?"

"She and Mom have been duking it out over a hoodie." Dot sipped her coffee. "I may or may not have unknowingly instigated that."

"You shouldn't be allowed near children," T.J. said as he settled on the other chair.

"I'll have you know, I'm very good with children." Dot braced her mug on the Adirondack's wide arm. "When they warm up to me."

"Be careful around that one inside. She has grandiose dreams of getting you and I married."

Dot gaped at him. "Come again?"

He chuckled. "Don't worry, I disavowed her of the notion."

"You better have." Before she could bring the mug to her lips again, he reached out and snagged it from her. Dot didn't bother to protest.

T.J. took a hearty gulp, gave a grunt of satisfaction, and slumped down.

The dogs, having fully inspected and marked the SUV to their satisfaction, had resumed their previous positions, heelers at Dot's feet and the guard dog patrolling.

"How's your arm?" he asked after a brief respite.

Dot lifted her bandaged arm. "Doctored up."

"What's Sloane doing?"

"What Sloane does best. Trace and investigate." Dot relayed what she'd learned from Cherry about Matlock and their family. "I don't know if she'll say anything to Larrabee about it."

"He'll want to know since it's going toward motive." T.J. stroked his beard, something Dot noticed he did when he was mulling. "Why wouldn't Matlock tell you this last night?"

"He might have been working up to it and the fireworks interrupted him." Dot studied the end of her cigar before taking another pull. She'd chosen the New World Puro

Especial flavor tonight, needing a bit more spice to her smoke. "Or by some misguided need, he was trying to avoid having more people involved in order to protect them."

Which brought back Dot's earlier misgivings of leaving her mother out there on her own.

"I'm no mind reader, but I get the sense you're worried about your momma," T.J. said softly.

"I shouldn't be," Dot admitted.

"How mad would she be if you rode up there and interrupted her client's hunt to drag her home?"

"I might be taller than her and too damn old for it, but she'd haul me over her knee and whack me good."

"If something happened to her?"

Dot stuck the cigar in her mouth and took a long pull on it, burning it down to her fingers.

"Regret isn't a place anyone needs to visit, Dot," T.J. said after the drawn-out silence.

She was reprieved by the screen door creaking open. Ashley stepped out.

"She passed out," she said and looked down at T.J. "There's food if you want it."

He groaned as he pulled himself upright. "Better have at it."

After he'd gone inside, Ashley ambled to the steps and sat in the puddle of light coming from the doorway. She drew her coat about her as she stared into the yawning dark.

Dot watched her while she smoked the last of the cigar. If they were going to have this conversation, Ashley needed to get the ball rolling. A bit later, Ashley reached up and cupped the back of her neck to massage it.

She sighed and shifted to face Dot. "Have either of them told you about me?"

Dot shook her head, then smashed the last of her cigar into the ashtray at her elbow.

Ashley seemed to consider her options before coming to terms with one. Dot guessed it was the truth.

"My name isn't Ashley Cooper—it's Rebecca Shumway. My father is Hyrum Shumway."

She waited for her words to sink in. Dot continued to stare at the younger woman.

"Do you know who my father is?" Ashley, or should she be called Rebecca, asked.

"Not off the top of my head, no."

Ashley's mouth made a perfect *O*. "Well, um, I think he's making a bid to run for Idaho attorney general."

"You think he is? Or he is?"

"I'm not sure. It's a guess really. But it makes sense."

"And you being the black sheep of the family need to return home so he can keep a squeaky-clean reputation?" Dot speculated.

Ashley shifted to face the yard. "Not exactly."

The night sounds of wild Idaho filled the emptiness hanging between them. From inside the house, Dot heard T.J. rummaging around. Hopefully, he was bringing her a fresh mug of coffee when he returned.

While Ashley ruminated in silence, Dot puzzled over the younger woman's small revelations. The last name. Her real last name stuck out to Dot.

"Where's your family originally from?" she asked.

"Utah. More accurately, Hildale, Utah."

"And they moved to Rexburg when?"

"When I was six." Ashley ran her fingers through her hair, disrupting the ponytail. "We didn't move. More like we fled. Father and all his *family*." She said *family* with air quotes.

What little bit Ashley was stating was beginning to piece the puzzle together for Dot. "Fuck," she whispered. "How old are you? Your real age."

Ashley took a moment, probably to gather her flagging wits. "Twenty-one." She hung her head, the loosened hair curtaining off her features. "I turn twenty-two next month."

Dot let the conversation lapse while she calculated Ashley's timeline regarding Bethany's birth. Their talk was interrupted by T.J.'s return, carrying two mugs of coffee. Ashley hopped to her feet and dusted her backside.

"I'm pretty tired. I better get some sleep." She darted for the door, not giving Dot or T.J. a chance to bid her goodnight.

T.J. stared back at the screen door, then handed Dot her mug.

"How much did you hear?" she asked, sipping the hot brew.

"Enough to rethink something." T.J. resettled in the other chair.

"Like what?"

"Like how much that kid doesn't look like the man claimed to be her father."

Dot lowered her mug. "How do you figure?"

"When you have to stare long enough at his mugshot, you catch on to some things. Makes it easier to pick him out even if he'd done any alterations to himself. I paid careful attention to Bethany today and noticed how none of her features, outside of what she got from her mother, are anything like Craig. He's not her biological dad."

The rustling of leaves alerted them to a party crasher. Sloane, seeming to lean heavily on her cane and favoring her right side, hobbled into view.

"He's onto something," she said by way of greeting. "I started a more thorough dig on Hyrum Shumway's background and noticed he's done a bang-up job of covering up his transgressions." Sloane labored up the few steps and managed to make it to the porch. "*Sister Wives* might be popular with the general populace, but no one wants a polygamist with questionable connections to a child rapist in their government, especially here in Idaho."

"I thought you were working on the phone?" Dot asked.

"It's being done. Doesn't happen by waving of a magic wand. By morning we should be in."

T.J. hopped up from the chair and jabbed a finger at it. "Sit down."

Sloane shook her head. "I can't. I need to stand and get the blood flowing."

"What you need to do is lie down and sleep," he admonished. "You've overdone it."

"Stop fucking babying me," Sloane snapped.

"He's not wrong," Dot said behind her mug.

Sloane looked at her sharply, but the shadow crossing her face diluted what was supposed to be an evil glare.

"We need shut-eye," T.J. said, breaking through the ice block inserted between the women. "It's been a long day.

Shit, a long week."

"Fine by me. You two get some sleep. I'll take first watch," Dot said. "And Sloane is not spelling anyone tonight."

T.J. made a noise, but Dot cut him off.

"No arguments. I'm used to sporadic sleep cycles. The dogs do a fine job with intruders, but we need a human presence out here to stop an incoming threat."

Sloane, leaning against the porch rail, pointed her cane at the items propped against Dot's chair. "Is that what the bow is for? Stopping the incoming threat?"

"Shooting an arrow is much quieter than shooting a rifle or a pistol." Dot snapped her fingers at T.J. "Give me your cup, and you two go back to the bunkhouse. You can relieve me in four hours."

"Three," T.J. insisted, handing her his mug. "You've already given it about an hour as it is."

"Four hours, and that's final. Now get. We have all day tomorrow to plot and interrogate."

The two hesitated a moment, then moved along after another bout of finger snapping from Dot. Once they had melded into the dark, she reached inside her wool coat and pulled out a packet of deer jerky. The heelers, upon getting a whiff of the dried, salted meat, jumped to their feet and plopped their rears in front of Dot.

"You two beggars aren't getting a bite until I say so."

Zip let out a low gruff and sneezed.

Dot stared back at him. "Cop an attitude with me boyo and you'll get nothing."

She took a bite of the jerky and chewed on it, staring at

the dogs. They didn't budge.

Their jerky standoff continued until a howl from the mountains pulled the heelers from their sentry position at Dot's feet. The first howl was joined by others.

This was no common coyote howl. It was all wolf. A beautiful chorus echoing over the ranch. Their song was broken up by the fierce barking of the livestock guardian dogs, soon joined by the heelers.

Dot let the dogs do what they'd been bred to do. Her thoughts drifting to a long off place in the Payette where her mother was bedded down for the night.

"*Ama*, watch your back."

Chapter Twenty-Four

S LOANE WOKE WHEN T.J. entered the bunkhouse after his rotation as sentinel. While he crashed on his bunk, she showered. The hot water helped ease the ache in her bad hip and relaxed the knots in her neck and shoulders.

She dressed in thermals, over which she wore a loose-fitting pair of pants and long-sleeved tee and a flannel button-up. She knotted her damp red hair in a messy bun on the top of her head, securing it with a pair of hair sticks.

Quietly, to avoid disturbing the snoring T.J., she checked on the progress of the cell phone decryption, finding it nearly complete. She returned to the table and her laptop, which had been left to charge while she slept. In the dim light of dawn, Sloane revisited her notes from yesterday.

Dot's reason for the land buyouts—Sloane wasn't seeing it. She'd stake her life on the fact there weren't large pockets of minerals of any use on those swatches of land.

She wasn't finding the evidence of interest leading to that assumption even as she dug further through state and federal government papers and invoices. That wasn't saying there wasn't, it just wasn't showing up in writing. With the parcels of land being close to a nationally registered—and protect-ed—forest reserve, no one with any lick of common sense in the government would allow any type of mining. In fact, Sloane had played around on websites and the dark web run by eco-warriors and environmentally likeminded and found no hype or stirrings about this area.

By the time she'd reached that point of her research, exhaustion had taken over, and Sloane slept on it.

An idea had struck her while in the shower, where all her best thinking tended to happen. Now, she was running with scissors.

T.J. had mentioned his suspicions on Bethany's paternal DNA. The more Sloane cultivated the thought, the more the idea germinated. If Ashley slash Rebecca knew what Sloane had done, the young woman would probably panic.

T.J. set a mug of coffee next to her hand.

"Thanks," she said as she glanced at the time on her screen and picked up the mug.

She'd been at this for three hours.

"What are you doing?" he asked as he sank into the chair opposite her, his own mug in hand.

"Lemme ask you this." She sipped the hot brew and relished the taste as it went down. "Where did this coffee come from?"

"Something Dot had. A veteran she knows started a coffee business, and she cashed in as a shareholder."

"You're going to buy in, too, and get this."

T.J. grinned as he shook his head. "Train get back on track."

"Fine." Sloane pushed away from her laptop and leaned into the chair back. "What do you know about fundamentalist Mormons?"

"I thought Mormons were all the same."

"Not by a longshot. There were a few splinter groups started after the main church decided to break tradition in order to have the state of Utah allowed into the Union. Some of these groups still held to the practice of polygamy, and for the most part they're fine. But there's a few of these groups who took it to a whole 'nother level and have a laundry list of unsavory ideologies. One sect splintered off from the core group that took these practices to their vilest depths."

"Like?" T.J. prompted after Sloane paused to gather herself.

"Like child marriages, rape, and incest."

He stared at her, then placed his mug on the tabletop and stood.

Sloane remained silent as he paced the floor. This was his way of processing, and she dared not interrupt. When he was ready to talk, he'd initiate. He spoke sooner than she expected—his rumbling voice startled her.

"I thought I saw a lot of disgusting shit during my tours. I know children being sexually abused happens here in the states. But…" He stopped pacing and looked at Sloane. "Is this what Ashley is running from?"

Sloane sat forward, placing her mug on the table. "I don't know for certain. I've scratched the surface on my research into this, and I can't find a connection between Shumway and these fundamentalist groups. You said Ashley told Dot last night her family originated from Hildale, Utah."

"Yes. What's significant about that place?"

"If you didn't know much about these sects, then I can assume you know nothing about Warren Smith."

T.J. pursed his mouth and shook his head.

"Thought so. Might be better if you read up on him yourself. Just the thought of repeating what I learned about him out loud makes me want to commit murder."

"That bad?"

She leveled a hard stare at him. "Worse. The only consolation is, he's in prison." She sighed. "It's a rabbit hole this Alice should have never fallen down."

"What about the information Dot got from Cherry last night?"

"I'm not finding what she's suspecting. But it doesn't mean she's wrong—it's just probably not for the reason she thinks."

T.J. resumed his seat and picked up his mug. "How so?"

"Someone is buying the land. Someone with pockets so deep, even I can't get access to the information. Yet," she added.

Her fantastic skills as a skip tracer and a private investigator did come with some knots in the strings. Sloane hadn't fully mastered the art of hacking.

"Where we at on the phone?" he asked.

"It should be done." She moved to get up and T.J. waved her off and went to the second computer she used for just such purposes.

He smiled as he scanned the phone. "We're in."

"And?" Sloane pressed.

He gave her a sly side-eye. "I think we've got our smoking gun here."

She beckoned him over with the phone. T.J. passed it off

and then circled behind her chair to peer over her shoulder. Sloane scrolled through the call log, all incoming, none outgoing, from a single number.

"Definitely a burner." Sloane left the call history and found the message app. "You did say there was another phone?"

"Yeah. Looked like his personal, and it had the face ID log in. That was the one I gave to Larrabee."

"Think he's managed to learn anything from it?" Sloane thumbed through the short list of texts, again from the same number as the calls.

"Probably. Doubt we'll hear from him anytime soon on what he knows." T.J. reached past her head and tapped the screen to stop her scrolling. "What's this?"

There had been a single outgoing text. *Target is alone and hungover.*

Reply: *Get it done.*

"Time stamp was an hour before Dot showed up at Matlock's," T.J. said. "Which gave the attacker enough time to get to the house and beat the shit out of him. How much you wanna bet they were staking out the Hargraves?"

"The calls and texts to this phone started three days ago," Sloane mused.

"About the same time I showed up here looking for Craig." T.J. moved around the table and stood to her left. "Wonder if that was the first time Alphabet man, aka Charles Smith, showed up?"

"I don't think this is his first time here in Euskadi. Dot said Ford acted like this guy has been around before. Many times."

"We've got to figure out who he is and who is pulling his

strings." He headed to the bunks.

"T.J., I keep having this reoccurring thought."

He wandered back with his phone in hand. He didn't say a thing, just waited.

"The bug, the break-in, and ransacking our rooms, the constant tabs from Shumway—this shit isn't normal for us."

"Our jobs aren't exactly normal. We hunt bail skippers and dig through the garbage that is people's lives."

"This goes way further than that. I'm by no means a conspiracy theorist, but this all smacks of some shady political maneuvering. Ashley doesn't have it wrong here. If her father wants the AG office, then he's going to do what he can to make sure that happens."

T.J. returned to the table, his phone dangling between his fingers. "You think he's behind this? Other than getting Ashley and Bethany, what motives would he have to eliminate Matlock Hargrave? I don't think it's all connected, Sloane. I think we've got two different situations playing out here."

"Maybe but hear me out." Sloane pushed up from the chair and limped to the bunkhouse door to shove it open. She pointed at the vastness beyond the Ybarra ranch. "Out here. Near the Payette Forest, we're isolated. We're close to a mountain range where one can hide illicit activities." She faced T.J. "Where you can murder people and make their bodies and their stories disappear."

An explosion of pain staggered Sloane. Seconds later the retort echoed through the valley.

T.J. rushed forward as Sloane, gasping for breath, sank to the floor.

Chapter Twenty-Five

D OT STOOD IN the kitchen, stirring a scoop of collagen into her coffee, something her physical therapist had recommended during her recovery.

She'd recharged on four hours of sleep. T.J. had been in the bunkhouse for the last three, hopefully getting more sleep.

She sipped the hot brew and stared out the window over the sink. Her vantage point was narrow from here, but she still had a good view of anyone coming toward the house. The heelers were bracketing the screen door, Gidget watching Dot, and Zip keeping an eye on the door. Outside, the animals were making a ruckus, ready for their morning rations.

Dot half rotated away from the window at the light, happy skips of a girl coming down the hall.

Bethany, wearing the black hoodie again, emerged. The heelers tensed but stayed at their posts. Bethany saved them the agony of missing out on pets and went to them.

"Morning," she cooed to each dog with a rigorous pat to their heads.

Ashley stumbled into the living area with a yawn. She nodded at Dot as she moved to the coffeemaker. "Do you have anything in mind for breakfast?"

"Don't bother. We have plenty of rolls and leftovers." Dot lifted her mug and paused, then lowered it as a glint caught her eye. "Ashley."

The echo of a gunshot reached the house. Dot saw the glint change directions and dropped her mug.

"Get down!"

The kitchen window exploded. Mother and daughter shrieked in unison. Dot, bent over, rushed to Bethany, and scooped her up from the floor as another bullet splintered the door. The heelers surged around Dot as she hauled Bethany through the house, a terrified Ashley right behind.

Dot shoved Bethany into her mother's arms. "Get in the hallway."

As they scuttled toward the hall, more windows were blasted out. The barrage seemed to come from all directions. The consistent rattle of gunfire indicated a weapon set on full auto with an extended clip. No way it was a single shooter, but there was no way to tell how many were out there.

Staying low, Dot scrambled to the center counter and sat with her back against the solid wooden boards. Her more effective weapons were near the front door, and her 1911 was by the sink, useless against an enemy too far off to see. Down the hall, Ashley and Bethany cowered, with the heelers pressed against them.

Biting her lip, Dot banged her head against the cabinet, flinching as the shooters strafed the house. She needed a plan. No! She needed to even the playing field.

T.J. and Sloane!

If they weren't in trouble themselves, T.J. would be hell-bent for leather trying to reach the house and picking off the attackers. The man was trained for this, not to mention wired for it. But without knowing what was happening to them in the bunkhouse, Dot couldn't rely on him to save the day.

She had to do this her own way.

Silence descended on the house. The eeriness of it rattled Dot. She couldn't hear the guardian dogs. They should be losing their minds with the intruders. Unless … Fury roiled through Dot. Unless those assholes had killed her dogs.

Dot scooted to the edge of the counter and peeked around. Her rifle lay on the floor near the shattered front door, far out of reach. She stared at the carnage, wondering how Bethany, the heelers, or she hadn't taken a bullet. There was nothing left of the screen door, and the main door was wide open. Dot risked exposing herself to the shooters if she made an attempt to get the rifle.

She looked to the hall where her charges were hunkered down. Dot had stored her bow in Angela's bedroom, and a multitude of arrows were boxed in her own bedroom. She'd have to forego the guns and bullets and have at it the old way.

Dot looked to the ceiling and smiled. If she could get the high ground, the shooters were easy targets.

She rolled onto her feet and stayed crouched down. "Ashley, get in the bathroom."

Despite her terror, the younger woman nodded and ushered her daughter and the dogs into the bathroom, where there were no windows and had solid walls standing between them and bullets. Once they were tucked inside the room, Dot shot through the living room and dove into the hall.

No gunfire ripped through the house.

If she were the shooters, she would be advancing on them. It was the most logical move.

She had to hurry.

She gathered the bow first and then grabbed as many arrows—most of them already fixed with tips—as she could carry in a quiver and her hand. Back in the hall, she stared up at the trap door for the attic. When was the last time she or her mother had gone up there? Had the hinges or any other metal components been oiled in the last God knew how many years? No way to know except to pull it down.

She hopped up and snagged the stout leather strap. The door came down easily, making a few cringeworthy creaks and groans, but nothing to screech out her intentions. She locked the collapsible hinges and peeked into the bathroom.

"Keep an eye out," she whispered to Ashley. "I'm going up."

She didn't give her a chance to protest. Dot scaled the ladder-like steps with ease. The attic held a few wooden crates filled with the history of the Ybarra family, along with long-forgotten Christmas decorations tucked into corners. Other than that, it was free of excess debris, and she had a clear path to her objective.

Dot crept across the sturdy floor to the lone portal at the end of the house, a ventilation door used only in the worst of the summer heat to keep the house cool. A larger version of the *lauburu* was carved on the outward part of the door. The door faced east. Most of the shooting had come from the west and south—hopefully the shooters hadn't circled the house where they could see her. She was also counting on the trees still laden with their fall foliage to create the blind she'd need to crawl onto the roof.

Before she unlatched the door, Dot situated her bow and gear across her body to free up her arms and hands for climbing. Then she carefully slipped the latches free and guided the door's swing toward her enough for her to peer outside.

A mist had rolled down from the mountains and hung over the valley, lingering just above the rooftops of the outbuildings. It would soon settle to the ground and shroud everything in a thick curtain, obscuring optics and making it difficult to tell friend from foe. The air was still, unusual for this time of the year but a blessing. Dot wouldn't have to adjust for wind speed. She could hear the horses' and goats' distressed calls, but still no guardian dogs' bark. Her earlier fury over the thought of her dogs being killed rekindled.

Across the yard and behind the barn, she could make out the bunkhouse. The door was standing open, and there was no movement coming from inside. Were T.J. and Sloane lying in their own blood? Damn them to the screaming pits of hell if they had killed her friends. She swallowed, took a deep breath. At this moment, her task was to keep Ashley and Bethany alive. Her way was clear. She slipped between the door and the frame and sat on the edge, then secured the heavy, looped rope over the aged metal hook that kept the door partially open but not enough to attract attention. After checking her surroundings for a second time to ensure she hadn't been spotted, Dot reached up and grabbed the edge of the roofline. Like a trapeze artist, she mounted the roof, a bit astonished she'd done it with such effortlessness after a year of being out of commission.

Once on top, she lay belly down on the rough shingles and did another sweep of the yard. Still no detection. The trees had done their job.

She'd no sooner begun to relax when gunfire rent the morning air. Hope sprang anew as she realized the shots were coming from inside the bunkhouse. They must have seen Dot crawling on the roof and were providing the distraction she needed to get into position. The ploy worked as return fire focused on the bunkhouse. As she cautiously walked, bent over, along the roof, she spotted two figures peel themselves away from the trees where they'd been sheltering about twenty yards out.

Dot knelt, pulled the bow over her body and settled it into position. She removed three arrows from the quiver and nocked one. Assuming the shooters were wearing Kevlar vests, Dot adjusted her aim lower.

So focused on shredding the bunkhouse, the two shooters stepped clear of their cover and stopped. Dot let the first arrow fly, and was nocking the second the moment the razor-sharp tip found its target in the lower back of the first shooter. He let out a startled cry and went down. His teammate stopped shooting and turned to his buddy. His worst mistake.

Dot released another arrow. It hit the guy just below the edge of his vest and between his hip bone. Liver shot. Down he went, grasping at the arrow shaft protruding from his body.

Two down. How many more to go?

Dot was moving again, pulling more arrows from the quiver. The two downed shooters gave up any pretense of stealth and were making a lot of noise. It helped draw out Dot's next target.

He stepped from the cover of the barn doorway. A larger man, with a full beard and huge arms covered in sleeve tats. No coat for this one.

Where the hell did these guys come from? Mercenaries-R-Us?

Dot dropped to her knee and reassessed her arrow choices for this guy, switching for a more lethal arrowhead. This guy was built like a Kodiak bear, and he wouldn't go down easily.

She was going to have to shoot quickly.

Despite his size, the guy moved on light feet, sweeping the yard like a professional. He was expecting the threat to be ground level. Not from above.

With a little twitch of her mouth, Dot lined up. Kodiak man stepped past a tree, his right leg moving out first. The arrow hissed past the string. Direct hit to the thigh. He spun, releasing his rifle. Dot nocked the second arrow as he bellowed and grabbed at his leg. Her bull's-eye exposed, she sent the next arrow. He died before he hit the ground.

Dot gathered herself and scuttled to the opposite side of the roof. The shouts of dying men were sure to bring the others out of hiding.

On a thrilling note, the gunfire from the bunkhouse had ceased. The two bounty hunters had done their due diligence. Now it was up to Dot to put this ambush in the grave.

She noticed the mist was heavier on the west side. It was descending faster than she anticipated. It would give her better cover but hinder her sights. She was about to peer over the edge of the roof to get a look at the porch when something tugged at her back.

The crack of a bullet passing the speed of sound reverberated over the valley.

"Shit."

She rolled away from the roof's edge and slipped over the roofline just as another bullet smacked into the shingles.

A sniper. Somewhere past the pastures. Probably perched up in a tree.

Dot flopped on her back and stared up at the thick fog. If she gave it a few minutes more, it would shroud the entire roof and cloak her from the sniper. But she didn't have a few more minutes to spare. The longer she dallied up here, the closer the remaining attackers would come to entering the house and getting to Ashley and Bethany.

"Fuck it," she said and rolled onto her stomach.

It was time to bring the fight down to their level.

She crawled to the edge of the roof, keeping a low profile. She checked on the three she'd removed from the board. Liver shot guy and back shot man weren't moving. Both were lying on their backs, long, gaping wounds at their throats. Someone had finished them off instead of allowing them a slow death. Kodiak man was dead, her arrow still protruding from the fatal wound.

There was another assailant on the ground. Where was he?

Dot was about to leave the roof when a figure emerged from the darkened interior of the barn. This one was wirier than Kodiak man but every bit as imposing. He didn't break the cover of the barn; he looked about. When his head began tilting, Dot slinked back onto the roofline, melding with the descending fog.

He scanned the top of the house. Dot stayed low, wishing she could ready her bow and end him. Seemingly finished with his recon, the man merged with the shadows cast by the barn's walls.

Unwilling to remain a sitting duck, Dot scooted away from her spot and went to the far end of the roof. Out of sight of the sniper and the fourth man, she readied herself to swing off the side and drop to the ground.

A shriek from inside the house turned her cold. Dot threw her legs over the side, dropped down by her arms, kicked out her feet to catch a support post and pushed off it, letting go as her body swung backward. She dropped to the ground in a crouch.

Her actions caught the attention of a man posted on guard outside the back door. He rotated, raising his rifle. He never got the chance to shoot. Three consecutive gunshots blasted from her right. His head whipped back, his body slammed into the house, and he slumped to the porch.

Dot glanced over and spotted T.J. advancing across the yard, his own firearm raised. He waved at her to go.

She darted into the house through the back door with bow in hand and another arrow nocked. More shrieking and the heelers' menacing bark came from the front of the house.

Dot raced forward. She breached the end of the hall and

burst into the living room.

Ashley and Bethany were crowded into the kitchen, the heelers making a protective wall between them and the man advancing on them. He was aiming at the dogs.

"Hey, asshole!"

He spun. Dot released the arrow. It buried itself deep in his pelvis. He screamed and tried to raise the gun once more.

Dot nocked another arrow and let it fly. This one caught him in the throat, nearly passing completely through. He went down.

"Move! Now!" she yelled at mother and daughter.

Ashley didn't hesitate. She grabbed Bethany into her arms then raced toward Dot, the dogs hot on her heels. Dot shoved them down the hall where T.J. met them at the back door.

"Get them to the bunkhouse. We still have at least one more on the grounds and a sniper out in the pasture."

"Sloane's been hit," he said before propelling the pair out of the house and across the yard.

Dot watched their back until T.J. had them inside the bunkhouse. She abandoned her post and returned to the house, where she discarded the bow and arrows and went for her 1911 and rifle, stepping over the now-dead man in the kitchen to retrieve her pistol.

The fog had drifted down far enough to obscure visuals, but the sun was rising and would soon be past the mountains, sending its bright rays to burn off the mist. If this was a smart sniper, which Dot figured he was, he'd move from his last position and head east to get the sun at his back. He could be on the move as she thought about it.

Her immediate threat was the man in the barn. She had to locate him. Now.

Taking a firmer grip on her pistol she headed for the barn, using her keen sense and knowledge of the grounds to guide her. From tree to tree she moved, finally reaching the barn, unharmed.

Dot lingered near the open doorway, listening to the distressed animals inside. With all the chaos, it was hard to decipher the horses' whinnies and snorts from *stranger in the barn* or *what the hell is going on*. If she were the man, she'd aim chest high and wait for her to breach the doorway.

So, she'd do the opposite.

She backed from the doorway and headed around to the goat shed and pen. She moved with the stealth of a hunter, avoiding things that would make a noise and give away her position. Reaching the rear part of the barn, she pulled up. Then slowly, inch by inch, she crouched down, keeping her back to the wall. When she was as low as she dared go, she took a quick breath, then poked her head around the corner.

No shadows. No man with a gun. Empty space.

She returned to her previous standing position and readied herself to move.

A gruff woof stopped her. She waited. Then there was another, farther away from the first. The goats bleated. Their affection noises were joined by the dogs.

Dot sagged against the barn wall. The guardian dogs were fine. Probably tranquilized to keep them from alerting Dot. It would have been quieter than shooting them.

They must have smelled her scent, as they started a friendly ruff. Her cover blown, Dot advanced on the barn's back door. She flung it open and pressed her back into the wall.

Nothing happened.

She rushed inside and quickly cleared the barn. No man with a gun. Not even a sign he'd even been in here. He had to have slipped away while she was breaching the house and saving Ashley and Bethany.

"Shit," she spat.

Dot emerged from the front of the barn and stopped. The fog had settled more, leaving the world about her half cut off. She listened. Focused past the sounds of the animals and listened for the signs of humans.

The swish of clothing made her turn suddenly, pistol raised.

"Friendly." T.J. materialized from the mist. "It looks like the rest have moved on."

Dot relaxed. "It's over."

"Today's skirmish," he said. "But not the war."

Chapter Twenty-Six

S LOANE WAS BAD off. They needed to get her to the hospital.

Dot knelt beside the bunk where T.J. had sequestered Sloane during the attack. He'd done his best with what little trauma care they had on hand.

"Did you get the fucker who shot me?" she wheezed.

"Maybe, maybe not," Dot said. "There were too many to determine who shot you. I do know at least two got away."

Two men who were a bigger threat in Dot's mind than the ones already eliminated. Now began the guessing game. Who sent them? Why? Was their main objective to kill? Or to retrieve? Or was it a bit of both?

Sloane clasped Dot's hand with her bloodied one. "You can't leave those two here unprotected."

"I've got to get you out of here. I know the faster routes."

"No. T.J. can do it." Sloane's sticky hand tightened on Dot. "Get them in the mountain."

"In the middle of hunting season? Have you lost your mind?"

"They can't come with us. It's too dangerous." Sloane bent closer. "They're sitting ducks here. Out there is your playground."

"It's a bad idea," Dot insisted.

"It's the last one we have."

"What aren't you telling me?" Dot asked.

T.J. squatted next to the bunk. "What Ashley has been hiding from us all along."

All eyes went to the cowering woman, who tightened her hold on her daughter.

"Tell her," T.J. ordered.

"What exactly am I supposed to tell them?" Ashley demanded, biting insolence in her voice.

This was a new development with her.

"How about you start with the truth," Sloane said in a reedy voice.

Dot noticed her grip slackening. "T.J., she needs to go." She met his worried gaze. "I'll handle things with Ashley. Get Sloane to the hospital."

"You in a helicopter would be a godsend right about now," he said.

She grimaced. Yes, a helo to load up everyone in and fly out of here. High above the range of any gun. Up where she was in control. If only she were able to make one appear out of thin air.

"Got a few million sitting around I could borrow?" she quipped.

"The fact you're even considering it is a good sign," T.J. said and rose. "Let's load her up and get out of here."

He'd driven their SUV over to the bunkhouse. Why the attackers had not disabled the vehicles to prevent their escape was mindboggling. It fell in line with tranquilizing the dogs versus killing them. Evidence would suggest they wanted to abduct the people on the Ybarra ranch not kill them. But they'd shot Sloane. A few inches more to the left and she would have been dead. They'd also attempted to shoot T.J. and Dot.

As she assisted T.J. with getting Sloane to the vehicle, Dot glanced at Ashley. The younger woman had bowed her head until her face was touching her daughter's hair. Bethany was clinging to her mother, her face buried in Ashley's chest.

They weren't safe here any longer. This dawn attack was proof enough. Sloane was right, those two were in danger no matter where they went. If they stood any chance of survival, it was to avoid civilization. Go off-grid.

With Sloane loaded in the back end, lying on the backs of the collapsed seats, T.J. gripped Dot's shoulders.

"Ride hard." He bent his forehead to hers and pressed into it. "I'll get Sloane safe, and then I'll come find you."

"No. Stay here and alert Larrabee. You would think by now he would have updates. He'll need to know about this. Someone will need to clean up the bodies."

"I'll handle it." There was a hard edge to his voice—he had a plan in place for their attackers.

They stared at each other a moment longer, then T.J. released her. "Watch your six."

Dot backed away as he got into the SUV and drove off. She turned at the scuff of feet against the wood porch slats.

"I'm sorry for getting you caught up in this," Ashley said, her voice hitching.

"We don't have time for regrets. We've got a hard ride ahead of us."

YEARS OF HAVING to bug out on a moment's notice taught Dot speed and efficiency. She had gathered everything they'd need and stuffed it in saddlebags or packs for the pack animals. In the house—stepping over bodies—she gathered her arsenal and more food staples than she thought necessary. All the while, she waited for a bullet to take her down. But none came.

She couldn't shake the feeling she was being watched. No doubt the sniper had stayed behind. So why not take a shot? Something was up.

Where were they? At least two had been spared from her counterassault. If she was being watched, the other might have left. Maybe to get reinforcements. Or rethink the strategy. This had not gone as planned. Whatever the plan had been.

Or, whomever ordered this assault had called them back to relay what intel they might have learned. There would be a second assault. All the more reason to get away from the ranch and do as Sloane had begged. Get into the mountains.

Dot located the spare satellite phones and texted T.J. the numbers, then left her cell phone stashed in the same place she kept her marijuana.

Horses and mule saddled, pack animals loaded, they were ready to go in less than two hours. Dot's final chore was to open the gate to allow the goats to free range in what was typically their summer grazing pasture, where she needed them to have easy access to a small pond and food. T.J., being from a ranching background, would have the wherewithal to check on them but let them be. She left a substantial amount of food for the dogs and shut up the chickens in their run with bucket loads of feed and water to protect them from predators.

"How long are we going to be out there?" Ashley asked as she settled Bethany on her horse.

"However long it takes." Dot double-checked the girth straps on all the horses, then moved to her mount, the two heelers trotting beside her. "I have access to an unused forest ranger station way up there. That's where we're going."

Ashley, with the use of a mounting block, climbed into the saddle. Once she was settled, Dot swung aboard her horse. She reined around her gelding and leveled a hard look at Ashley.

"We have a long ride. Plenty of time for you to tell me everything."

Ashley glanced at her daughter.

"Nope," Dot barked. "She isn't your excuse any longer. Time for her to know the truth."

Ashley attempted and failed to stare down Dot. She would not be a gatekeeper to her secrets. Dot would get the truth.

This act of defiance squashed, Dot pointed her gelding toward the mountain. "Let's go."

Chapter Twenty-Seven

As T.J. FLEW down the road, he called Larrabee.

"My partner's been shot. There was an assault on the Ybarra ranch, at least five dead. I'm getting Sloane to the hospital. Dot is getting the mother and girl off-grid," he barked out as greeting.

"Whoa, Roman, back the trailer up. What did you just spew at me?"

T.J. took a quick breath and glanced in the rearview mirror. Sloane was holding a compress to the place on her chest where the bullet had blown through her. Her chest wasn't rising and falling as normal as T.J. liked.

"Sloane was shot," he said firmly into the cell. "I'm getting her to the hospital."

"Who shot her?" Larrabee asked, his voice sounding odd, like he was moving about.

"Unknown. Far as we could tell, it was seven-man assault team sent in. Five are KIA and two AWOL—those are the ones we are aware of."

"Who KIAed them?"

"Dot took down a few. I got one. But she'd only wounded two of them, someone else made sure they wouldn't talk."

Ahead, T.J. could make out the town limits. If he stayed

on the eastern edge and away from residential, he could circle around and get to the hospital without causing a scene.

"Where's Dot now?"

"Hopefully, getting the mother and child to safety."

"Where?" Larrabee pressed.

"I can't say. We made it a point not to discuss it for protection."

"Shit, Roman," Larrabee spit. "I suppose you want me to go to the ranch and clean up the mess you left behind."

Movement to his far left caught T.J.'s eye. He chanced a look and spotted a vehicle veering onto the road behind him.

"Where you staying at?" he asked as the blue lights lit up.

"At the rundown road motel east of Euskadi."

"Saddle up and ride like hell to the hospital. I'm just now passing you, and I've got the local five-o on my ass."

"Shit, Roman," Larrabee spat again. "Just don't kill anyone."

"Too late for that."

T.J. ended the call and stashed the phone in the console. "Sloane, hang on. We're going to be coming in hot."

She didn't reply, but he spotted her lifting a bloodied finger. She'd heard him.

The SUV's engine roared as he gave it more gas. The county deputy's vehicle lagged as T.J.'s shot away. Seconds later, the sirens flared to life, and the deputy gave chase.

An idea struck T.J. He called 9-1-1 and the dispatcher picked up after the first ring, rattling off the universal response.

"This is T.J. Roman. I'm en route to the hospital with a severely wounded woman. Get your dog off my ass."

"Wait? What?"

"Ma'am, no disrespect, but keep up. I have a gunshot victim in serious need of medical attention, and I'm coming in hot to the ER. Alert them now. And get this county mountie off my ass."

"Hang on," the dispatcher screeched.

T.J. saw the sign to the hospital. "I don't have time to hang on." He ended the call. "Sloane, gotta take a hard left like I'm at the Brickyard."

She moaned her response.

T.J. hit the brakes and prepared for the slide. Then he saw the oncoming tractor trailer.

"I swear I'm not trying to kill you!" he hollered.

He yanked the steering wheel left and cut in front of the semi. The SUV squealed around the corner and missed the huge front end of the tractor by inches. The semi driver blew his horn and shot past, blocking the pursuing deputy. T.J. adjusted for the slide like a dirt track driver and righted the SUV in time to avoid hitting a parked car along the street. Once out of the skid, he gunned the engine.

Barreling down the street, he peeked in the mirror. "Sloane, ya dead?"

"Fuck … you," she managed to get out.

He grinned.

The three-story hospital loomed ahead. He spotted the red sign to the ER and slowed the SUV. He took the turns at a more reasonable speed and hurried behind the building. Once he parked under the canopy, the doors slid open, and a pair of nurses came out rolling a gurney.

He rattled off Sloane's injuries and what he'd done as he

laid her on the gurney. Blood was now leaking from between her lips.

"Sloane…"

The wailing police siren cut him off.

"We'll take care of her," one of the nurses said, and they headed for the open doorway.

T.J. was about to follow when there was a shout to stop. He turned to face the deputy and was tackled instead. They crashed into the pavement, T.J. barely avoided getting a road rash on his face.

"You motherfuckin'…" The deputy struggled to find T.J.'s arms.

T.J. recognized Deputy Wall's voice. With a feral grunt, he heaved off the ground, the lanky deputy grappling on for dear life as T.J. climbed to his feet despite the man on his back. Then T.J. backpedaled and slammed Wall into the side of the SUV. Wall's grasp on his body slackened, and T.J. shook free.

"This ain't a fight you want to pick today, *deputy*."

Wall went for his gun. T.J. moved faster. He slapped away the man's hand, then backhanded him. Wall staggered, and given his punch-drunken state, T.J. disarmed him and chucked the gun far from them.

"Don't try it again."

Wall swiped a fist across his bloodied mouth. "I'm going to wreck you."

"You're five foot nothing squaring off against me?" T.J. asked incredulously.

"You evaded police and resisted arrest. I will take you in."

"If this how we're doing it." T.J. shook his arms, then settled into a fighter's stance. "Be my guest."

With a bellow, Wall rushed him, swinging his right arm.

T.J. blocked the punch and landed one of his own to Wall's torso, following it up with another to Wall's cheek. Wall staggered, shook his head, and came at T.J. again, this time lower.

T.J. stepped aside at the last second and grabbed Wall by the back of his coat. Using the forward momentum, T.J. swung him around and tossed him into the side of the SUV. Wall slumped to the pavement on his knees.

"Stay down," T.J. said.

Wall pushed upright, using the SUV for leverage.

"I told you to stay down."

Wall rotated, his body weaving as he faced T.J. "Fuck off."

The dumb son of a bitch. T.J. waited for Wall to make the next move. It came, albeit a bit slower than before. Wall charged, swinging wildly. T.J. dodged the flying fists, catching a glancing blow to his chin from one errant strike. Wall left his center open, T.J. pushed on his chest. and as Wall wheeled backward. T.J. threw a hard punch to his jaw.

Wall slammed to the ground. T.J. straddled him, grasping the front of his uniform in a fist and lifted his upper half from the ground.

"Cry uncle."

"Fu..."

"That's enough! Get off him!"

T.J. released Wall with a little push, letting him fall to the concrete, then stepped back and raised his hands. He rotated slightly, facing the man who'd ordered him away from Wall.

Sheriff Ford's service weapon trembled, and his face had a purple hue.

"Better ease up there, Sheriff, or you're going to have an aneurysm," T.J. drawled.

"Shut up, you red dirt hick!" Spittle flew from his mouth.

Wall moaned and tried to move, only to flop down and lie still.

"He's going to need medical assistance," T.J. said.

"Fuck off. You're under arrest."

"On what charges?"

"Attacking an officer of the law."

Breathing heavily, T.J. shook his head and lowered his arms. "He attacked first. Unprovoked. I was defending myself."

"That's not how I saw it."

He pointed at the SUV. "Want me to pull the footage from the security cams on my vehicle?"

Ford glanced at the metal beast, then jerked his service weapon toward T.J. "You were speeding and evading a law officer."

"I called your dispatch and told her what I was doing. My partner is in there right now fighting for her life. She needed medical attention hours ago."

"That's what ambulances are for."

"She didn't have time to wait for an ambulance!" T.J. shouted. "We were under fire."

Ford steadied his firearm, and he braced himself. "I don't

give two fucks. You're under arrest."

"Sheriff, you need to stand down." Larrabee emerged from behind T.J.'s SUV. "Let me handle this."

"This matter isn't your concern," Ford shot back.

Larrabee moved to stand between T.J. and Ford. "It is."

The finality to Larrabee's voice brought a deathly silence to the standoff. Even the battered Wall didn't make a peep. T.J.'s tunnel vision widened, and he spotted a few gawkers watching the whole spectacle, phones raised and recording every second of this altercation. T.J. knew he'd get painted as the hero in this situation and the sheriff and his deputy as the enemy. The power of social justice warriors.

Slowly, Ford lowered his firearm. He glanced about, then carefully holstered his weapon. "The dispatcher didn't tell me there was a wounded passenger."

T.J. recognized the stench of a political ploy when he smelled it. "As I'm sure you didn't realize there was an attack on the Ybarra ranch early this morning."

Larrabee shot him a censoring look, but T.J. ignored it. No way was he keeping this under wraps. Not when he had an audience.

A murmur passed through the small gathering at his announcement.

Ford's snake-like eyes darted about. "What attack?"

"Don't try to save face," T.J. snarled. "That attack nearly killed my partner."

"Roman," Larrabee said under his breath.

T.J. pushed around him. "Play dumb all you like, Sheriff, but a good woman is fighting for her life. Instead of being in there to keep watch over her, I'm out here dealing with you yahoos."

"Is it Dot?" someone asked from the group of onlookers. "Your partner? Are you talking about Dot? Is she the one?"

The questions drained the blood from Ford's face. "I don't know about any attack on the Ybarra ranch," he said, his voice sounding strangled.

"Likely story," T.J. snapped.

Larrabee hooked a hand into T.J.'s elbow, hauled him back, and propelled him toward the sliding ER doors. "Roman, you've said enough. Get in the hospital and take care of your partner. I'll handle this."

"He's behind it," T.J. insisted.

"Let me be the judge of that." Larrabee released him, thrusting him to the opening doors. "He's right. You should be arrested for assaulting the deputy."

"Ain't like he didn't get what he deserved."

"Roman, for God's sake. Shut up and get in there."

T.J. gave Ford and Wall a parting look, then turned his back on the whole lot and strode down the corridor toward the unknown.

Chapter Twenty-Eight

"MOMMY, I'M TIRED."

Dot peered down at the young girl riding between herself and her mother. She looked exhausted, hunched over the saddle horn.

"How much longer?" she asked, her voice holding a note of whining.

"I don't know, sweetie." Ashley looked to Dot.

They were two hours into the ride and had another three to go. Ahead of them, the pack goats picked their way over the rocky edge of the path the horses were following, stopping to nibble at this branch or that yellowing foliage. The heelers were keeping up with the goats, but they would need to rest soon.

"We'll stop for a break in about half an hour," Dot said.

She reached over and took the reins from Bethany, who had done a fair job staying focused on her riding and keeping up with Dot's and Ashley's mounts. Reins in hand, Dot tucked them through the gap between her saddle seat and the horn. Then she held out a hand.

"Come here."

Bethany peered up, uncertainty glowing in her small face.

"I've got you," Dot assured.

With a glance at her mother, Bethany gripped Dot's hand, then swung her leg over the saddle, relying on Dot's strength to change horses. The moment she settled in front of Dot, chest to chest, the young girl hugged Dot and relaxed. Through the whole switch, the mare kept a steady, plodding pace, unbothered by the now-empty saddle.

Another few hundred yards and Bethany was sawing logs, her arms drooping. Dot tucked the girl close and kept a steadying hand on her back.

"She's asleep," she said to Ashley.

When they'd first rode out, Ashley had given child-appropriate details of her family history—her birth and childhood in a large community of like-minded people in Hildale, Utah, with a father who had six wives and more than fifty children. Ashley talked about the move from Utah to Rexburg when she was still a child. She remembered a ripple of fear through the adults before they left Utah, but she didn't really know the reason. Too young to understand it all.

After they had set up a new home and compound on the outskirts of Rexburg, things began to change within the group. The ideology of the compound's founders shifted to a belief that anyone outside of their family meant to harm them. Children were scared into believing if they ever left the family, they would burn in the pits of hell. Yet, boys and young men of certain families were disappearing.

God's favor was bestowed on the elders who had many wives, of which Ashley's father was one. Ashley suspected her own mother may have been her father's cousin.

Bethany asked what a cousin was, and Ashley ended the discussion, moving onto a topic about all of Angela's dogs.

With Bethany sleeping, it was time for Ashley to get the truth out.

"Craig's not her biological father, is he?" Dot popped the can of worms.

Ashley bowed her head and gave the barest of nods. "I'm not sure who her biological father is."

Dot waited, hoping Ashley's explanation was the opposite of what Dot was thinking.

Giving a sniff and a sigh, Ashley looked up. "Three of my father's sons from his first wives … lured me and one of my half-sisters out to an … unoccupied house at the edge of the compound." She gave a strangled moan before blurting. "They took turns raping us."

Something hot and ugly formed deep in Dot's chest. She curled her arm tight to the sleeping child.

"I was fourteen. My sister was twelve."

Dot released a shuddering breath. The leather reins creaked under the pressure of her crushing grip.

"When my father found out," Ashley continued, "he forced me to marry another man in the compound. I think he was a brother of Father's. He trapped me in his home for weeks. Never once touched me, but he and his wives took every chance to verbally abuse me. Told me it was my fault they did it. I was damaged goods. No man in the family would take me now, and he was stuck with me."

The gelding snorted, veering to the right. He was sensing Dot's foul mood. She tried to relax, for his benefit and hers.

"Your sister?" Dot asked.

"Married off to another man. I don't know what happened to her." Ashley released a sob. She bit down on a knuckle, smothering the cries.

Dot let her cry. While Ashley composed herself, Dot resisted the urge to dig out a pre-made joint and smoke it. She needed to be clearheaded. The horses were depending on her to guide them through the winding mountain paths to the old ranger station.

Ashley cleared her throat. "I found out I was pregnant a month later. Not long after, I managed to escape."

"How?"

"I had heard about other women doing it. Escaping. I picked the right time and ran."

"Where did you go?"

"To Boise. I had no money. I didn't know what I was doing. Didn't know where to go. I was frightened of everyone I encountered. Scared they'd know who I was and tell my father. If he found me, he'd take me back and I'd be punished."

"Where does Craig come into this?"

"I was moving from one homeless shelter to the next. I'd just turned fifteen and was seven months pregnant by then. He took pity on me and asked if I needed help. I was a stupid, naïve girl looking for any handout I could get. I knew Father and the other men had to be after me, so I accepted his help." Ashley swiped the cuff of her coat under her nose. "We pretended to be married. He took care of me. Got me a doctor. Found us a place to live until I had Bethany. He even helped me change my name and get me all the proper IDs to turn me into Ashley Cooper."

"Then the honeymoon ended," Dot said.

"A year after Bethany was born. He started working for some dealer, then got into taking the drugs himself. He'd never touched me, never demanded sex from me. We just were." Ashley swiped at more tears. "As bad as he got and no matter how many times he hit me, he never raped me." She turned her head to look away. "It's why I stayed for so long. Until he went to jail." She looked at Dot. "By then I'd learned enough and had stashed enough money aside. So, I ran."

"And concocted a story to protect yourself and Bethany."

"It worked for two years." Ashley stared straight ahead, letting the horses move them farther along the path before speaking again. "I don't know why he came here. I don't know why he took Bethany."

Dot thought back to the moments before Craig was killed by Deputy Wall. The things he said didn't make sense at the time. Comments she'd brushed off as the ramblings of a desperate man who had a drug problem.

They had gotten to Craig. They'd figured out where Ashley had gone and used Craig to get what they wanted. Sometime in the years Ashley had been with him, her father and his fellow fundamentalists—Ashley's husband most likely one of them—put the screws to Craig and demanded he turn over the two. But Craig's shitty lifestyle got to him first, and Ashley ran.

"Ashley, did they know you were pregnant?"

"I don't think so." She withdrew into herself, her head making jerky tics back and forth. "Craig and I always made sure to claim her as his. I kept my pregnancy hidden while I was running." She lifted her head and pulled her horse to a halt. "They want my daughter."

"Maybe. But you're a threat to your father's political machinations. The only way he can take a state office in Idaho is if he's relinquished all of his wives and disowned his children. You and Bethany are proof enough to voters that he's unfit."

"I can't go back," Ashley sobbed. "I can't go back."

Dot maneuvered her gelding around and rode up beside Ashley. She gripped the younger woman's shoulder and shook her. Ashley ceased her crying and gaped at Dot with red-rimmed eyes.

"You're not going back." Dot leaned closer. "I won't let them. I swear it."

"I don't think you understand how dangerous my father is, or you wouldn't make a promise like that."

"I don't think your father realizes how dangerous I am. Sloane's right. Out here is my playground. We play by the mountain's rules. Not man's."

"They'll get to you. Through your friends. Your mom."

Dot gave a derisive chuckle. "God help them if they go after *Ama*."

"What if she comes back to the ranch before we do?"

"T.J. will explain everything."

"Does she know where we're going?"

Dot shook her head, then reined the gelding around. "The ranger station has gone by the wayside. Not even the current forest service has it on their list of stations."

"How do you know about it?"

"It's a place my *aitona* and I stumbled upon when we were moving sheep to summer grazing. Anyone in the know has long passed away. It's just you, me, and the kid."

Chapter Twenty-Nine

S HERIFF RICHARD T. Ford wanted to kill the man seated before him calmly eating his midday meal of a juicy, medium-rare ribeye, potato, and salad.

The man known only to him as Charles Smith was unbothered by Ford's rage.

Here they sat in Millie's Diner while the owner herself remained in Boise, where her only son was hospitalized and holding on to life by a thread. The diner was empty except for Ford and Smith and the handful of staff Millie employed to keep the place going while she was away.

"Wall is in the hospital. Beaten so badly by that recovery agent, it's a wonder he's even able to breathe."

Smith lifted a dripping bite of steak to his mouth and merely glanced at Ford before eating it.

"Did you send men out to the Ybarra ranch?"

Smith chewed in silence, staring at Ford. Carefully, he placed his fork and knife on the plate and wiped his mouth with a paper napkin, never taking his steely gaze off Ford. He set aside the napkin and leaned onto the tabletop.

"Sheriff, if you'd done what had been asked of you, there would have been no need for any intervention on my part."

"You told me twenty-four hours," Ford hissed. "Twenty-four hours to make a decision."

"That's what you were told. You've been dragging your feet from the moment you were given instructions to eliminate the Ybarra woman, the girl, and her child. I gave you every opportunity to act on these orders. Each time, I sensed hesitation in you." Smith pressed his body into the chair. "This spectacle has gone on long enough. He expects results in a timely manner. You've failed at every turn."

"This was not what I came onboard for."

Smith slammed his fist against the table, rattling the tableware and Ford's already wracked nerves. "You were brought into the fold with the full expectation to do whatever it took to make the progress we needed. If that meant getting your hands bloody, then so be it."

Ford gnawed on the inner side of his cheek. Smith might be the mouthpiece of the man he worked for, but he also enforced the rules. The boss sent Smith to do the dirty deeds when the deeds needed doing. This was why Ford had looked the other way when troublemakers and annoyances disappeared. Smith did what Ford would not, could not do.

Now Ford was being informed that the rules had changed.

"You told me twenty-four hours," he insisted. "I would have made the deadline."

Smith sat back, adjusting his sleeve cuffs. "The deadline changed."

"You couldn't tell me this?"

Smith's eyes seemed to darken, giving Ford the impression he was facing down a shark. "You should have run."

A lesser man would have lost his bowels right then and

there. Ford managed to keep some semblance of self-preservation intact. From some corner of his charred soul, he pulled out one last attempt at bravado.

"You are aware that this attack failed. Spectacularly, I might add. You lost five." Ford cleared his throat. "Scratch that. Six men to Dorothy Ybarra. Now she's in the wind."

Smith picked up his knife and fork and resumed his meal. "Plans are in motion to make that a moot point."

"You gravely underestimate that woman."

Smith speared a potato wedge. "Each move on the chessboard is a learning experience." He ate the potato.

"What's that supposed to mean?"

Smith swallowed, his shark grin in place once more. "She reveals her secrets with each move she makes. I know more about your niece than even you do."

A gut punch had never knocked the wind from Ford like Smith's statement did.

"I will be handling this situation from here on out. You are relieved of your duties, Sheriff." Smith cut into his steak. "Now leave."

Ford rose and, on shaky legs, left the diner. He rounded his truck to the tailgate, bent over, and vomited. When all that remained were dry heaves, he sank to his knees, staring at the yellowish puddle.

For more than thirty years, he had kept Angela Ybarra's secret hidden. Despite her animosity toward him, he had done this for the love of his younger brother. A brother who'd knocked up the prettiest girl in the valley and then run off to war. A war he never came home from.

Angela had hidden the identity of her daughter's father.

She had never been aware that Ford knew, but it hadn't stopped her from taking out her wrath on him at being abandoned for the army by a man she'd thought she loved.

No one knew.

Until now.

How had Smith figured it out? What stones had he located to overturn and learn the darkest truths in Ford's life?

Maybe it wasn't important how he'd learned it. Maybe what Ford needed to consider was how Smith would use it against Ford and Dorothy.

Angela was Dorothy's weakest link. The chink in her titanium armor.

And right now, Angela was a moving target.

Wiping his mouth with the sleeve of his coat, Ford stood. He kicked dirt over the puddle and hobbled to the driver's side.

With Wall out of commission and the rest of the deputies in the office out of the loop, Ford would have to go it alone.

His misdeeds were miles long. If he could right one single wrong, then let it be to save Angela Ybarra.

Chapter Thirty

T.J. WAS HALF aware of Larrabee's arrival in the hospital waiting room, where he paced a well-worn path in the floor.

The hospital staff was trying to get Sloane stabilized long enough for a flight to Boise. She had lost so much blood they couldn't get her blood pressure to level out for the trip. T.J. was beginning to believe he could have made the drive and gotten her to Boise faster than this.

Larrabee hovered in the doorway.

T.J. stopped his pacing. "What?"

"Any news?" Larabee asked in a voice too calm for T.J.'s liking.

"Nothing that warrants a mention. As you can see, we're still here. She needs to be in Boise, and they can't get her damn body to cooperate long enough for the trip."

Larrabee crossed the floor in three long strides and gripped T.J.'s shoulders. "Sloane will be fine. She's too stubborn to go out like this."

"For someone who uses our services sporadically, you know her too well."

Larrabee grinned. "You'd be surprised what I know about Sloane Cross."

Even in his distraught state, T.J. picked up on the odd inflection in Larrabee's voice. Now wasn't the time to pick apart the man's connection to Sloane.

Shrugging free of Larrabee's hold, T.J. backed up. "Have you IDed the dead man who attempted to kill Matlock Hargrave?"

"We have and we haven't," Larrabee said. "He's gone by a few different aliases, and none of them led us to a definitive answer. What I do suspect is his connection to an outfit from Arizona that has some ambiguous ties to the old Las Vegas mobs."

"What about a connection to some shady Mormon fundamentalists?" T.J. asked.

Larrabee considered his question. "Why would you think that?"

"Before Sloane was shot, we were hashing it all out." T.J. pushed past Larrabee and checked the hall, then closed the door to the waiting room. "The woman and girl Dot is protecting have ties to a radical group that moved into Idaho about the time Warren Jeffs went to prison. She thinks her polygamist father is making a bid to run for attorney general for the state of Idaho. He hired Sloane and me to find his missing daughter."

"And you're thinking your bounty case and this missing person case are connecting with my case?" Larrabee asked.

"It's starting to look like it." T.J. moved to the center of the waiting room. "What did you find out at the ranch?"

"Nothing."

T.J. scowled. "Come again?"

"I'm serious. We found no bodies. They were gone."

"You're saying someone came in and cleared out the bodies?"

"Unless Dot did it herself. The only thing we found was blood left behind where bodies had been."

"This is wacked. Dot wouldn't have had the time to dispose of them. She was getting out of there." He checked his watch. "There's been enough time for one of them to hike out, relay what happened, and come back with reinforcements to remove the evidence." He rammed his fingers through his hair, then jerked his hands down to his sides. "Fuck. Which also means the other could have stayed behind to watch the ranch and keep tabs on Dot. They could be trailing her right now."

"Do you have a way to contact her?"

T.J. pulled out his cell. "She sent me the number to her satphone before she left, but she's not going to turn hers on until she absolutely needs to."

"Do you have any idea where she's going?" Larrabee demanded.

"She wouldn't say because we didn't want there to be any chance someone overheard or figured it out."

"Yeah, well, genius, that idea just backfired in your face if you think they're tailing her and her charges." Larrabee pulled out his own phone. "We have no way of tracking her. And no way on God's green earth am I involving any search and rescue people."

T.J. stared at the text message Dot had sent him not long after he'd arrived at the hospital with Sloane. It was two numbers. Why would she have given him two numbers? Unless, one was hers and the other was...

"Angela."

"Angela? Who's Angela?"

"Dot's momma. One of these sat numbers is Angela's. She would know. She would have to know." He tapped on one of the numbers. "Let's hope she kept her phone on."

The first number didn't even bother to ring, instead going straight to a flatline tone. T.J. tried the second number. This one rang.

After about a dozen rings, someone answered his call.

"Who is this?" Angela's hushed voice demanded.

"Ms. Ybarra, it's T.J. Roman."

"Mr. Roman, why are you calling me while I'm on a hunt with clients?"

"We have a problem. And I think Dot is in serious trouble."

There was a moment of dead space, then he could hear the distinct sound of Angela's voice informing her client they needed to move. She came back a second later.

"Mr. Roman, give me about five minutes, then call me back."

"Yes, ma'am."

They disconnected and he stared at Larrabee, who stood several feet away with a woman in dark blue scrubs.

"Mr. Roman?" she asked.

"Yeah?"

She introduced herself as Sloane's attending doctor. "We've got her stabilized enough to get her on a life flight to Boise. You might want to start the trip now. The helicopter will be here in ten minutes."

There was a slight ease in the tension pulling on his

body. Thank God he hadn't killed Sloane in his reckless attempt to evade Deputy Dipshit in getting her here. T.J. had kept at bay the self-recriminations of what losing Sloane would mean by pacing the waiting room. She still wasn't out of the fire yet, but at least he could breathe a bit easier.

"Thanks," he said.

The doctor nodded and left.

Now he had a bigger problem. "I can't go to Boise," he said to Larrabee. "I have to find Dot."

"Who's Sloane's health care proxy?"

"Shit. I am. But I swear she has someone else."

"And that person would be?"

T.J. pawed around in his coat. He'd stuck Sloane's phone in there somewhere. "I think it's her lawyer friend." He found it, tucked in an inside pocket and pulled it out. "Let me call and update her."

"Sloane Cross is friends with a lawyer?" Larrabee asked incredulously.

T.J. paused in bringing the ringing phone to his ear. "She likes you, too, for some reason."

Larrabee seemed to mull over the revelation.

The other end connected. "I'm in the middle of walking into a courtroom, Sloane. You'll have to make this quick."

"Vivian, this isn't Sloane. It's her business partner, T.J. Roman."

"Mr. Roman, why are you calling me?"

"Sloane's been shot, and she's critical."

There was a long pause. In the background, T.J. could make out the sounds of people talking and wood creaking, then it was suddenly quiet.

"Where are you?" Vivian Montgomery asked.

"In Euskadi. The hospital here is life-flighting her to Boise. I'm in the middle of a situation that has the lives of four females at stake, and I can't be there for Sloane. We're going to need you to be her proxy."

"Euskadi? Why is Sloane back there?"

"We're on a case. Make that two cases that collided and brought in an old friend of hers."

"Dot Ybarra?" asked.

"You know her too?"

"She's my cousin."

And that was how Sloane knew and befriended Vivian. This was no small coincidence. Having only met Vivian Montgomery once before, T.J. couldn't equate the polished, professional with a penchant for expensive pantsuits being related to backwoods, rough-and-tumble Dot Ybarra. He should never discredit stranger things.

From his station next to the door Larrabee eyed T.J., no doubt waiting to hear what the response had been to his question. T.J. scowled at him and turned his back.

"How long before they get Sloane here?" she asked.

"Less than an hour."

"Should be enough time for me to ask the judge for a continuance and get to the hospital. Keep Sloane's phone and keep me posted. I have a feeling I'm going to be called there soon."

"I'll do what I can, but this situation is getting uglier by the second."

"Well then, Mr. Roman, you best get to making the ugly pretty again." Vivian ended the call.

T.J. tucked the phone in his pocket and faced Larrabee. "So?"

"So, Sloane's covered. And I'm heading into the mountains to find Dot." He checked his watch. "Shit. Angela." He pulled his phone out again and called Angela.

The satphone didn't ring through, going straight to the steady hum of a phone not in service. A tendril of fear slithered through T.J.

"Something happened to her." He lowered the phone and killed the attempted connection. "Her phone isn't online."

"You said she's a hunting outfitter?" Larrabee asked.

"Yeah."

"She'll be easier to locate. She has to report her route to the forest rangers." Larrabee moved to the door. "Update the doctor. And let's ride."

Chapter Thirty-One

D OT REINED IN her gelding at the peak of the trail. The pack goats were nibbling on the leaves of a sagebrush, oblivious to the dogs crowding at their heels. Behind her, the pack horse blew out a tired breath.

"Yeah, I hear ya," Dot said to the old guy.

She twisted in her saddle to check their trail. Still empty. Yet, she sensed the niggling of watchful eyes. Maybe the wolves she'd heard last night. The goats would have attracted their attention.

Yeah, right. You know better. Those aren't wolves you sense.

Bethany, who had resumed riding her own horse after her nap and their rest break to eat two hours ago, gave a sigh of wonder.

A few hundred yards ahead of them, nestled between a stand of juniper and pine, was the old ranger station. Over the years after discovering the old place, Dot and Samo had renovated it and made the place as functional as one could out in the middle of nowhere. They'd built a small, ventilated shed for the gas-powered generator to protect it from the elements and large wild animals. A small paddock connected the cabin to a lean-to for the horses. The trees provided a natural canopy to hide them from prying eyes of the overhead kind.

"It's rustic," Dot said. "But it'll do for now."

"When was the last time someone was up here?" Ashley asked.

"Me, four months ago," Dot said, urging her gelding forward. "Let's get these horses unsaddled and settled in."

The goats abandoned their afternoon snack and followed Dot to the paddock.

After the animals were unpacked, fed grain, and munching away on the flakes of hay Dot had stored in the shed with the generator, she had Ashley haul their equipment into the cabin. She carried one of the two gas cans she'd brought to the shed and started the generator.

With everything in place outside and the dogs on guard duty, Dot entered the cabin.

Ashley had made short work of setting up house for the three of them. Bethany stood by one of three windows in the cabin and talked to the horses. The mare she'd taken a liking to thrust her nose into the open window and lipped the girl's hand, sending Bethany into a giggle fit.

That child had been through one horror after another and still she seemed unfazed by it all.

"How is your daughter not screaming in terror?" Dot asked Ashley as they watched Bethany blow kisses into the mare's nostrils.

"I don't really know. She's been around bad stuff most of her life." Ashley looked at Dot. "Maybe she's grown immune to it."

"She won't in her sleep."

Bethany stepped back with a squeal when one of the

goats jumped up, stuck her head into the open window, and bleated.

"Why did you bring goats?" Ashley asked.

"They make great pack animals and are good predator alarms." Dot looked around the cabin. "As you can see, we don't have any refrigeration out here, but we can always get milk from them."

"Oh."

Dot turned to the door. "Finish up in here. I'm going to set the perimeter."

"Set the perimeter for what?" Ashley shook her head. "I don't even know what that means. Never mind."

"It's a military term." Dot paused in the doorway. "I'm just making sure that if we have visitors, I know about it before they get too close."

Ashley clutched a canvas bag. "Visitors? You said no one knew about this place."

"Of the four-legged kind. There are bears and wolves out here, and we brought tasty treats."

"Oh."

Dot had to hand it to Ashley—she'd led a sheltered ex-istence for the majority of her life and had only ever known control and abuse. She was naïve and ill-prepared for the realities of life in this world. But at least she was willing to try and learn. Samo had taught Dot to never discredit someone trying to be better than they were raised, and she carried that motto with her through her own life.

"I won't be far," Dot assured her.

This placated Ashley. In truth, Dot had never been far from either of them when danger encroached. Mother and daughter were beginning to rely on Dot to rescue them.

Stepping out into the wilds of the Payette National Forest, Dot realized she would always rescue them. The need to help people ran deep in her veins. She'd been raised to put family and others before herself.

It was why she'd befriended a girl like Sloane Cross. Why she'd defied her *ama* and joined the army. Why she'd chosen the path of a helicopter pilot when she enlisted. After getting out, she'd gone right into a job with the forest service to help.

Despite the crash, the yearlong recovery, and the trepidation that poked its head up now and again, Dot's desire to protect and aide had not been crushed.

She hadn't given much thought to Sloane's and T.J.'s proposal to join them. They'd sold the idea as Dot being a suitable partner to T.J., but they hadn't touched on the other side of the job. The innocents.

Coming up to the first tree where she'd placed a distance marker, she paused. She touched the reflective marker punched into the bark. It wasn't noticeable to the naked eye if one didn't know where it was located. Only traceable when she was looking through her scope on the bow or rifle. Someone wearing night vision goggles might spot them, but they'd be hard-pressed to figure out what it was for.

There were fifty, give or take, of these at varying distances and angles surrounding the entire cabin. Dot had spent the better part of a week placing all the markers and then trail cams. She'd done it with the intention of coming out here and roughing it when she needed solitude. Never had she dreamed this would become a safehouse.

She moved on to the next marker and the first trail cam.

Sloane had taken a direct hit to the chest. If she passed, what then? Would T.J. continue on with their business, or would he return to Oklahoma and set up shop there? And if Sloane made it, she'd have a long recovery. She wouldn't have the energy or the physical capabilities to do the job for at least a year. Or ever.

Dot stopped next to the tree with the trail cam.

She and Sloane hadn't spoken or seen each other in years. They'd just reunited. What if Sloane died? Dot struggled to get the camera off the casing. If Sloane died…

"Damn it." Dot smacked the device. It aligned and resettled into place, then popped right off the backing.

Her friend was too bullheaded to die. But the reality of her wound could force Sloane to step away from her job as a recovery agent for good, possibly end her career as a PI. T.J. would need a partner.

Dot could do the job. They'd both assured her it wasn't difficult to learn the trade of bounty hunting. Hell, she'd practically been doing the job on the fly in the last few days as it was. Her crash course was bringing her to life. In fact, *Aitona* hadn't visited her in his ghostly form since right before Ashley dropped out of the blue into her lap.

Dot switched out the digital photo cards, pocketing the one taken from the camera to check through the photos later. She replaced the trail cam, then moved on.

The heelers tracked her progress around the cabin; they'd done their own recon and territory marking to ward off predators. Gidget found a half-eaten elk antler shed and carried it around. Jealous that his favorite sister wouldn't share, Zip tried to pick a fight and brought out the bitch in Gidget. Getting his butt soundly thrashed, Zip, his tail end tucked under him, resumed his own search for a tasty chew toy.

An hour later, Dot had gone about halfway through her perimeter check and was nearly a klick out from the cabin when she stepped into a small clearing. She'd followed a path through the trees and was out of sight of the cabin. This was the perfect place to pull out the satphone and turn it on.

Once it booted up, she sent two texts—one to T.J. and one to Angela. She had made certain her satphone's GPS and any other tracking app were turned off on her phone and as an extra precaution—the law be damned—had retrofitted hers with a blocker. The people likely to follow her didn't give two shits about the law and were most likely in cahoots with them anyway. They would use any means necessary to find her. Any means.

While she waited for her recipients to respond, she studied her terrain. The clearing was wide enough and flat to the point where she could have set a small helicopter down. If the men after them wanted to get here quickly, this would be how they'd do it.

The aircraft wouldn't be big enough to carry more than two or three extra men. But a fleet of them could bring a whole squad. She looked skyward. To save time and reduce the risk of being caught, the smart thing would be to have the infiltrators rope down from a larger copter and then spread out.

Dot doubted the people after them were military-equipped. She scowled. No, but they had the money to bring in some kind of special security group. No, she needed to amend that—it was a mercenary team sent in this morning. Big money. People who thought themselves above the law and were willing to pay whatever it took to achieve whatever goals they had.

Either way, Dot would booby-trap this whole area and around the cabin. They were on her turf now.

The satphone rumbled. A message from T.J.

You might have been followed. Angela has gone dark. Going to find her. Stay alert.

A special kind of ache strangled Dot around the throat.

Ama going dark could mean one of many things, none of them good. Angela never turned off her satphone when she was with clients on a hunt. She had to be able to reach someone in case of an emergency or to send a report to forest service or natural resources officers.

If something happened to her mother … damn it, Angela had not signed up for this clusterfuck.

The satphone vibrated in her hand. Another message.

Don't panic. I've got this. Focus on the girls. Shut down your phone.

T.J. knew her too well.

Dot did as he ordered and tucked the satphone away.

No news about Sloane. She'd take that as a good sign and not think too badly of T.J. for not updating her. To be frank, she was rather grateful he was more worried about her mother. If Angela was in trouble, having T.J. on the way was the best alternative to Dot herself.

She faced the path back to the cabin. If his warning and her sense she'd been followed did pan out, she shouldn't get too far from Ashley and Bethany.

Dot called to the dogs and started back.

Booby-trapping could wait. It was time to teach Ashley how to defend herself.

Chapter Thirty-Two

"I'VE HEARD FROM Dot," T.J. said, and brought Larrabee up to speed.

Larrabee ensured that the girth strap on his saddle was snug. "Now we find her mother."

With all of the Ybarra horses gone, they had found two reliable and fast mounts through the local conservation officer and brought them to the ranch. Larrabee was plenty comfortable around horses.

"What did you do before you became a cop?" T.J. asked as they led their mounts to the pasture.

"That's a mighty personal question coming from you, Roman."

"PI. Private investigator. Nosy is implied in the title."

Larrabee grunted. "So is dick."

They paused near the fence line.

"I grew up in a family of cowboys and cowgirls who settled here in Idaho dating back to the Buffalo Soldiers." Larrabee grinned. "Guess you can say riding and policing have been strong threads throughout our history."

"Whose idea was it to name you Cassius?"

He chuckled. "My daddy was a fighter who loved boxing."

T.J. clicked his tongue. "Good to know I've got a reliable solider with me."

Larrabee's response was halted by the arrival of a flashy, black sedan. They scowled at each other, then watched as another car followed the first into the ranch drive. The two vehicles parked. The driver of the second car exited and opened the back passenger door. A dark-haired man in a pair of black slacks and a white button-up emerged.

"Fuck," T.J. said under his breath. "Hang tight and keep your badge and gun out of sight."

Larrabee gave a grunt of acknowledgment.

T.J. strode over to the cars. Upon drawing closer, the other man bypassed his driver and met T.J. near the lead car.

"Mr. Roman?"

The voice was familiar, one T.J. had heard over the phone many times. But it didn't match the image he'd conjured of the person behind the search for Ashley. If this was her father, he was doing a bang-up job of managing to ward off the aging process.

"Mr. Shumway, what are you doing here?"

"I warned Ms. Cross I would be checking back with her. She hasn't been answering her phone, so this is me checking back."

T.J. frowned. He had silenced Sloane's phone to stay focused. It was possible Hyrum Shumway had been calling. But why didn't he try T.J.? Because, as he suspected, Shumway thought he could control and browbeat a woman versus controlling a man.

"How did you know where to find us?"

He knew Sloane wouldn't have revealed their location,

and he had not said a word. So how did Shumway know they were here in Euskadi?

"I admit, I was able to track Ms. Cross's cell phone location after our last conversation. It wasn't something I wanted to do, but I have not been receiving adequate updates from either of you. Forgive me for wanting to make sure I'm getting what I paid for."

"Right," T.J. growled.

He wanted to call the man a liar, but why expose his hand? Sloane had all manner of protections on their phones and electronic devices to keep people tracking her the way Shumway claimed he would. Maybe he was the one behind the GPS tracker on the SUV? Certainly would explain it.

"Still doesn't explain how you were able to get out here."

Shumway flashed a smile, one that held no warmth or amusement. "It's not hard to ask the locals."

T.J. could smell bullshit a mile away, and this one reeked of it. He might not be from Euskadi, but the people here liked their privacy and knew their neighbors did too. No one was revealing any information to an unfamiliar man. Except for money. Money did have a way of greasing the gossip wheels.

Shumway peered past T.J. to the horses. "Are you going somewhere?"

Moving into the man's line of sight, T.J. recaptured his attention. "Why are you here? My partner and I have this under control."

"That's not how she made it sound yesterday. Now I hear that there's been some trouble in town. Most of it stemming from this ranch."

T.J.'s situational awareness tingled, the sense of being watched. Closely. He glanced to the car next to him but could barely make out the driver and his front seat passenger through the tinted windows. From what he saw, T.J. didn't recognize the men. He did, however, sense the cold calculations of the two. Security.

What he sensed was more. More chilling. More malicious. Someone else was studying him, and it was coming from the second car.

"I don't know who you've been talking with"—T.J. focused on Shumway—"but I'd advise you to stick with discussing things only with myself and my partner."

"Where is she?"

"Running down a lead."

T.J. returned the man's hard stare with one of his own. He knew the type, had dealt with it through a lot of his career in the army and in his PI work. Shumway was a man used to getting what he wanted, whether by intimidation or by force. Hence the security detail.

If Ashley was correct about his bid for a political position, and a high one at that, Shumway would be the worst man for the job.

"Call her," he said, his tone brokering no rebuttal.

"Can't," T.J. shot back. "She's in an area where her phone won't work."

"What area could that be it where it would lead to the loss of service?"

T.J. lifted his hands and gestured to the world around them. "Pick a spot. Any spot." He lowered his hands. "This whole county is prone to service outages. Tower shortages and whatnot."

Shumway leered at him. "You're not a very cooperative man, Mr. Roman."

"Yeah, guess that's why the army was the only branch of military willing to have me." T.J. pointed at the sleek sedan Shumway had rolled up in. "Why don't you head on out of here and let me and my partner do the jobs you paid us for. We'll call when we have what you want."

"By nature, I'm not an accommodating man." Shumway leaned toward T.J. "My patience has run thin, Mr. Roman."

"Push harder, Mr. Shumway. See where that gets you."

The man's face twitched. T.J. was riled and ready for another fight. A fight he didn't have time for.

Seconds passed, and Shumway stepped back. His gaze flicked past T.J. again, then back to him. "I expect an update by tomorrow morning."

"You'll get what you get and that's it." T.J. waved his hand. "Bye."

There was an intense moment of Shumway glaring at T.J.—to which he thought that fight would actually go down—then Shumway returned to his car. Once he was seated inside, his driver closed the door and resumed his position behind the wheel.

T.J. watched the two vehicles circle the drive. As the second car passed, the passenger side facing him, he tried to see the occupants inside. The tinted windows prevented him from making out anyone but the driver.

As the sedans drove away, Larrabee joined him.

"Who was that?"

"The radical Mormon I told you about. Did he seem too

young to be a twenty-odd year-old woman's father?"

"Amazing what plastic surgery can do these days." Larrabee frowned. "I didn't think they would be into those kinds of medical procedures."

T.J. started back to their horses. "There's not a whole lot I know about the group as it is. Sloane was digging into all of that before she was shot."

"Speaking of which. Any updates on her?" Larrabee asked.

"No." T.J. put foot to stirrup and swung aboard the dark sorrel he chose to ride. "At this point, no news is good news in my mind. Vivian will take care of it. Sloane trusts her enough to make her medical proxy, then I will too."

Larrabee, astride his bay, settled the reins comfortably in his left hand. "We better get going. We're losing daylight and time."

Chapter Thirty-Three

DOT SUPERVISED ASHLEY as she filled a pistol clip. Behind them, Bethany sat on the ground, playing with the stuffed horse Dot brought to her their first day on the ranch. The girl wore a pair of earmuffs to protect her hearing while her mother practiced firing a pistol.

Dot had set up a makeshift range, firing away from the cabin and the animals. So far Ashley couldn't hit the broadside of a barn, owning up to her nerves and fear of the weapons. Dot was able to convince her that the more she practiced with it, the less anxiety would hold her back. By the time the third clip had been spent, Ashley lost her petrified outlook and managed to wing one of the target boards.

"Being familiar with the weapons will make you respect them more." Dot nodded at Bethany. "She'll be taught too. A child brought up to respect sidearms will not mistreat them. A girl taught to shoot will greatly reduce the chance she ever becomes a victim later in life."

Ashley laid down the filled clip and looked Dot in the eyes. "She's already a victim."

"So are you. We can't undo what's already been done, but you're changing the course of your life, and hers."

A contemplative expression passed over Ashley's features. "What about you?"

Dot eyed the younger woman. "What about me?"

"I can see the demons you try to hide. You're a victim too."

Dot crossed her arms and stared at Ashley. "How so?"

"You were attacked when you found your friend. Then you saw what was done to him. I bet his family blames you for what happened to him. Now Sloane's been hurt." Ashley resettled her earmuffs over her ears, then picked up the pistol and clip. "You've had to kill people." She slid the clip into the grip as she'd been taught. "Your mom told me you were in the army. Flew helicopters. Something happened to make you leave."

Dot's muscles tightened to tensile strength. Ashley had just laid bare her fears and anxieties. If she really pushed to the heart of the matter, Dot might break.

Ashley hesitated as she was chambering the first bullet. "Your mom never asked you why. She was afraid you'd leave her again if she did. And you almost died in the crash a year ago, that could have left her permanently alone."

"For someone who knows nothing about our family, you sure know an awful damn lot," Dot said loud enough for Ashley to hear as she plugged in her earbud protectors.

The deceivingly perceptive woman chambered a round and flicked the safety off. "Guess your mom needed someone to talk to, and I'm a good listener."

When she met up with *Ama* after this was over, Dot was going to remind her mother what loose lips and all that nonsense tended to do.

Ashley fired off two rounds, hitting targets this time. Dot instructed her on her stance and redirection. She fired again. One of the targets spewed wood chips.

"Oh my God, I hit it."

Dot smiled. "Gives you bit of an adrenaline rush, doesn't it?"

"Hell yeah." Ashley slapped a hand over her mouth and looked back at her daughter, her cheeks turning bright red.

"She couldn't care less," Dot said and took the pistol from Ashley. "It's going to be dark soon. We should wrap up and get inside."

Dot took aim and fired the remaining rounds into the rest of the targets, obliterating them. She dropped the clip, ejected the last spent cartridge, and handed over the empty pistol.

"Now you get to learn how to take care of a firearm after use."

Ashley removed the earmuffs and took the gun. "How do you do that so well?"

"Decades of practice." Dot removed her earbuds and pocketed them in her shooting vest. "Along with a healthy dose of dedication."

RICHARD FORD HAD a great relationship with the conservation officers. As sheriff, he had to maintain a workable association with them because he never knew when they would need to call on his office for backup. Maintaining that connection also gave him the ability to ask after Angela's numerous hunts into the national forest and surrounding areas.

That meant he knew where her general location was and who she was with. As part of her contract with the conservation office, Angela had to keep records of her hunting licenses, the clients who had licenses, and ensure everyone was properly tagged. Most of the people who used Angela's outfitting business were longtime clients. One of the names on the roster he recognized as a repeat hunting patron. The others on this trip were new.

Those new names worried Ford. If Smith knew about Dot and Angela's connection to him, then so did Smith's boss.

Ford had saddled both of his horses then hauled them up on a fire road he'd used earlier when they were tracking down the criminal. He parked at the end of the road and left the rig, wondering if he'd ever see it again.

He rode as fast and hard as he could through the mountain trails before nightfall. Once darkness hindered his ability to follow the trail, he would switch mounts. His second horse was younger and had better night vision. The young horse had also been one of a handful rounded up from a wild herd from the area and was familiar with the trails. Ford trusted him.

He'd been halfway to his destination when sporadic gunfire pulled him up short. His horses shied at the reports echoing through the rocky passages and trees. Settling them best he could, he dug out his GPS.

It was hunting season, so the sound of firearms shouldn't bother him. What disturbed him was his location. Far as he knew, and as far as the forest service and the conservation service knew, there was nothing out here. This was not a great area to hunt for elk.

There was a long delay in shooting. Should he check it out or move on? Night was about to fall, and he still had miles to go to get to Angela.

As he redirected his horse in his original direction, more gunfire cracked through the air.

"Damn it," he spat, wheeling the horse around and rode headlong toward the sounds.

Twenty-five minutes later, he found them.

Keeping his horses far back in the trees and using the rocky outcroppings as a blind, he watched Dot and a younger woman with a small girl in tow head back to a cabin.

"Son of a bitch," he whispered.

Ford had never heard of this place. The setup was distinctly old school forest service cabin—probably a fire observation center—but the lean-to for the livestock and the small shed were new additions. Someone had long forgotten about this place and left it to rot. Dot Ybarra had found it and made it her own.

Once the women and girl were inside, Ford dismounted and led his horses to a spot where they were out of range of detection by Dot's animals. He pulled out his GPS and checked his location, then tracked it from where he stood to where Angela had notated where she'd taken the hunters. On the map, it looked like the Ybarra women were a few miles apart. In reality, they were nearly twenty miles apart, with the forest and mountain looming between them. There was no direct route out here, only winding, twisted paths taking you up and then down and around.

Just like those paths and trails, Ford was twisted inside. Continue on his way to Angela and save her from whatever peril was coming her way? Or stay here and keep watch over Dot and her charges?

He looked to the sky where stars were just making their appearance, and the blue-black fingers of night were plunging through the vestiges of orange and pink. He had no time to get back to where he deviated from before total darkness ruled. Common sense kicked in, warning him that a ride through the forest reserve was an idiotic idea at best, fatal at worst.

Smith had alluded to knowing things about Dot that Ford himself was not privy to, and this cabin could be one of them. If it was the girl Smith's employer so desperately wanted, then this would be where they came. Dot would need backup, like it or not. With her friend shot and fighting for her life and that bastard Roman holed up with her, Dot was on her own.

Devil's advocate told him to just walk up there, take down Dot, and haul the woman and her child out of here, depositing them into Smith's hands. It was time to be done with this bullshit. If he could get rid of the woman and her daughter, then all of these cutthroats and undesirables would leave town, and Ford could get things back to the way they were.

Who the hell was he kidding? None of this was going back to normal. Ford would be damn lucky to get out of this ordeal with a still-beating heart.

No. The immediate concern was right here with Dot.

His niece. The last thing left of his brother.

At his first choice to camp, he spied the trail cam and stopped before triggering it. He paid close attention to the surrounding area, making sure to not run across any other cameras. Not sure if the cam was functional, and not wanting to find out, Ford redirected his path.

He found a spot to tie the horses and set up a cold camp for himself where he could still keep an eye on the cabin but not be detected.

Now he waited. For what? God only knew.

Chapter Thirty-Four

A FIRE CRACKLED in the small woodstove, keeping the cabin pleasantly warm. While Ashley cleaned and oiled the pistol, Dot was combing through the photos from the trail cams. There were quite a few nice photos of deer that passed through here. Some of a bear with her cubs. And a lot of photos of wolves.

The packs were moving closer to the valley. This was not a good sign.

Bethany had barely kept her eyes open as she ate. She was curled up on the bottom bunk fast asleep. Every now and again, she'd twitch and whimper, then resettle. The heelers slept under the bed. Dot glanced over every so often to check on the trio.

Was Dot a victim, as Ashley had implied? She refused to believe it. She was not made of glass—this would not shatter her.

Still, truth rang in Ashley's statements, especially when it came to *Ama*. Dot had never been able to bring herself to tell Angela why she'd left the army other than the easy answer— her enlistment was up, and she decided not to return. The real reason stayed with those involved in the Afghanistan pullout and T.J., who had mostly guessed until he got it right.

Starting the day Dot had announced she'd enlisted and was leaving, Angela had been cold and distant with her. The longer Dot remained away, the more Angela's passive aggressive attitude diminished, and she became more like her former self, loving and protective of her daughter. She still refused to discuss why Dot's time in the army was such a disgraceful topic, ranked right up there with the non-discussions of who Dot's father was.

Aitona, *I really wish you'd been more open about your daughter's life to me.*

Silence met Dot's plea. Samo Ybarra's spirit remained elusive.

Learning that Angela had talked about their dark family secrets with Ashley, someone outside their family circle, was grating. Ashley wasn't wrong about Angela looking for a sympathetic ear—Dot hadn't exactly been open or talkative with her mother. A nasty little trait that had rubbed off from mother to daughter.

"Done," Ashley said.

Dot looked up from the photo she'd been staring at for the last fifteen or so minutes. The younger woman placed the pistol on an oiled rag and looked expectantly at Dot, a gleam of pride in her road-weary eyes.

Dot set aside her laptop and inspected the work. "For someone who hasn't handled a firearm before, you did a nice job of this."

"No different than some of the things I was meant to clean and take care of when I was growing up." Ashley's proud features turned sour. "Females were expected to do hard labor and have minimal education. Especially in certain areas."

Dot set the sidearm down on the rag. "Don't discredit yourself. You've done a fine job of bucking the stigma." She nodded toward the sleeping girl.

Ashley peered over her shoulder at her daughter.

A fleeting smile dispelled the bitterness. "If not for her, I'd be dead."

It was a sobering thought. One Dot could understand.

Ashley sighed and draped the corner of the large, oiled rag over the top of the gun. "Doing busy work with your hands gives you time to think and consider things."

"Like what?"

"Like I don't think it's my father who is looking for me."

Where the hell had that come from? "How so?"

"He was already an older man by the time I came along." Ashley shifted in her chair, seeming to look for a more comfortable position. "When I escaped, he was much older. I don't know what his exact age is, but he's got to be over seventy."

"What about his brother, your uncle, the one he married you off to?"

"He was older than my father and not a lawyer."

"Your father was a lawyer, right?" Dot asked.

"Yes. He made one of the older sons become a lawyer."

"Which one?"

Ashley turned silent. Dot saw the gradual morphing of the younger woman's features as realization dawned on her, then she turned a deathly shade of gray. Dot waited, her own brain trying to comprehend whatever it was Ashley had figured out but wasn't saying.

Then it struck Dot. "One of your rapists?" she asked quietly.

Ashley's breathing increased. She shuddered, then wrapped her arms around her. "The oldest one," she said, the words coming out choked.

Dot bent forward and grasped Ashley's shaking elbow. "Don't go there."

Blinking, she gaped at Dot. Ashley reached over with her other hand and grasped Dot's.

"If it is him, could he be after Bethany and not you?"

Ashley nodded then shook her head with jerking motions. "Our family believed they were the direct lineage of Jesus Christ. Our blood was to remain pure."

Dot mulled over this. "Why would he want her? What if he's not her father? You said there were three of them."

"It doesn't matter. She belongs to the family. She didn't willingly flee—I did. If they think she's a daughter to any one of them, they believe they have divine right to take her."

And to do whatever they wanted. Dot wasn't sickened. No, she was pissed.

Ashley swallowed a sob. "By the time I ran away, they were desperate for more females." She squeezed Dot's hand. "They'll never want me again. But she's still young enough to brainwash. If it is him, he'll use her to pawn off to one of his sons from another wife. Or another family member."

"I need names."

"Ephriam—he's the oldest, the lawyer—Samuel, and Daniel."

Dot released Ashley's hand and stood. She picked up the

satphone. "Stay here."

She went outside and stood by the paddock. Once the satphone powered up, and she'd been joined by the goats checking out what she was up to, Dot dialed a number she knew by heart and sent a text.

Call me at this number. Now!

Then she waited. A minute later the satphone vibrated. She answered.

"Thanks for being prompt."

"Anything for you, coz." Voices and other odd sounds came from Vivian's side of the connection.

"Where you at?" Dot asked her cousin.

"At the hospital with Sloane. T.J. told me there's been trouble, and he couldn't come, so I'm next up to bat."

"I didn't know she was still in contact with you."

"If you'd spend more time in Boise and hang out with me more instead of tapping me every time you find yourself in a spot of legal trouble, then you'd be in the know." Vivian's cultured voice couldn't hide her Boise upbringing. She'd gotten her law degree from Stanford but refused any and all offers for laws practices in California and moved back to Idaho.

"Touché, *lehengusina*." Dot rubbed her face. "What's Sloane's status?"

"Don't know. She's in surgery right now." Vivian paused. "We're on hour three since she went in. The surgeon sounded optimistic, but Sloane lost a lot of blood before they got her here."

Dot's misgivings about Sloane's chances crept back in. Doctors always tried to stay upbeat and hope for the best—

but it didn't mean they were right.

"Keep me posted. I won't have the satphone on, but you can still send texts, and I'll get them the next time I turn it on."

"Why are you using one, anyway?" Vivian asked.

"Back to my reason for this call. I've got a woman and her daughter in mortal danger, and we're off-gridding it until this can be resolved."

"Mortal danger being the reason Sloane was shot in the first place?"

"You could say that," Dot said. "What can you tell me about a certain fundamentalist Mormon family named Shumway?"

"Nothing right now. I'd have to do some research."

"Okay. What have you heard, if anything, on a man named Hyrum Shumway running for attorney general?" Dot asked.

"Again, nothing," Vivian said. "Far as I know, our current AG is running unopposed."

"Would you do me a solid and research that and a few others from the Shumway family?" Dot rattled off the names of the sons.

"I can make some calls, but I don't want to leave the hospital for the serious stuff."

"Vivian, do whatever you can without leaving Sloane. I'm doing my damnedest to keep more people from being sent to Boise."

There was a pause, and Dot could once again make out the sounds in the background.

"Dot, I saw the Hargraves here. What happened?"

Vivian was intimately aware of Matlock and his family, as she'd visited the summer Matlock and Dot spent way too much time alone together. What Cherry was not aware of was the amount of time Rowdy and Vivian had spent together, alone. God, they'd been such hormonal sex addicts back then.

"Someone tried to kill Matlock by beating him to death. I put an end to it by killing the man who did it."

"Oh my God. Do you need a defense lawyer? I can recommend one."

"No. It was self-defense, and the law isn't pressing charges. We don't even know who the guy was yet."

"Is Matlock's near death related to what you have going on?"

"Don't know for sure. It's all one big clusterfuck." Dot swallowed hard. "I think the sheriff is in cahoots with whoever is behind it all."

"Never liked that asshole," Vivian said in a low voice.

"I'm starting to agree. Guess my mother's hatred for him was always justified."

"You need to get off the phone and power down. Let me work my magic and see what I can come up with. Give me two hours and check back in."

"Two hours? Are you sure?"

"Oh, coz, don't doubt my skills."

Before turning off the satphone, Dot checked for any incoming messages from T.J. None.

She leaned on the fencing and stared at the sky. It was as cold tonight as it had been the night before, and here she stood with no coat on.

She listened to the night sounds, familiarizing herself with them and the forest around her. So far everything was safe and sound. For how long?

Assured they were not going to be ambushed, she turned for the cabin and pulled up short.

Ashley stood in the cabin doorway, backlit by the firelight. "What do we do?"

"We wait."

Chapter Thirty-Five

T.J. AND LARRABEE were within one klick of Angela's last known location when full darkness took over. There was a gradual descent from their position to the lake where she'd reported her camp set up.

"Dark, my favorite woman in black," Larrabee said as they reined in their mounts at the edge of the trees.

Beyond this point the trees were gone and it was only rocky shoreline, leaving them exposed. T.J. lifted his night vision binoculars and scanned the lake's shore.

"See anything?" Larrabee asked.

"Nothing so far. There's a glow over on the far side of the lake." T.J. lowered the binos. "Could be a campfire."

"Maybe they moved?"

"Maybe." T.J. looked around.

A waning gibbous moon hung low in the sky, giving enough light to see with the naked eye and expose any of their movements.

"If you were a mercenary trying to keep a low profile and corral a woman to use her as a bargaining chip, how would you work this setup?" Larrabee asked.

"First, I'm not a mercenary, so I'm not going to think like them." T.J. stowed his binoculars. "Second, I'd stay put and wait for further instructions if I have her corralled. They've got to find Dot and the girls before they can make a play with the hand they've got."

Larrabee's horse shifted under him and blew out a bored snort. "You're the one with army experience. Now what?"

T.J. wheeled his horse uphill and pointed him in the direction he'd seen the light. "We go hunting," he said, sliding his rifle from the scabbard.

Halfway around the lake, they dismounted and secured their horses in a thick stand of trees. From there, they went on foot with T.J. leading the way.

The slight glow he'd spotted before gained in brightness the closer they drew to the point on the shoreline. T.J. halted when he sensed they were about fifty yards out.

"Set up here and cover my six," he told Larrabee. "Make sure no one sneaks up behind me." He handed off his rifle with the nightscope.

Larrabee hoisted the heavy weapon and settled it on his hip. "If they do?"

T.J. secured his lighter rifle to the gun sling strapped across body. "Neutralize them. I'll try to save us a witness to interrogate."

"At this point, we don't know who's friendly and who's the enemy. Are you sure you want to make that call with these unknowns?"

T.J. removed his hat and held it out to Larrabee, not wanting the brim to hinder his sights. "That's why I'm going in alone for more recon. Once I know the lay of the land, I'll come back here and relay. We'll decide from there."

"If all hell breaks loose before you can do that…"

"Move closer and help me out. Enemy will make themselves known by who's firing on me."

Larrabee touched the brim of his hat with the rifle muzzle. "Aye, aye."

"That's navy. Get it right," T.J. groused as he walked away.

Behind him, Larrabee gave a low chuckle.

T.J. eased through the forest like the hunters of old, staying far out of the line of firelight. He was light-footed over the debris-littered ground, careful to stick to large rocks to muffle the sound of his approach.

The lakeside camp came into full view. Four tents horseshoed a blazing firepit. The tents, and a line draped by canvas, helped to block the fire from the opposite points of the lake. One man sat by the fire with a barreled cup in hand and a rifle leaning against his leg. Two other men stood, rifles in hand, walking back and forth on the perimeter. The horses and mule were tied to a line attached to three trees at the edge of the shoreline. All seemed to be dozing.

T.J. calculated in his head how many men he'd seen Angela leave with the day before. Her client and three other men. Angela and her client were not in sight. T.J. couldn't tell if the three men in sight were the same three men who were part of the original hunting party. He checked his backside to make sure no one was sneaking up on him, then moved positions to another point fifteen yards over.

He found a spot against a wide tree and took a knee. Until he had eyes on Angela, he was not making any further advancements. He noticed her dogs were missing.

God, he hoped these men hadn't killed them.

T.J. checked his watch for the time, then settled in. When a half hour passed, he shifted onto his other knee and adjusted his rifle.

The men continued to rove the camp, and their compadre remained seated, emptying whatever was in his cup and setting it aside.

After another half hour passed, T.J. decided he'd lay prone. As he was adjusting himself to lie down, a flap on the far-left tent flicked back. Angela emerged. Through the firelight, T.J. made out the blood-stained shirt and dark streaks across her arms and face. The old, familiar sensation of intense anger whipped to life inside him. If they'd so much as left a scratch on her...

"If we don't call in for a helicopter, he's going to die," Angela barked at the seated one.

The man tilted his head back and peered at her. The other two paused their patrolling and watched.

T.J. lifted his rifle, shoving the butt into his shoulder, and settled his cheek into the weld to look through the scope. The moment any of those men made a move to shoot Angela, he would preemptively strike.

"He wouldn't be in his current predicament if you'd just done what you were told," the seated one said, his gruff voice carrying over the lake.

"You killed two of my dogs," Angela snarled. "I should gut you for that offense alone."

Seated one chuckled. "You don't stand a chance."

Angela shifted to move closer to the man but was stopped short when he lifted a pistol from his lap and aimed it at her.

"I have orders to keep you alive," he said, the malice in his voice reverberating over the distance. "Frankly, I couldn't give two shits if I shoot you now or later. If you so much as take one step closer to me, I will end you."

T.J. took a bead on the man, his trigger finger twitching against the trigger guard.

"Give me a reason," he whispered.

At the scope's edge, he caught Angela drawing herself upright.

"You have no idea what kind of hell you are bringing down on yourself," she said, her voice iron hard.

"Lady, I've been doing this type of work for the better part of a decade. Ain't no one able to fluster me with empty threats."

"My threat is not empty, *ergela*. If you kill me, my daughter will ensure you never see another full rotation around this earth." Angela cocked her head, her long, dirty braid sliding from her shoulder. "Out here, you'll be forgotten 'til you disappear."

The seated man stared at Angela, his stony features slipping a fraction before shoring up. He lowered his side arm. "Empty threats."

T.J.'s rage simmered, but he was able to smile through it. Angela had struck a blow to the seated one's ego.

A man's agonizing cry came from the tent. She turned to it, then glared back at the seated man.

"If he dies..." She left her own threat hanging and returned to the tent.

Seated man looked back at his companions. "She's batshit crazy."

They all laughed.

T.J. lowered his rifle and rose from his kneeling position. He'd seen what he needed to see. Time to update Larrabee and plan their move.

Chapter Thirty-Six

A FEW MINUTES past the requested two-hour mark—after she did a quick walk around the cabin—Dot stood out by the corral, this time wearing a coat, and powered on the satphone.

Found your mom. Will take care of it. Danger Ranger.

She readied a response, and the phone rang. Dot sent the message, then answered the incoming call.

"Coz, girl, what the hell have you gotten yourself caught up in?" Vivian asked by way of greeting.

"That's why I called you." Dot switched hands and rubbed her gelding's forehead. "Is there an update on Sloane?"

"She's out of surgery. They're optimistic but cautious. Also, they called in an orthopedic for some reason. He told me he found a hairline fracture in her bad hip. Do you know how she fell when she was shot?"

"I wasn't there when it happened. T.J. was, but he's gone dark."

"Well, either way, if she doesn't suffer any complications from the other surgery, she's laid up longer than she would have been because of the fracture. He's not sure how she's going to come out of this. She was already on borrowed time with her injuries from before. The bullet and the blood loss have severely weakened her."

Dot ceased scratching the gelding and pressed her forehead into his and breathed in the tangy scent of horse. The gelding lipped her coat and gave a contented sigh.

Sloane had been through the meat grinder in the last decade. Dot should have never left her behind. Alone.

"If you're giving yourself a mental ass-kicking over Sloane's predicament, you damn well better stop," Vivian chided.

"Can't help it. She's my oldest friend, and I feel like I failed her. Like I failed my mother." Like she had failed those people killed or severely injured in the bombing at Abbey Gate. She had only been a helicopter pilot, helping shuttle people out of there. She was not in any way, shape, or form responsible for security or policing, but it didn't stop her from going there.

"Dot, I mean this with all the cousinly sincerity I can muster. Shut the fuck up. You are not responsible for other people's actions. You are only responsible for the mistakes you make."

"Vivian, I mean this with all my cousinly heart. Go to hell."

"Well, now that we have that out of the way, listen up. You stepped into a rattlesnake's nest of trouble. That man you asked me to look into, he's dead. If it's the same guy."

Dot lifted her head from the gelding's and stepped back. "How long?"

"Three years it looks like. I managed to connect with someone in the FBI who has been watching this group closely for the last fifteen years, and she told me they found out Hyrum Shumway passed and not long after his brother died, too. She suspects foul play, but no one can touch the family and get any answers to prove it."

"Did one of the sons take over?"

"His third eldest was shifted into his place. Seems Hyrum Shumway was removed as an elder about six years ago. Sounds like he and his brother Silas were kicked out of the family."

About the time Ashley had escaped. Had her freedom caused her father's and her quote unquote husband's downfalls in the group?

"What was the third son's name?"

"Daniel. From all outward appearances, it was a peaceful shift in power. 'Course, when the guy you are replacing has been removed and can't object, what do you expect? Then Hyrum and Silas died."

"What happened to the Shumway family afterward?"

"Here's the juicy part. They're gone. The compound where they were living is still intact and continuing with their secretive lifestyle, but the Shumways have scattered to the four winds. Everyone, poof, gone."

Dot rubbed her forehead. "Why?"

"The FBI isn't sure. They're searching for some family members, but they're certain everyone has changed their names. Best the agents assigned to this case can tell is there was a power shift within the group, and it appears the Shumways were the recipients of the short end of the stick. My guess is they're looking for a different place to set up a new compound and probably more remote than before."

"Out here makes the most sense," Dot said. "Near the mountains and the forest reserve."

"Where one can hide and never be seen again if they so choose," Vivian said.

"So, who is the person claiming to be Hyrum Shumway?"

"I wasn't able to find out a whole lot on that one. I talked with the current AG, and he told me he'd heard rumblings of someone thinking of running, but the election is another two years off, so it might be only rumor."

"Or a convenient ploy to have as an excuse to look for someone who doesn't want to be found." Dot looked back at the cabin.

Or the workings of a paranoid imagination. Ashley had been the one to suggest her father's supposed run for attorney general. Why make that assumption when she knew her father was too advanced in age? She'd also been the one to think it was a half-brother after her too.

Was Dot being led astray? Craig had been adamant that Ashley was a lying bitch, a woman not to be trusted. Or were those just the ramblings of a drug-addled man desperate for escape?

Dot pulled the satphone from her ear and pressed it against her forehead. She closed her eyes and stilled her wild thoughts. Even if Ashley had conjured the idea from thin air, Dot had to remember, this was a young woman raised in what could only be described as a cult. She'd been manipulated and brainwashed the majority of her life. Her predicament hadn't been any better upon escaping. She had no way of knowing whether what she was saying was truth or fiction. How could she tell the difference when she'd been lied to?

"Dot, you there?"

She returned to her call with her cousin. "Is there anything else you can tell me?"

"Only one thing I was able to learn. My FBI contact informed me this sect had a Las Vegas mob association. Shocked nearly everyone involved with the investigation. Apparently, it was a money connection. This isn't your average fundamentalist group. They used to have extremely deep pockets and long-reaching ties with an assortment of unscrupulous folks. No one thinks that's the case now."

"Would explain the mercenaries," Dot said in a low voice.

"What do you mean, mercenaries?" Vivian demanded. "Is that who shot Sloane?"

"*Lehengusina*, stay on task here."

"Dot, trained killers are nothing to trifle with."

"I'm aware of that. I've already tangled with them twice now."

"Then let's hope T.J. and his law connections can take care of the rest before you have any more involvement. You better lay low."

"I find it highly unlikely this ends with me not getting into another scrape," Dot said.

There was a frustrated snarl from Vivian's end. "You never could follow direct orders."

"Only from those who have the authority," Dot reminded her cousin. "By the way, T.J. and Sloane offered me a chance to join them as a bounty hunter."

"They did what? You're not seriously considering it, are you?"

"Yeah." Dot massaged the back of her neck. "I actually am."

"Dot, are you out of your mind? You barely returned alive from war and miraculously lived after a helicopter crash. There's no way this can be a good idea."

"Vivian, leave my life decisions to me. Be glad I told you at all."

"Does your mother know?" When Dot didn't answer, Vivian growled again. "Whatever grudge she held against you when you enlisted in the army will be nothing compared to the grudge she'll hold if you do this."

"Guess we'll see, huh?"

"I'm getting off the phone. We've been on too long."

"Don't worry, I've got my safeguards in place."

"Just the same," Vivian said. "Better safe than sorry. Check back with me in the morning. Hopefully I won't have to send an army out to help you if trouble comes knocking."

Dot powered down her satphone after checking for a response from T.J., of which there was none.

When revealing her family dynamics earlier, Ashley seemed to be telling the full truth, as best she could with innocent ears listening in. Not to mention, Dot knew from personal experience that when a victim or witness recalled a tragic event in their lives, details were skewed or left out. Memory was a fickle thing.

So was a young woman with little to no life experience whom Dot just imparted knowledge on how to handle and shoot a weapon. A woman running scared. A woman from a family of liars.

Damn it, Dot, Ashley's not the enemy.

She leaned on the top fence pole and let her body sag. She was working on less sleep than usual, had overexerted herself earlier that day in defending Ashley and Bethany, and then the hard ride here to the cabin. Dot wanted to crash, but she had to stay alert. Had to watch for attack.

Drawing in a deep breath of the bracing air, she allowed the cold to invigorate her. She pushed up from the wood pole, feeling the aches and burn in her body. The pain masked the random throbs from the cut on her arm, a somewhat good thing yet also bad, because she forgot about it.

She looked heavenward, past the alpine forest surrounding her, at the clear night sky. Stars glistened against a backdrop of midnight blue.

"*Aitona*, I could certainly use your wisdom right about now. Maybe even a little ghostly visit."

Dot wished like hell he hadn't slipped away so long ago. His was the only male influence in her life, guiding her into womanhood with Basque wisdom born of centuries of experience. He had taught her skills most women her age were negligent in learning, and a few most were not privy to. One of his life's mottos was do right, fear no man. This was ingrained deeply into Dot.

Always, he'd reminded her she was stronger as a woman born of adversity. She hadn't fully understood his meaning, believing he meant she had to go through adversity to remain strong.

"Or did you mean something else?" she asked the sky.

Dot looked in the direction she believed her mother to be. Where T.J. was positioned to aid *Ama* if she needed it. Dot should be there.

If anything happened to Angela and Dot was not there…

"You are where you are most needed, *biloba*."

Dot glanced around. He wasn't there. But it had distinctly been his voice.

Aitona was right. Here was where she was needed. T.J. was a man better suited to rescue Angela if needed. Dot trusted Angela's safety and care to no one, aside from herself, more than she did T.J.

Dot stared at the cabin where a tiny girl and her terrified mother slept. She alone stood between men hell-bent on evil intent and those two. Tonight, this was a dark trail she had to ride solo.

Chapter Thirty-Seven

T.J. WAITED TO make his move after the leader had gone to bed. The man spoke to each person left on guard duty, then disappeared into the tent on the far-right side, opposite of the canvas curtain. By this point, T.J. had the sentries' walk patterns memorized. The first mistake was having so few men. The second was being predictable.

Larrabee was posted with the rifle up the hill just to T.J.'s right. T.J. still suspected there was another man involved, but this fourth man had yet to reveal himself.

When both sentinels were certain their lead man was tucked in for the night, they converged near the fire, their backs to the tents. T.J. moved.

He circumvented the tents, heading for the lake and the backside of the encampment. He had to slow his approach when he reached the rock-strewn shoreline. The sound of the stones sinking into the sandy beach would carry over the lake's wide expanse. T.J.'s needed a careful tread.

Once behind the tent where Angela was housed, he crept up to the backside. From within he could hear the labored breathing of the injured man and Angela speaking Basque to him in low tones, the lantern hanging from the center forming shadows that danced along the walls. T.J. made out

Angela's position next to her injured client lying on a cot. Dead center of the tent.

T.J. removed the ripped sheet of paper with his note. Quietly, he squatted next to the canvas wall and rolled up the edge. He stuck his hand with the note under the wall and crinkled the paper. Angela's voice faded. T.J. smiled as the woman resumed her normal volume and rose.

He left the note inside the tent and waited. Seconds later, Angela was kneeling opposite him in the tent's interior.

"Mr. Roman, there are two other men," she said softly through the canvas.

"Where are they?" he asked, as he slipped his pistol inside to her.

"I'm not certain. After they shot my client and my dogs, they rode away."

"They're the messengers," T.J. said. "Ms. Ybarra, get your client on the ground and you stay there with him. Use that gun only if necessary. Where are the rest of the dogs?"

"With me."

"Keep them there. Don't move until I come through those flaps."

"If it's not you?"

"It'll be me. And for God's sake, don't shoot me."

T.J. shifted into predator mode. He was going at this with the silent approach—hands and a knife, his backup tucked inside a holster at his back. If he could avoid any shots fired, all the better.

While Larrabee would be the more effective and faster choice on the rifle, T.J. did not want the report from the shot bringing any attention to what was about to happen here. It was good intel to know there were two unaccounted men, and they were still a potential threat. Stealth was ideal for this operation.

He circled the tent, coming up the side cast in shadow. The sentries had moved from the firepit and were back to their patrolling.

Hunkered down, T.J. lingered at the junction of the two tents, waiting for the one guard to make his pass close to this location. His half-fingered gloves tightened over T.J.'s knuckles.

The guard paused beside the entry to Angela's tent, staring at the flap. He lifted his rifle barrel and poked it between the loose canvas. As he began to lift one of the flaps aside, T.J. moved.

His appearance startled the sentry, who was too slow to cry an alarm as T.J. silenced him with a slash of his knife across the man's throat. He caught the dying man's crumpled body and laid it on the ground.

The second guard had his back to them, walking toward the opposite end of the encampment. T.J. stepped over the bloodied dead man and rushed up behind the other sentry just as he passed the leader's tent.

He brought his knife hand around the front of the man and brought the blade across his throat. T.J. was laying the dying man on the ground when gunfire ripped through the trees.

He glanced at the hill and spotted the bright flashes of light. Bullets began peppering the ground, racing toward him.

T.J. dove away from the strafing bullets, landing hard

inside the tent. The canvas trembled under the onslaught.

"What the fuck?"

He looked up from his prone position as leader man hopped out of his cot. The two men stared at each other, realization dawning on the leader at what was going down. He reached for his pistol.

T.J. was on his feet and rushing the leader instantly. The man had no chance to aim his weapon before T.J.'s hulking frame plowed into him. They flew into the backside of the tent, the canvas bowed out but held their combined weight.

The men grappled, the leader trying to get his weapon around to shoot and T.J. attempting to disarm him. Their fight was making the tent cave. Finally, the leader found a hole in T.J.'s hold and slipped free.

Grabbing the leader's arm as he passed propelled T.J. out of the canvas's cradle. He smashed his free fist into the leader's chin, staggering the man. The pistol dangled precariously in his hand. T.J. went to grab it and was met with a blow to his temple.

More bullets strafed the tent, sending both men diving to the ground. T.J. scrambled forward and pounced as the leader swung his side arm toward him. T.J. sensed more than felt the bullet's impact. It didn't stop his momentum, and he landed on top of the leader. They struggled for control over the weapon, the gun going off twice more, the leader's finger on the trigger.

T.J. locked his arms around the other man's and flung his own body to the side, dragging the leader with him. The smaller man flew up, T.J. released his grip, and the man's body hurtled through the tent flaps, landing outside.

T.J. rolled to his feet and rushed between the flaps. The leader was straightening to his full height when T.J. emerged. The man had lost his gun.

"Who the fuck are you?" the leader barked.

T.J. rolled his shoulders, feeling the first heated bursts of pain coming from his midsection.

Getting no response from T.J., the leader settled into a fighter's stance. "Why the fuck do I care who you are? You're a dead man." He charged.

The crack of a gun jolted him to a stop. He looked down, reaching for his chest.

T.J. saw the blooming spot on his shirt. When the leader pulled his fingers away, they glistened in the firelight.

There was another gunshot, and the leader jerked sideways.

T.J. followed his gaze and watched Angela lower the pistol he'd given her.

"Two dogs. Two bullets," she said.

The leader staggered toward her. "Bitch," he slurred.

He reached for her, but Angela batted his hand away. The force of her deflection sent him spinning, and he tripped and fell into the firepit. As the flames engulfed him, he began to scream.

With a calm T.J. had only ever seen in Dot, Angela put the man out of his misery.

"He was going to die anyway," she said, as if that was reason enough.

"Ms. Ybarra, remind me to never double-cross you." T.J. grunted, as fire tore through his body.

She moved to his side as he bent over. "Let me see," she ordered.

"It's just a flesh wound."

"Stupid male pride," she muttered and rolled up his shirt. "That's going to need stitches."

T.J. studied her, watching for the signs of reality kicking in that she'd killed another human being. "Angela?"

She ceased fussing with his wound and looked directly at him.

"Have you done that before?"

"Killed a man?" she asked. "No. But he had it coming to him."

T.J. realized there was silence all around them. "There were other shooters."

"Taken care of." Larrabee emerged from the dark, holding his hands up. "Friendly, don't shoot." He, too, looked like he'd gone a few rounds with a heavyweight, his clothing ripped and dirty, scrapes and cuts bleeding on his face.

Angela lowered the pistol. "Announce yourself sooner."

"Can we take that man's body out of the flames?" Larrabee asked. "I'm not fond of burning human flesh."

"Be my guest," T.J. said and grimaced as another flare of heat hit him. "I'm just going to…"

Angela helped guide him to an upright log and sit. "Do either of you have a way to call in a helicopter?"

"I do," Larrabee said as he dragged the dead man out of the fire. "I was able to get through to the forest service before we pulled off our rescue mission. Have one en route as we speak."

Angela squatted in front of T.J. "You're not going to like this, but you're out for the count."

"No, we still have to get to Dot."

"You are going nowhere but on a flight out of here with my client and to the hospital," Angela ordered. "I will get to my daughter."

"Ms. Ybarra, Angela, we don't know where she took Ashley and Bethany."

Angela smiled. "Titus, I know exactly where my daughter took them." She looked back at Larrabee. "Call in another helicopter for transport."

"Transport where?"

"To my daughter."

"How do you propose to help them without manpower?" Larrabee asked.

She looked up at the towering state policeman. "You're a man, and you have power. What do you think?"

Larrabee nodded. "I see where Dot gets it."

"You'll need to hurry." T.J. grasped her arm. "I don't know how long we have before they make their move on her. If they've figured out where she's gone."

"Helicopters move faster than horses."

Chapter Thirty-Eight

THE COLD PRESS of metal at the junction of his jaw and neck startled Ford out of his nap. He stiffened as the bearer of the gun shifted into his line of sight and crouched down.

"Paint me all sorts of surprised to find you out here, Sheriff."

The forest's deep shadows obscured the man before him, but his voice was unmistakable.

"Smith. How did you find me?"

More men ringed Smith, none of them paying attention to them.

"Not important," Smith said. "What disturbs me is your presence out here and not a word was said to me about it."

"According to you, I was through. So why bother?"

Smith's chuckle was void of humor. "I think you're more concerned with saving your niece from my handiwork." He pulled away the pistol and tapped it against his own chin. "Yet, here you sit, up on a hill, far from her sight. What did you hope to accomplish, Sheriff?"

Ford swallowed. "Nothing."

Though he couldn't see him, Ford knew Smith was studying him with that predatory glare. Given the small red dot in the center of Smith's forehead and the same dots on the men around him, Ford was certain they all wore night vision goggles.

One of the men shifted closer to Smith. "Boss."

Smith rose and turned to his man, who pointed downhill.

"See it?"

"Well, isn't that interesting," Smith said. "Thoughts on what they're for?"

"It could be for any number of reasons. Target is a hunter."

Smith turned back to Ford. "Maybe uncle dearest knows and can enlighten us." He reached down and gripped Ford by the armpit and jerked. "Get up."

Ford's aging body struggled to move as fast as Smith demanded. Once on his feet, he was forced to look downhill.

"Tell us what is in all those trees ringing the cabin?"

Ford peered through the dark. "I don't see anything."

"He won't be able to see them," the man said, then tapped his vision equipment.

"Exactly," Ford said.

Smith grunted. "Gentlemen, I think we're going to send the sheriff down there. If the Ybarra woman has booby-trapped the area, he'll be the first to find out."

"Now hold on there, Smith."

Smith jerked Ford closer. "I'm done holding on. We will come to get what we were sent here for and put an end to this mouse chase. If those are triggers for traps, you will be the one to trip them, and I'll kill two birds with one stone."

"Dot's not that kind of hunter," Ford insisted, trying

desperately to keep the terror out of his voice.

He hoped like hell he wasn't lying, and that Dot hadn't changed her MO.

Smith seemed to consider Ford's words. "Alpha One, what do you think?"

"Intel on the target suggests he's correct. However, she's a known associate of special operations and she's killed four of my men already."

"With a bow and arrow," Smith finished.

Ford recoiled.

"Appears our sheriff is not onboard with my strategy," Smith said. He checked his watch. "We have two hours before daylight. Let's adjust the mission perimeters." He jerked Ford toward the front of the group. "The good sheriff here is going down there. If he makes it down unscathed, he can knock on the front door and get himself let in. Then we'll move."

Ford shook his head frantically. "It'll never work. She isn't sleeping. She's been coming out every half hour and patrolling. I'll be dead before I even make it to the corral."

"All the better for us. She'll expose herself, and we'll put an end to this for good."

"Dot isn't that stupid." Ford looked around, counting six men total in this hit squad, with Smith making seven. "She has an arsenal in there. And she was teaching the woman how to shoot."

Alpha One sniffed. "There's shooting, and then there's killing people."

"None of which I anticipate the woman being able to do on such short notice." Smith shoved Ford forward. "March,

Sheriff. Clock's ticking."

Ford tripped and fell to the ground; his body skidded a few feet down the hill, stirring up loose rocks. The clink of rock on rock echoed through the still early morning air. Ford lay on his stomach after his body stopped sliding, intently listening and staring at the cabin several hundred yards off. There was no movement or sound coming from the corral or the cabin, and he let out the pent-up breath.

Slowly, he pulled himself to his feet. He glanced back at Smith and his men, finding they had melded into the darkest recesses of the forest. Carefully dusting himself off, Ford picked a path down the hill. He rashly thought about moving in front of Dot's trail cam to trigger the photo flash, only to nix the idea when he considered who would be shot in his endeavor.

Best course was to get to the cabin unscathed and somehow convince Dot not to kill him before Smith and his men stormed the cabin. Keeping a low profile and using the trees as cover as far as he could, he managed to make it within ten yards of the corral.

The horses had sensed his presence and turned restless. Their shifting woke the goats, and they let out a throaty bleat.

Ford squatted next to the small shed to catch his breath. The first thing to catch his attention was the sudden quieting of the animals. Next, he caught the scent of cigar smoke.

From inside the lean-to a shadow shifted, drawing his attention to the small orange glow.

"Dorothy?" Ford whispered.

The glowing ember moved lower. "I always knew you

were a fucking scumbag, Ford."

The backside wall of the lean-to faced the hill where Smith and his men were stationed. Unless they had infrared sensors, they would have no idea Dot was inside the shed and not the cabin. How much had she'd heard of the men's conversation? Out here sound traveled, and as still as this night was, it traveled even farther.

"It's not what you think," he said. Hopefully Smith couldn't hear him.

"Oh, it's exactly how I think," Dot whispered back. The orange glow flared, then it fell to the ground where it disappeared, probably under Dot's boot. "How many?" she asked.

"More than you can handle."

"Not what I asked."

Oh, God, she was going to turn this into a showdown at the OK Corral. Unlike Wyatt Earp, she didn't have brothers or friends to aid her in a shootout. She was alone.

"Dorothy, don't do this. Just give them what they want."

"For fuck's sake, Ford, do you honestly think they're planning to let me walk away alive?"

He hung his head. "No. They don't plan to leave me alive either."

"That's the bed of fleas you chose." There was the distinct click of a safety being switched off. She was not going about this with a bow and arrow this go-around. "For the last time, how many?"

He sighed. "Seven. All military-trained. Those were the only ones I saw."

There was a prolonged silence. Ford braced for a bullet.

"Better run along, Trojan Horse."

"Dorothy, please."

"Begging doesn't become you, Sheriff. If you want a chance to the see another sunrise, leave now."

"They won't let me. I'm sure as dead the second I leave my hiding spot."

Another prolonged silence.

"There's a window facing the corral. It's open. You get inside there; I'll give you a pass."

"It's a lot of ground to cover."

"Your only option." The shadow shifted again, stepping out from under the lean-to roof.

Ford's breath caught. There was no way Dot could pull off the impossible. They were out here alone, no backup, and no one aware of where they were. How did she think she'd get out of this?

She moved to the wall of the lean-to, bringing a long-barreled rifle to her shoulder.

"Run."

He bolted for the fence the moment she fired the rifle. It was like he moved in slow motion. This had to be a dream. He hit the bottom rung of the fence and threw himself up and over it.

The instant his boots hit the ground inside the corral, there was a loud pop, then the entire early morning sky exploded in bright strobing lights.

Disoriented, Ford staggered, trying to shield his eyes from the fireworks. He slammed into the cabin wall. Through the barrage, he found the open window and fell inside.

A startled shriek at his unceremonious drop greeted him.

Once he was able to adjust to the semi-darkened interior, he made out the young woman and her daughter clutched in her arms. He held up his hands as the woman extended a wobbling pistol at him.

"I'm not here to hurt you."

A rifle cracked, and she ducked.

"Stay low," he said and scrambled to his feet. "Where's another gun?"

The young woman shook her head, clutching her pistol to her chest. "Dot has all of them on her."

"Shit," he spat and looked at the open window above him.

They were all going to die.

Chapter Thirty-Nine

DOT'S FIREWORK DISPLAY ended, leaving fires burning all along the perimeter, giving her the much-needed light to pick off the men coming to kill her. Her main objective had been to eliminate the men's use of night vision, blinding and disorienting them.

She was no fool thinking they'd just stumble out of the tree line and expose themselves, but she could hope.

Now that Ford was out of sight and Ashley was hunkered down inside with strict instructions on what to do, Dot could focus. To avoid her animals getting caught in the crossfire she'd confined them to the lean-to, and after lighting up the sky she had moved to the opposite side of the storage shed. The generator had been relocated to a spot behind the cabin to avoid an unnecessary firebomb.

Ford's path down the hill gave her a starting point to look for the men. His headcount was enough to work with, but like he said, there could be more out there. The one she most worried about was the sniper. If he wasn't already set up, he'd be looking for his spot. Hopefully, right into one of her traps.

Dot scoped the hill and noted with satisfaction that her barrage of bombs had taken out one assailant, his lifeless form left to burn next to a shredded tree. She spotted movement coming from near the body. She lined up and fired.

Without bothering to watch if her shot hit its mark, she rolled to the other side of the shed. Once she was resettled in the prone position, she hit the bolt, ejecting the spent cartridge, then scanned the hill again.

A second man writhed on the ground where she'd dropped him.

Two down and five to go. If seven was the accurate number to work with.

Where was that sniper?

Except for the crackle of the fires, silence lingered over the area. Dot kept on the scope, watching for any movement other than the dying man along the hill. No one moved. She placed her trigger finger along the guard and tapped off the seconds.

"Dot Ybarra!"

The man's voice echoed over the hollow. No way to pin down where he was stationed.

"You can't win this," he bellowed again.

Dot settled deeper into the cheek weld of the Winchester, tucking her finger inside the trigger guard.

"The wisest course of action is for you to give up the woman and the kid."

This one liked to hear himself talk.

At the edge of the scope's field, she spied a shadow. Dot adjusted for the distance. The shadow moved. Someone was getting antsy.

"Last chance!"

The moment the echo from the warning faded, the shadow stepped out from behind the tree he was using as a shield. Dot registered a second too late the grenade launcher he held in his hands. She pulled the trigger at the same time a brilliant explosion came from the barrel of his weapon.

If her shot hit or not, she didn't know. She abandoned the rifle and ran, her flight dogged by the silent death hot on her heels. The grenade hit the shed and detonated.

The explosion yanked Dot from her feet and flung her forward. She hit the ground, flipped, and rolled until her body slammed into the cabin wall. She lay there, head spinning from the concussive blow.

Warbled sounds of screaming penetrated the thick blanket of silence filling her head. Muffled pops followed. More screaming.

Dot felt her body curl on itself. She heard the garbled cries and pleas. The scent of scorched flesh and fresh blood slammed into her. She clutched her head, covering her ears. She couldn't see it. She couldn't relive it.

The screams faded, but the smells persisted. Dot peeled her eyes open. Through a watery haze she made out the climbing flames. Dark shadows passed before her. One reached back, calling to her.

A girl.

Dot's vision gradually cleared, and she saw Bethany crying for her over the shoulder of a man. Reaching her small hand out to Dot. Then they disappeared past a wall of flames.

They had Bethany.

Dot forced her arms under her battered body and shoved

herself upright. She patted her leg holster, finding the 1911 still strapped inside.

Someone rounded the corner of the cabin. As he was bringing his rifle up, Dot drew the 1911. Their shots went off simultaneously. The shooter's bullet grazed her arm and struck the cabin wall. Hers found its mark, center mass. His chest protector stopped the bullet, but he staggered back from the impact. Before he could recover and try again, Dot fired two more rounds, aiming for his head and hitting her target. He went down.

Overhead, a distinct *whomp, whomp* drew her attention. Helicopter lights passed over the area.

That was how they were getting the girls out of here.

Dot ejected the 1911's half-empty clip, replaced it with a full one, and holstered the gun as she staggered to the lean-to. The horses and goats were going crazy, except for Dot's trusty gelding. She threw open the gate, and the animals surged out of the building into the corral.

Dot grabbed up the stored bow and quiver, strapping the quiver across her back. The gelding snorted as she approached, shifting but not shying from her reach. Cooing words of assurance, she gripped his mane. Her touch eased his shiftiness. She vaulted onto his back, grinding her teeth against the pain shooting through her arm from the bullet graze.

With only her knees and hand wrapped in his mane, Dot guided the gelding out of the corral. Once free of the fencing, she pointed him in the direction the girls' kidnappers would take to the clearing and gave the gelding the command to run.

He bolted as if breaking from the starting gate.

Her balance precarious because of the injuries, Dot had to rely on her legs to keep her steady on the gelding's back as he raced over the rough terrain. She settled into his rhythm. Fighting past the pain of her injuries, she nocked an arrow and readied her bow.

Years of practicing this on horseback brought back all the muscle memory. Before she'd discovered her love of flying, Dot had competed in shooting horse competitions where they would shoot everything from single shot pistols and pump rifles to bow and arrows. This time, she would not be aiming at balloons or paper targets.

The gelding flew out of the makeshift yard and raced down the trail. She heard the commotion of men ahead.

Adjusting to the gelding's rocking head, she aimed the bow. A body appeared in the murky haze of dawn and smoke. Dot released the arrow.

The man wheeled, grasping at the protruding shaft in his neck as Dot and her horse flew by.

She was nocking the next arrow as the gelding continued.

By her calculations, it would take two men to carry out Ashley and Bethany. The one with Bethany wouldn't be as hindered in his escape; he should be farther ahead.

Another form stepped into the path, leveling a rifle at Dot.

She didn't have time to make a precise aim, she shot the arrow. It struck the man in chest and bounced off. But the botched shot threw him off and he stumbled, lowering his rifle.

Dot drew the 1911, and as the gelding closed in on the

man, she aimed and fired as he was readjusting. The bullet struck him in the face, and he was down.

Dot slung the bow over her back and kept the 1911 in hand. She urged the gelding onward.

Ahead, she could hear Ashley screaming. Hopefully, she was putting up a fight and hindering her captor. If Dot didn't hurry, he'd give up and kill her.

The smoke lessened, parting and revealing what was in front of Dot.

A clear path.

The echo of Ashley's screams came from Dot's right. They were on the other path. The more treacherous one.

Dot slowed the gelding, and she commanded him to stop. He halted, inches from where the ground turned rocky. Unwilling to risk seriously injuring him, she dropped from his back and shoved him toward the cabin, then slapped his rump. The gelding bolted.

Shoring up her reserves, Dot darted into the unknown.

Chapter Forty

T ENDRILS OF SMOKE from her fires and the fires left by
the explosion coiled and rolled through the forest
underbrush. Like the fog from the day before, it would serve
to mask her progress. But not for long.

Dot holstered the 1911 and returned to her bow and arrow. She needed to reserve her ammo as long as she could.

Ahead and to her left, Ashley let out another cry.

Dot redirected her path and hurried forward, staying
low.

Overhead the thump of rotary blades passed, the lights
from the helicopter illuminating the forest around Dot.

Yards in front of her, she made out the struggling forms
of three people. One too small to be a man was lodged
between the others.

Ashley.

Dot shot forward, leveling the nocked arrow with the
deadliest tip. When she was within eyesight of the men she
halted, steadied her body, and released the arrow.

The man closest to her dropped, screaming, an arrow in
his thigh.

The second gaped at his partner for two seconds, then
flung Ashley away. He was bringing his rifle across his body

when Dot's next arrow struck him in the groin. He dropped his rifle and hit his knees, roaring in pain.

Dot came abreast of the two men, 1911 in hand, and ended their terrorizing ways. That was seven. There had been more. She was missing the loudmouth—which was probably Smith—and the sniper. None of these men looked like the wiry man from the first attack. That left at least three unaccounted for.

Sitting in the dirt feet away, Ashley gaped at her. "Dot?"

Dot holstered her 1911 and thrust out her hand. "We don't have a lot of time before they get Bethany out of here."

Ashley grasped the offered hand. "They killed the sheriff," she choked out as Dot hauled her upright.

"He knew it was coming." She grasped Ashley's face and checked her over. "Are you hurt?"

"No."

Dot released Ashley's chin. "Was Ford the only one killed in the cabin?"

"Yes."

Shit. She had to find that sniper.

Dot took Ashley by the arm and turned her. "Let's go."

The helicopter passed over again. This time there were no lights and the oddity of it brought Dot to a halt.

She looked skyward as the mechanical bird circled. Its rotary wash cleared the smoke around them. Dot noticed the shape of the helicopter. This was not the same one as before. It was larger.

"Fuck."

Ashley looked up with her. "What?"

This helicopter had to be bringing reinforcements.

"More trouble." She tugged on Ashley's arm and they raced down the path. "How many men took you?"

"Four."

Two on Ashley. One to carry Bethany. And a fourth to watch his six.

"Ashley…" Dot's statement was cut off.

A wet thwack registered, then Ashley was yanked from Dot's hold and flung sideways. Dot gaped as the woman went down, a dark blotch high on her chest blooming. Ashley slammed into the ground and rolled away.

Dot reeled back and threw herself behind a tree as another bullet whistled past. She gasped for breath and pressed into the sharp bark.

"There's no use hiding, Ybarra."

This man wasn't the loudmouth, and it wasn't the sniper. No sniper worth their craft would ever give away their position. It had to be the fourth man to drag Ashley and Bethany into harm's way.

Dot propped her bow against the tree, then unclasped the quiver and set it beside the bow. Behind her, she heard Ashley come to with a cry of pain. She was alive. There was no time before the shooter finished what he started.

With her 1911 in hand once more, she readied herself. Dot swung out from behind the tree and fired in the direction she'd spotted him. Her gunfire was answered with his own. Dot felt a bullet find its mark as she ran forward.

The shooter materialized through the forest gloom. Dot readjusted and found her mark, but he vanished behind a tree. Dot did the same.

She dropped the empty clip and replaced it with her second to last one. Her objective to direct attention away from the wounded Ashley accomplished, she had to think of a better way to take this guy down. Her brief glimpse of him was enough for her to recognize him as the wiry man who had escaped through the barn after the attack on the ranch.

Pain throbbed from her thigh. She reached down and touched where blood was pulsing from a hole. She had to have caught him by surprise with her counterattack. He had probably been lining up to take the final kill shot on Ashley and wasn't able to adjust for a direct hit on Dot. She'd take a leg shot over being dead.

The smoke grew thick around them, finally hiding Ashley from the shooter's sights.

"Ashley," Dot yelled out. "If you can move, do it."

"You should have never involved yourself with them," the shooter said, his voice raised above the noise of the helicopter making another pass over them. "You and your mother didn't have to go down like this."

Dot let the comment about Angela slide. By this point, T.J. should have made good on his promise to rescue *Ama*, and she was out of harm's way.

"Drop this ridiculous notion to be a hero and be done with it," he said.

She found a hole in her shirt and made it larger, ripping a long strip out of it. The sound of the helicopter changed midair. Dot looked up and saw it coming about. She doubled up her makeshift bandage and wrapped it around her leg wound, tying it off to stanch the blood.

The helicopter made another pass over their spot. Gunfire from her left startled Dot.

She chanced a peek around the tree and saw the sparks from activated gunpowder falling from the tree where the shooter had hidden. He was aiming upward.

Dot wrenched back into her hiding spot. The helicopter was not one of theirs. She looked up as it buzzed the treetops. Through the moving boughs she made out the white underbelly of the bird, and a strangled laugh burst out of her.

It was a forest service helicopter. The calvary had arrived. Once the helicopter was out of range, the gunfire ceased. As long as that bird remained in the sky, it would keep the other one away or grounded.

Dot had time to rescue Bethany.

She just had to get past this scumbag.

The 1911 holstered, she studied her precarious situation. She needed to get back to the tree where she'd left her bow and quiver. And she needed height. Over the years, first Samo and then Dot had trimmed the lowest growing limbs on all the trees along these paths. A lot of the trees were stout enough to hold her weight.

Plan in place, she waited for the forest service helicopter to make another pass. If the shooter stuck to plan, he'd try again to scare off the pilot.

It came back around, making a higher run. And, true to form, the shooter let loose with another round.

Dot ran.

Hindered by her injury, she wasn't as fast as usual. She had just made it to the tree when strafing rounds chased at her heels. She slammed into the rough bark, her face meeting the sharp edges of the wood.

"They can't help you!" he yelled.

Dot returned the quiver to her back and draped the bow across her body, leaving her hands and arms free to climb. She peeked out into the path.

Ashley was out of sight. Dot just hoped the young woman didn't bleed out before Dot could put an end to this man's terrorizing.

Dot relished the feel of her shooting gloves flexing around her hands. She prepared her body and, with a mighty heave, jumped up vertically and grabbed the lowest branch. With her boots planted into the side of the tree, she hauled herself up.

Thankful she'd picked the stoutest tree to hide behind, she braced her feet on the thickest part of the branch and reached for the next two limbs. Her leg and arm wounds burned as she worked upwards, overpowering the rest of her injuries.

Overhead, the copter disappeared. Dot paused and looked down.

Daylight was getting stronger, making visibility easier. She spotted Ashley lying under a downed tree. Assured she was safe, Dot checked for the shooter's position.

He was making a bold move, emerging from his hiding spot.

She was as high as she was going to get. Dot wedged her back into the tree and braced her boots on two limbs. The tree shuddered under her weight, and she stilled. The shooter hadn't noticed it.

Slowly and carefully, she pulled the bow over her head and removed an arrow from the quiver. Arrow nocked, she lifted the bow and drew back the string, bringing the bow sight into line with her eye.

The shooter, rifle leveled at the point where Dot had run, crept forward. She waited as he inched into her sights. When he was as close as she wanted him, she let out a whistle.

He gave a slight jolt and looked up. Her released arrow was the last thing he saw.

Chapter Forty-One

D OT ROLLED ASHLEY into a sitting position.

"Is he dead?" Ashley asked, weakly.

"Yes." Dot peered at the wound. "You're in luck. It's just your shoulder." She leaned Ashley forward. "A through and through. No bullet to dig out."

"I don't feel right."

"You're losing blood." Dot helped her out of her coat and wadded it against the wound. "Hold it there. I've got to get Bethany."

Ashley grasped her arm. "Don't die."

Dot smoothed back the younger woman's wild hair. "I don't plan on it. Stay here and stay out of sight. There might still be a few stragglers."

Confident of Ashley's comfort best she could be, Dot took off for the clearing.

She could hear the whine of the engine idling as she came to the clearing. The first helicopter had landed. But the constant buzzing of the forest service one kept it grounded.

Dot stopped behind a tree at the edge of the clearing. She had a good line of sight on the pilot. The thought of putting an arrow through the window and into the pilot crossed her mind. But seeing as there was no sign of Bethany and her captor, Dot didn't want to risk the chance that the girl was onboard and the pilot did something rash to jeopardize the bird and cause an accident.

She swapped weapons of choice and area of incapacitation. The fuel tanks would do just fine. No explosion, no fire, just holes draining it out. She would have preferred her rifle for this, but the 1911 would work just fine.

As the forest service helicopter flew over again, she fired four rounds. Two in the tank under the blades and two into the side panel behind the pilot's seat. Aviation fuel should be leaking into the compartment and filling the cockpit with fumes.

As Dot waited, she ejected her clip and replaced it with the final one. She had two arrows left in the quiver.

A moment later the engine whined down, bringing the blades to a stop. There was hesitation on the pilot's part before he yanked open his access door and fell out.

"Don't shoot!" he screamed as he scrambled to his feet, hands up.

Dot wasn't concerned about him as she angled herself around to get a line on the opposite door.

But the pilot's attempt to save his own ass ended when his passenger shot him as he emerged from the pilot's door. Bethany, clutched in the man's arms, screamed.

Dot halted her progress and adjusted her aim. She glared at the man called Smith as he stepped clear of the door.

He leveled his sidearm at Dot. "You're like a goddamn cockroach, Ybarra!"

"Let her go."

"You and I both know that's never going to happen. One

way or another, she will be returned to her father. This won't end with me."

Fire rippled through her leg, setting her off-kilter as it weakened. She didn't know how long she had before the blood loss and her other injuries shut her down. Dot strained to keep the bow pulled taut and the arrow on target.

"I'm leaving," Smith said. "And I'm taking the kid with me."

"Your options of freedom are gone," Dot replied.

"You can't seriously believe I don't have backup contingencies."

"Oh, I know you do. But what you're underestimating, as you've done so far, are the countermeasures already in place in the event this would happen."

Smith dared to look around him, then back at Dot. "You've booby-trapped this whole area." He gave a harsh laugh. "You're a goddamn Rambo."

A noise to her right pulled her attention away from Smith, and she lowered her bow. Taking her eyes off him would have signed her death certificate, but the lumbering figure emerging from the haze slammed into her, throwing her forward and making her release the arrow. She hit the hard ground at the same moment the fired shot echoed over the wide clearing.

From the ground Dot gaped as a bloody Ford staggered a few steps forward then collapsed, blood leaking from his mouth.

"Well, fuck, Ford. Who knew you had a soft spot for your niece," Smith said. "Too bad your effort was for nothing."

Ford mouthed something that looked a lot like *I'm sorry*, and then the life left his eyes.

A burst of gunfire jolted Dot. She held her breath, waiting for the pain to register. Nothing came of it. She looked toward Smith. He was staring at the far side of the clearing where a body tumbled from a tree.

Once the body hit the ground, three forms emerged from the trees. Relief spilled through Dot as she recognized T.J. and Larrabee, and... "*Ama?*"

Dot scrambled to her feet, leaving her bow where it lay.

"Release the girl, Smith!" Larrabee ordered. "There's nowhere for you to go. Well, except to jail."

"You fucking believe I'm just going to give up?" Smith bellowed at Larrabee.

At one point during the whole exchange, Bethany had stopped screaming and was keeping her eyes on Dot. With Smith surrounded and weapons leveled on him, and the last remaining threat to her life gone, Dot made a rash decision and stepped forward.

"Bethany!"

The girl's eyes widened, and she tipped her disheveled head up.

Dot kept going as Smith faced her. "Bethany, what did I tell you about the *lauburu?*"

"Ybarra, stay the fuck back!" Smith yelled.

"Tell me, Bethany."

Bethany grasped the dirty hoodie, despite her predicament. "Luck," she managed to get out.

Smith backed toward the now-defunct helicopter, his pistol leveled at Dot.

"What else?" Dot pressed.

She could see the glint in Bethany's eyes. The child was no longer afraid.

"Family."

Smith had wedged himself inside the open cockpit door. He gave up aiming at Dot and pressed the pistol into Bethany's head. "Not another step."

A shadow passed over the window on the backside of the helicopter.

Dot smiled. "You got it, Roman?"

"Got it."

Smith chanced a look back to see T.J. with his sidearm leveled on Smith's head. When the man faced Dot again, defeat was etched into his features.

"Family," Dot said to Bethany.

He released the girl, and she bolted into Dot's arms. Just as they had in their first meeting, the two wrapped around each other as Dot, despite her injuries, lifted Bethany into her arms.

Larrabee rounded the back end of the helicopter. "Drop the weapon and move away from the cockpit."

Keeping his steely gaze on Dot, Smith dropped the weapon and slowly lifted his hands as he stepped away from the open door. "I'm not wrong. This doesn't end with me."

Dot glared back. "I'm not through yet."

Chapter Forty-Two

DOT CLUNG TO the strap and let the wind from the open door whip her face. She and T.J. had hitched a ride with Ashley and Bethany on the forest service helicopter, while Angela had gone to the cabin to take care of the animals. Another helicopter with federal marshals on board had taken custody of Smith and were hauling him to Boise. Not far behind them came Larrabee and a few of his men who hadn't been left behind to do clean up.

"You should be going to the hospital too," T.J. said into the headset.

Dot reluctantly peeled her eyes open and canted her head around to look at him. She hadn't been in a bird since her crash and subsequent flight to the hospital afterward. God, how she'd missed this. She didn't want it to end.

T.J. looked down at her bloodied leg and then met her gaze. "I'm serious."

"Not until I nail the fucker to the wall," she said.

"You're certain it's one of the sons and not the father?" he asked, glancing at Ashley on the stretcher, strapped to the floor of the helicopter.

Bethany lay beside her mother, staying out of the way of the medical personnel and paraphernalia keeping her mother alive. Ashley's good arm was curled around her daughter, her forehead pressed to Bethany's. They had refused to be separated.

Dot would see to the end of the terror wrought on these two. No one would touch them or hurt them ever again.

"Vivian confirmed via FBI that the father is dead and so is the uncle slash husband. It's one of the sons who raped her." Dot returned to watching the patchwork of trees, mountain, and fertile valleys passing by under her. She could see the outline of Euskadi on the horizon. "Once he's in custody, I'll go to the hospital."

ONE OF LARRABEE'S men had been tasked with tracking down the Hyrum Shumway imposter. It didn't take them long to confirm that the man claiming to be Hyrum was, in actuality, Daniel Shumway—the third eldest son. And, according to the FBI agent aiding Larrabee's team, the most sadistic one.

Daniel and his security detail were located at a hunting lodge thirty miles southeast of Euskadi.

Dirty, bloodied, broken, and pissed off, Dot approached the door.

She had announced her intention of walking right in, an idea both the injured T.J. and an insistent Larrabee failed in talking her out of doing. Dot's single concession to their objections to her asinine idea was for her to wear a vest. T.J., Larrabee, and two of his men surrounded the cabin's entrance, weapons aimed at Dot's back. At the rear of the cabin were stationed four of the federal marshals. Daniel had nowhere to run.

Dot beat a fist against the door from the side, using the thick pole walls to safeguard her, and eased away from the doorframe.

"Open the fucking door, you prick!" she yelled.

Through the earbud, she heard Larrabee groan. "So much for the diplomatic approach."

When no one came to the door, she beat on it again.

"Let's go, Shumway! We know it's you."

The interior door opened on quiet hinges.

Before anyone could react, Dot forced her way inside, grabbing the man who'd come to the door and using him as a shield. His body absorbed the shots coming from behind him. She continued to propel him backward, shoving him into a second man.

The two were forced into the back of the lodge where Dot released the now-dead man onto his partner. The partner collapsed to the floor, pinned under the weight. Dot mounted the men and stepped down on the second's gun hand, feeling the fragile bones crunch under her boot. She swept the gun into her hand.

She turned and threw the weapon at the man trying to escape through the backdoor. The pistol hit him in the head, and he stumbled to a stop.

Dot crossed the floor and grabbed Daniel by the shirt. With a mighty heave, she hauled him around by the collar, choking him as he went, and flung him into the sparse furniture. He crashed into the table, sending it, the chairs, and any contents on the table skittering across the floor.

Daniel lay among the wreckage.

Dot stalked toward him. His eyes widened at her approach, and he tried to scramble out of the mess. She bent down, grasped the front of his shirt, and dragged him upright, bringing him face-to-face with her.

"I should gut you for what you did," she snarled.

"You … I'll see the end of you," he said.

Dot smiled. "Not likely."

She studied his face, seeing what she'd hoped she wouldn't. The little details lost in a sea of innocence in a girl who had been conceived in an act of incestuous violence.

Dot relinquished her hold on him and took a step back. "I have a message for you."

He frowned.

She brought a stiff roundhouse punch around, clocking him in the cheek. He toppled over, lying on the floor on his side.

Dot gave him a few seconds to recover, then kicked him in the groin. He rolled to his back, gasping and whimpering and grasping at his abused manhood.

Dot straddled him and bent down. "That's for Rebecca and her sister. And for the child you tried to kidnap."

Through a haze of agony, he gaped at her, only uttering pitiful moans.

"Okay, I think that's enough," Larrabee said, gently taking hold of Dot's arm. "We'll handle it from here."

He guided Dot out of the lodge and left her standing on the small porch.

Her chest heaving, she stared out across the miles of sagebrush and grasses, watching how the midday breeze ruffled the tops. With weakened steps, she dismounted the porch and staggered into the middle of the yard as men surged around her. She dropped to her knees, then situated herself to sit cross-legged on the ground.

Dot closed her eyes and tilted her face to the sun's warm autumn rays. After a brief moment of enjoyment, she sensed T.J.'s familiar presence.

He eased down onto the ground next to her. They sat there for a few minutes in silence.

"Is it over?" she asked him.

"It's over."

"Good."

Epilogue

THE FIRST SNOWFALL of the season covered the yard. Bethany was running around, squealing with delight, while the dogs chased her.

Ashley, bundled from head to toe in every warm winter item available, sat in an Adirondack chair watching her daughter play. Two months after being shot she was recovering and gaining strength, nearly ready to tackle the task of being Angela's line camp cook.

From her spot propped against the barn doorway, Dot observed the quaint scene. She couldn't remember the last time she'd seen someone so excited to play in the snow.

She had just returned from a trip to see Matlock. He'd been released from the Boise hospital two weeks after his attack, and Millie had moved back into her old residence to see to her son's continued recovery. Embarrassed at what she called her unreasonable behavior toward Dot in the initial day of Matlock's injuries, Millie had apologized. Dot tried to downplay the need for it, but the matriarchal Hargrave would hear nothing of it and after a bit of a browbeating, Dot accepted. Matlock was still a long way off from being able to resume his duties as a deputy, if he wanted. Dot had assured him that she knew what he was going through and offered her assistance for as long as she was in the area.

They never got around to discussing what Cherry had revealed to Dot about Matlock's suspicion surrounding his father's death because Millie was always around. After everything that had gone down with Ashley, Dot began to believe the situation with Matlock was not related. But it was a mystery to work out at a later date.

The shuffle of boots against the hay-strewn floor made her look over her shoulder. Angela joined her. Together they watched their adopted family.

Dot reached out and hooked an arm around her mother's shoulders. "You still have me through the winter. I won't officially begin the job until I've been cleared from my injuries. And T.J. has everything worked out with Sloane."

Having barely survived her shooting, and learning that her once shattered hip was getting worse, Sloane had decided to retire from the PI and bounty hunting business. She planned to move back to Euskadi and, between bouts of rehab and another round of future medical procedures, she would assist Cherry at her bed and breakfast. Dot gave that venture about three months before Sloane got stir crazy or drove Cherry to violence.

"I'm not worried about that." Angela tilted her head toward Dot. "It's Ashley and Bethany. The worst of their ordeal might be over, but there's still the trial."

"Vivian is handling it. She's assured me that, other than the DNA test, Bethany will never see the inside of a courtroom and be subjected to any cross examination. Ashley, on the other hand, will." Dot sighed. "She's stronger than she looks."

"You made her that way."

Dot looked at her mother and smiled. "I had a good teacher."

"*Alaba*, you are the heart of the Ybarras. Your *aitona* did good by you."

Dot resumed watching Bethany and the dogs. She had delayed asking her mother the truth of what Smith had jeered at Ford as the man died. Used one excuse after another to put it off.

With the revelation of Ford's corruption while he was sheriff and the fallout of his death, Dot decided not to put it off any longer.

"*Ama*, who is my father?"

Angela stiffened.

"Please don't be angry. And don't lie to me again. I'm well past that stage of denial."

Her mother stepped forward, shedding Dot's hold on her shoulders, and faced Dot. "It is a painful thing for me to talk about."

"Are you saying I'm like Bethany?"

Angela's eyes widened. "No. Nothing like that." She cupped Dot's cheek with a gloved hand. "You were very much a product of love. But your father loved something else more than he loved me." She stroked the prominent cheekbone that had been a feature of Dot's, one that Angela always stated made her beautiful. "He never wanted to stay in Euskadi. The army had always been his dream. I would never be enough for him, so he left."

"Did he know about me?"

Angela shook her head. "I didn't know until months later. By then it was too late."

"Too late for what?"

"He was killed in combat." Tears filled Angela's eyes. "His brother refused to bring his remains here, opting to have them buried in Arlington. Thousands of miles away so I would forget."

"His brother? Ford?"

Angela nodded. She lowered her hand and looked toward the mountains. She brought her gaze back to Dot. "I am a daughter of this land. As you are. I never wanted you to leave, because I feared you would never return to me."

Dot grasped her mother's shoulders. "I will always return to you, *Ama*. It is my wish to be buried here with my family, nowhere else."

Angela's watery smile did not reach her eyes. "You have always been the strong one. Your trials have proven that."

"I'm not as strong as you believe."

Angela took her face in her hands and gripped her. "You are. You will face many things going forward. None of them will stop you. This is my vow. It was your grandfather's vow. And it is the vow of our ancestors." She dragged Dot into her arms and squeezed her.

Dot closed her eyes and reveled in the warmth of her mother's arms.

Angela thrust her back and smiled at her. "Now go, with my blessing. Do this job T.J. has asked of you. There are more people like Ashley and Bethany out there who need help and your special skills."

"*Eskerrik asko, Ama.*"

"*Maite zaitut.*"

"I love you too."

"Dot!" Bethany squealed. "Come help me make a snow-man!"

Dot smiled at her mother. "Coming!"

With that small statement, Dot knew she would always help. No matter who. No matter what. No matter when.

She would always do right and fear no man.

The End

Author's Note

This book and the entire series to come was born on a cold winter's day in 2021. I sent a random text to editor Julie Sturgeon asking her what she thought of a modern woman bounty hunter series. She came back with, "Come up with a concept and pitch it." The concept didn't fully come about until nearly two years later. I was elbows deep into my Benoit and Dayne series and wanted to keep that momentum flowing.

On a trip in October of 2022 with my husband and the local FFA chapter to the FFA national convention, I took a few breaks from all those teenagers and met up with Julie. Together, we created a rough, working idea for this series. She wanted this series. I wanted this series, but I was leaning toward a male lead. From this T.J. was born, and so was Dot. But those two, back then, were not what you were introduced to in this book. The initial concept fell flat, and it was back to the drawing board.

Fast forward to 2023, when the success of the Benoit and Dayne series catapulted me into a revamp of the bounty hunter idea. A few switched concepts, and this time we put the hat on Dot. Thus was born the badass woman before you now.

In the early stages of development, I decided to make her

different than any of my previous characters. I recalled reading a Craig Johnson Walt Longmire book that covered the intriguing culture of Basque people in the West. This was a people I had never heard of before. Blame it on the insular culture of the Midwest, but the thought dug in. In my research of Idaho, I learned there was a huge Basque community, and it fit so perfectly into my idea to flex my character development skills. I gathered as much research as I could, videos, documentaries, websites, and books, *The Basque History of the World* by Mark Kurlansky being my deepest dive into the culture. They are fascinating people, and I hope Dot and her mother will help facilitate more interest in their rich history and strong family ties.

Toward the end of 2023, I attended the Midwest Mystery Conference in Chicago. One of the author panelists, Cindy Fazzi, spoke on her debut novel *Multo* and how she created her bounty hunter character. She mentioned books she used in her research that I bought the moment I returned home. Both books are by Bob Burton and one, *Bounty Hunter*, is the more condensed version of the two. It's a surreal job, and at the time of his writing the books, the world of bounty hunting was very basic, nothing like the Old West versions we all were brought up on.

I'm a podcast devourer, always looking for a new show to listen to when I'm burned out on reading or writing. In my research on modern day bounty hunting, or more accurately fugitive recovery, I stumbled across a pair from Georgia that had done a podcast called *Wanted*. Alex and Jon did deep dives into some of their cases and what it's like to be a bounty hunter in our modern world. Though the podcast is only three seasons long, it was still enough for me to glean a great deal from. It even gave me ideas for the upcoming books.

At the time of Warren Jeffs' arrest and the subsequent fallout, I was dealing with deployment and young children, so this type of cult was not on my radar. Over the years and as more things became public knowledge, I poked around in the history of the polygamy fundamentalist movements but did not really become serious about it until recently. As I continued to delve into Ashley's character development, I found myself leaning away from what I was used to and wandered down this path. Special interviews with escaped members of the FLDS and victims of Jeffs' reign pulled me from my writing for a bit. My beta reader Rachel has long followed this situation and was thrilled when I began pulling this into the book. She urged me to watch *Keep Sweet: Pray and Obey* on Netflix, which I did. I created a fictional group, but it follows closely with Warren Jeffs' twist on the polygamy fundamentalist movement.

I truly hope you all enjoy Dot's entry into this world and follow along with me into her future. More will come out about her time during the Abbey Gate bombings, and her and T.J.'s ties to the army will play vital roles in future books.

Until book 2.
Signing off,
Winter Austin

Acknowledgements

I'm a faith-based woman, and with that comes the assurance that everything I write will touch readers in whatever way, shape, or form it needs to. I always give thanks to the Almighty Who cultivated this gift and drive to write.

My family has long since flown the coop, and in their place have flooded in nephews and nieces who keep my husband and myself hopping. I marvel at the gift of being the aunt able and willing to always be there when they need her. I loved researching the Basque way of life and really tried to thread in their strong ties of family into Dot and Angela. In all ways, I think we should all take a page from the Basque and treasure our families deeply.

The one person alive who is allowed to remind me that I'm procrastinating and goofing off is my husband. As much as it pains me that he reminds me of this, I love him still. Now if he'd only stop sending all those videos and memes in my Facebook messenger so I can focus on writing.

Writing a book is a taxing endeavor, and it's not possible without some kind of cheer squad or, in my case, prodders to keep me going. My editor, Julie, never wavered in her belief that I'd come through with this book. She might have received the worst draft I've ever given her, except maybe the very first book we ever worked on together, but receive this book she did. To her credit, she gave me too much credit on how little work there was to be done on it during the editing process. But the book you hold before you is one we spit shined and polished.

Along with Julie were my beta readers Jenn and Rachel, whose long-distance loathing toward me for not having a new chapter sent to them drove me on.

I couldn't have asked for a better dream team than the one at Tule. From the promotion team to the cover art team, this group is a fantastic one to work with.

I belong to a wonderful organization that aids authors in so many ways. Sisters in Crime and my local chapter SinC-Iowa have been a great motivator in the last few years for me. It's always a good thing when I can make a meeting in person, but belonging to this organization always fuels me and keeps me dialed into the mystery/crime fiction world.

I have made great connections with Iowa-based bookstores and look to expand into surrounding states. I will always support our independent bookstores and local libraries, even the little share libraries that have popped up in your hometowns.

Finally, I'd like to acknowledge all the readers who have supported me in reading and reviewing all of my books so far and continue to come back for more. Welcome to all the new readers I gain each year; come find my backlist and catch up. Most of you are strangers to me, some are actual family members, but you are all great in my eyes for being readers. Continue to support us authors by reading, reviewing, or just plain spreading the word. It means a lot.

More Books by Winter Austin

Benoit and Dayne Mysteries

Book 1: *The Killer in Me*

Book 2: *Hush, My Darling*

Book 3: *Straight for the Kill*

Book 4: *A Requiem For The Dead*

Available now at your favorite online retailer!

About the Author

Winter Austin perpetually answers the question: "were you born in the winter?" with a flat "nope," but believe her, there is a story behind her name.

A lifelong Mid-West gal with strong ties to the agriculture world, Winter grew up listening to the captivating stories told by relatives around a table or a campfire. As a published author, she learned her glass half-empty personality makes for a perfect suspense/thriller writer. Taking her ability to verbally spin a vivid and detailed story, Winter translated that into writing deadly romantic suspense, mysteries, and thrillers.

When she's not slaving away at the computer, you can find Winter supporting her daughter in cattle shows, seeing her three sons off into the wide-wide world, loving on her fur babies, prodding her teacher husband, and nagging at her flock of hens to stay in the coop or the dogs will get them.

She is the author of multiple novels.

Thank you for reading

Ride a Dark Trail

If you enjoyed this book, you can find more from all our great authors at TulePublishing.com, or from your favorite online retailer.

TULE